Unicorn

A
Phoe

Dana Simpson

Andrews McMeel
PUBLISHING®

Hey, kids!

Check out the glossary starting on page 172
if you come across words you don't know.

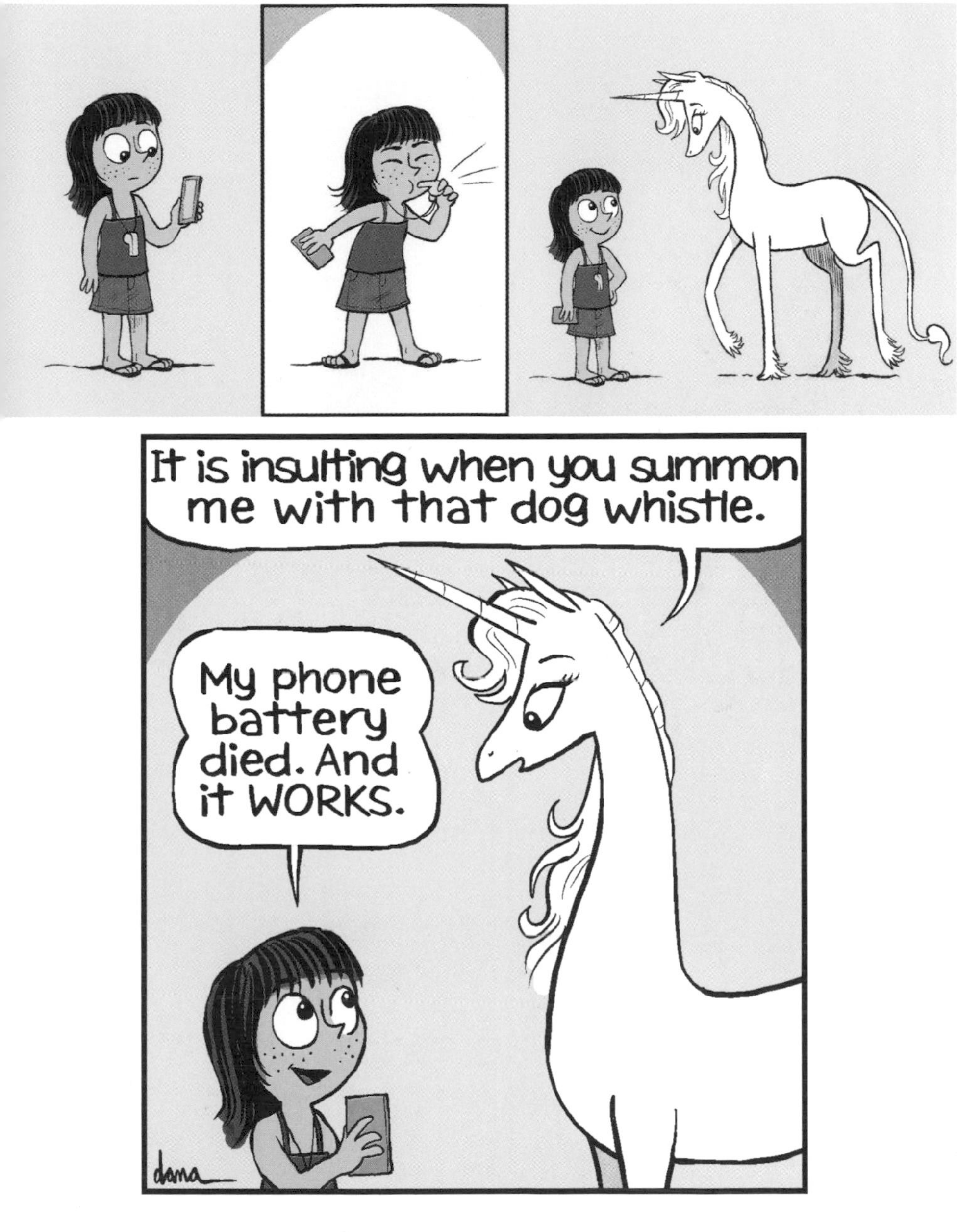
It is insulting when you summon me with that dog whistle.
My phone battery died. And it WORKS.
dana

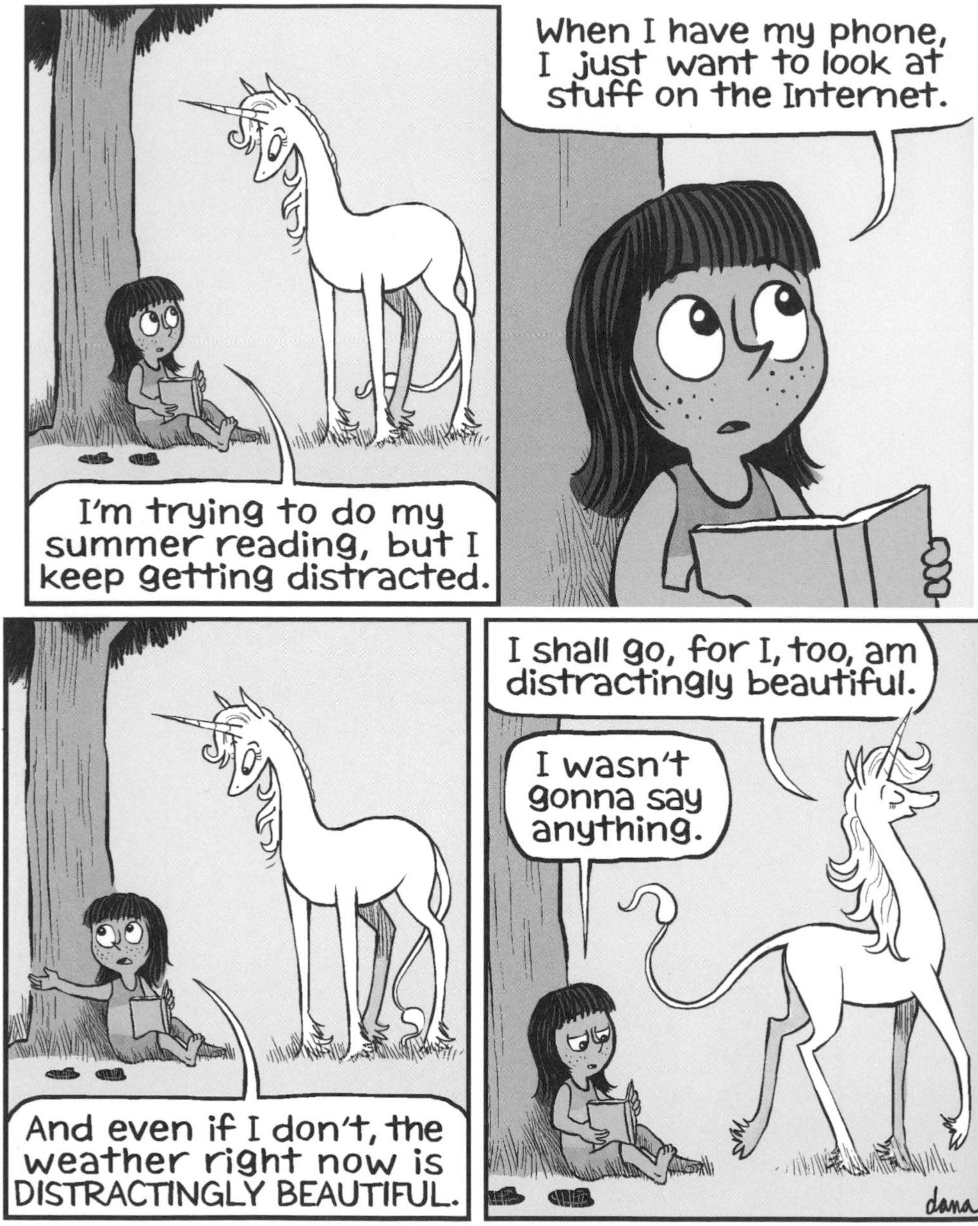
I'm trying to do my summer reading, but I keep getting distracted.
When I have my phone, I just want to look at stuff on the Internet.
And even if I don't, the weather right now is DISTRACTINGLY BEAUTIFUL.
I shall go, for I, too, am distractingly beautiful.
I wasn't gonna say anything.
dana

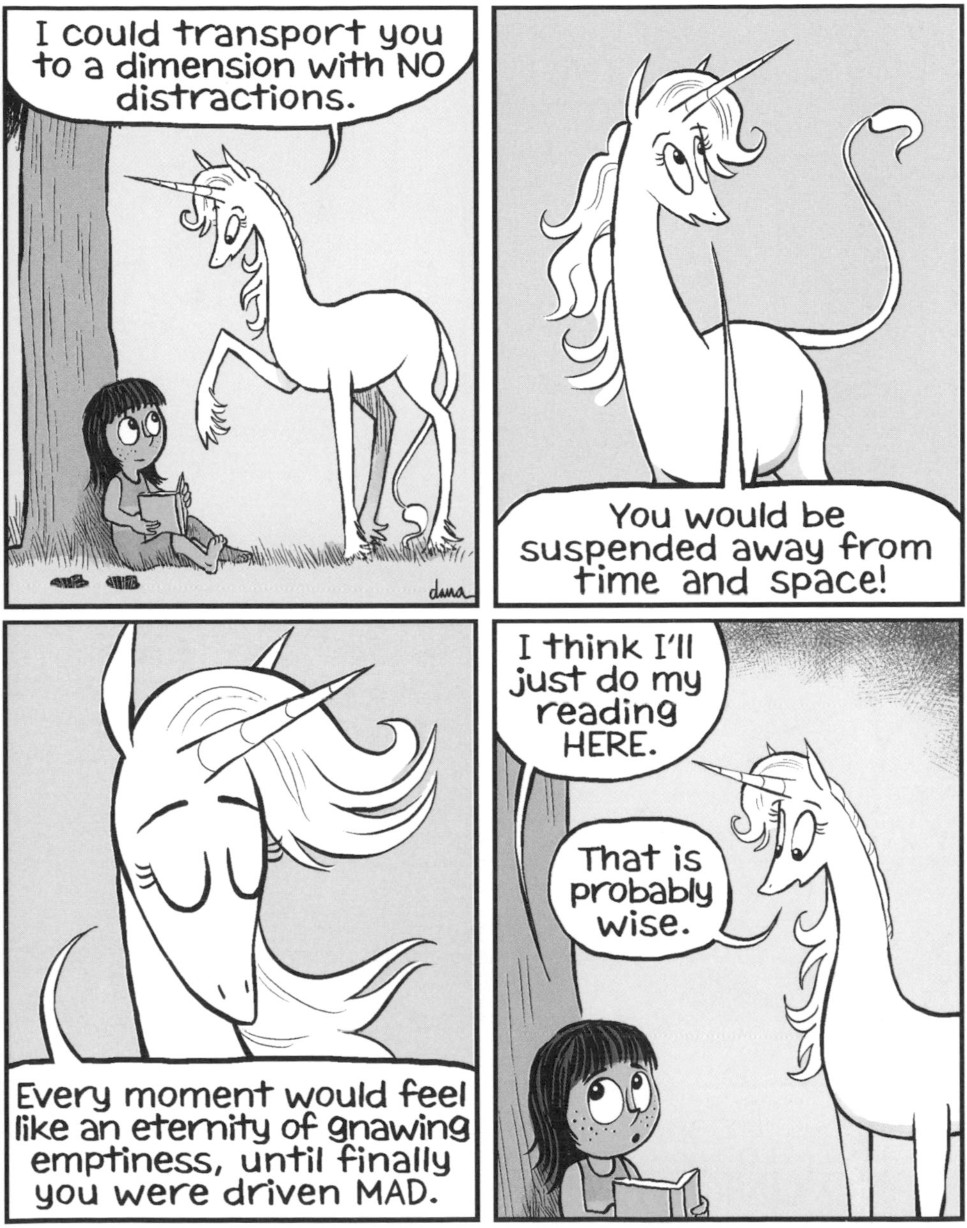
I could transport you to a dimension with NO distractions.
dana
You would be suspended away from time and space!
Every moment would feel like an eternity of gnawing emptiness, until finally you were driven MAD.
I think I'll just do my reading HERE.
That is probably wise.

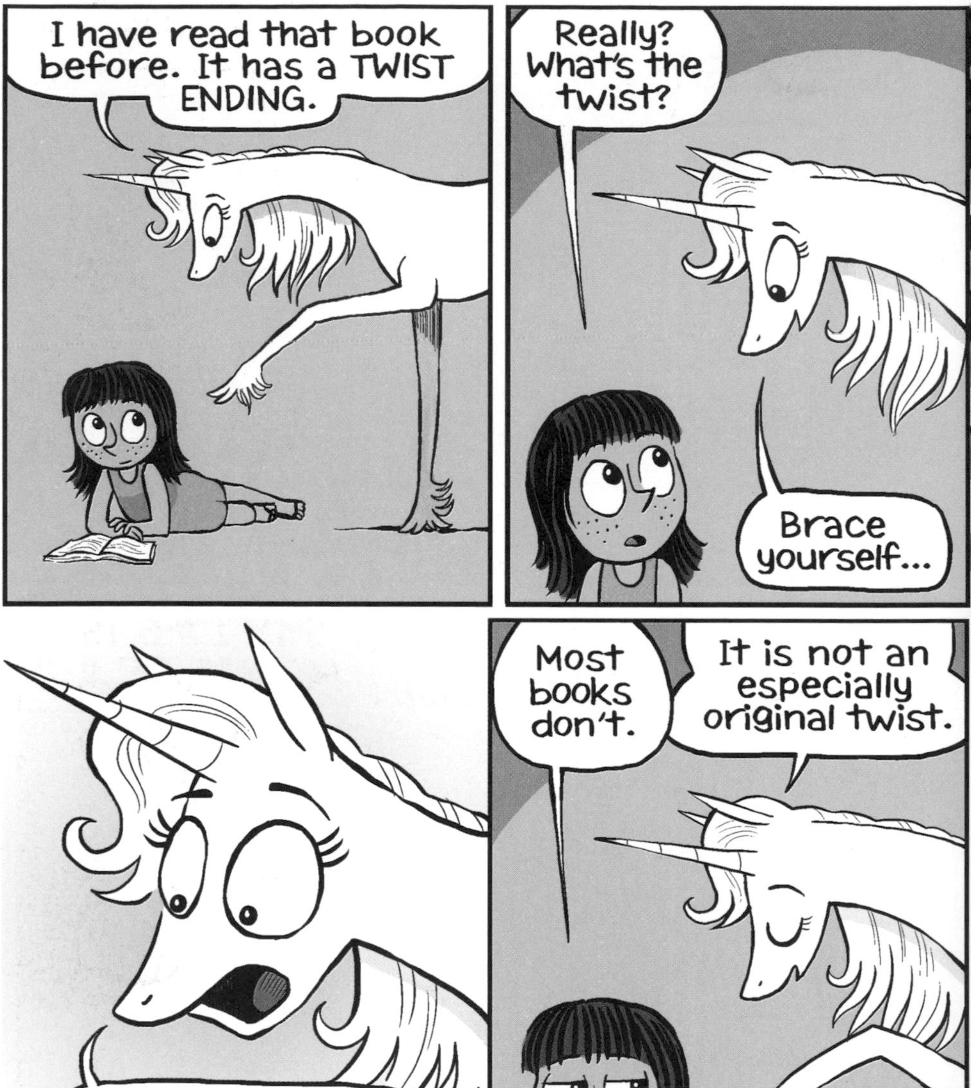
I have read that book before. It has a TWIST ENDING.
Really? What's the twist?
Brace yourself...
The twist is that the book has NO UNICORNS.
Most books don't.
It is not an especially original twist.
dana

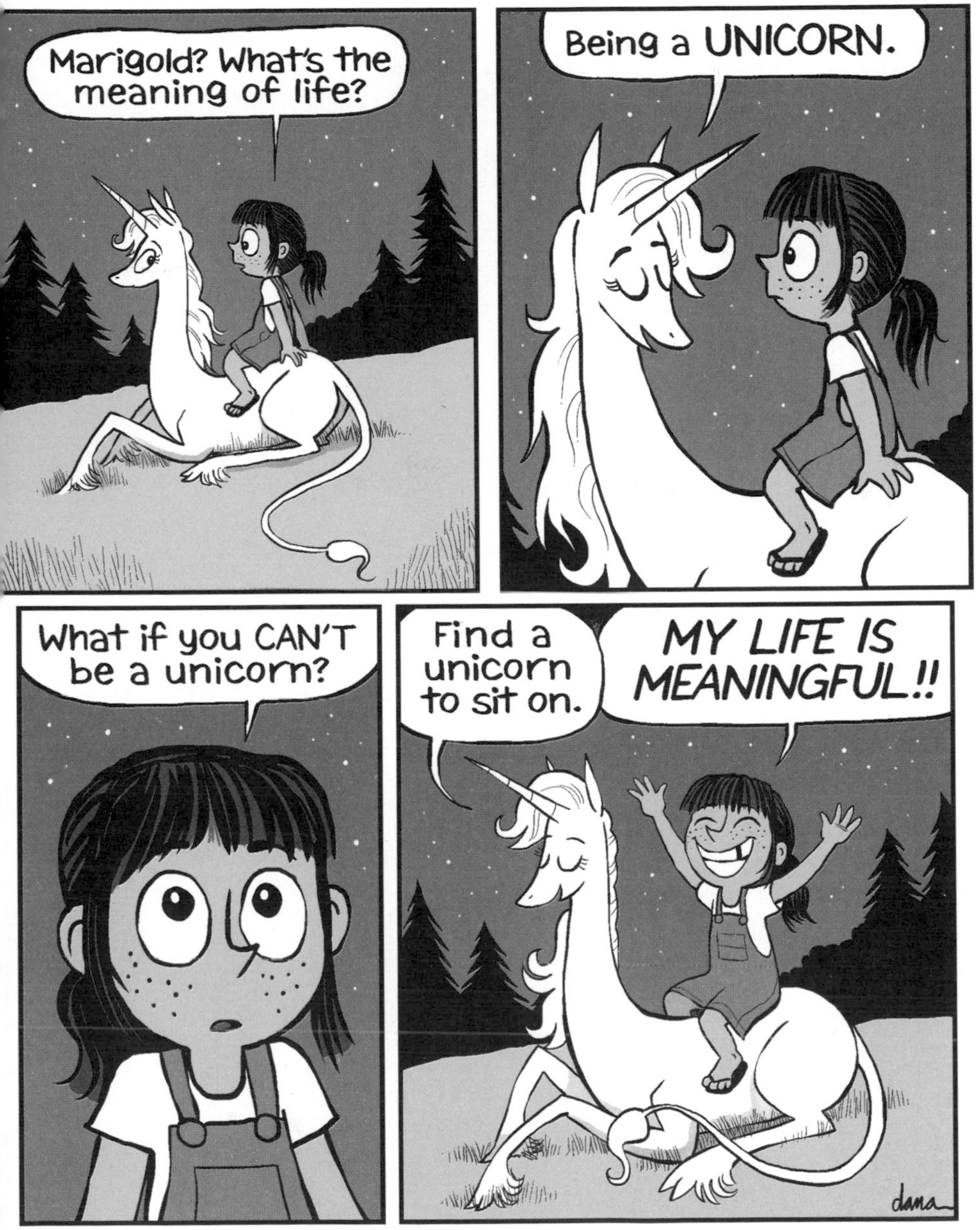
Marigold? What's the meaning of life?
Being a UNICORN.
What if you CAN'T be a unicorn?
Find a unicorn to sit on.
MY LIFE IS MEANINGFUL!!
dana

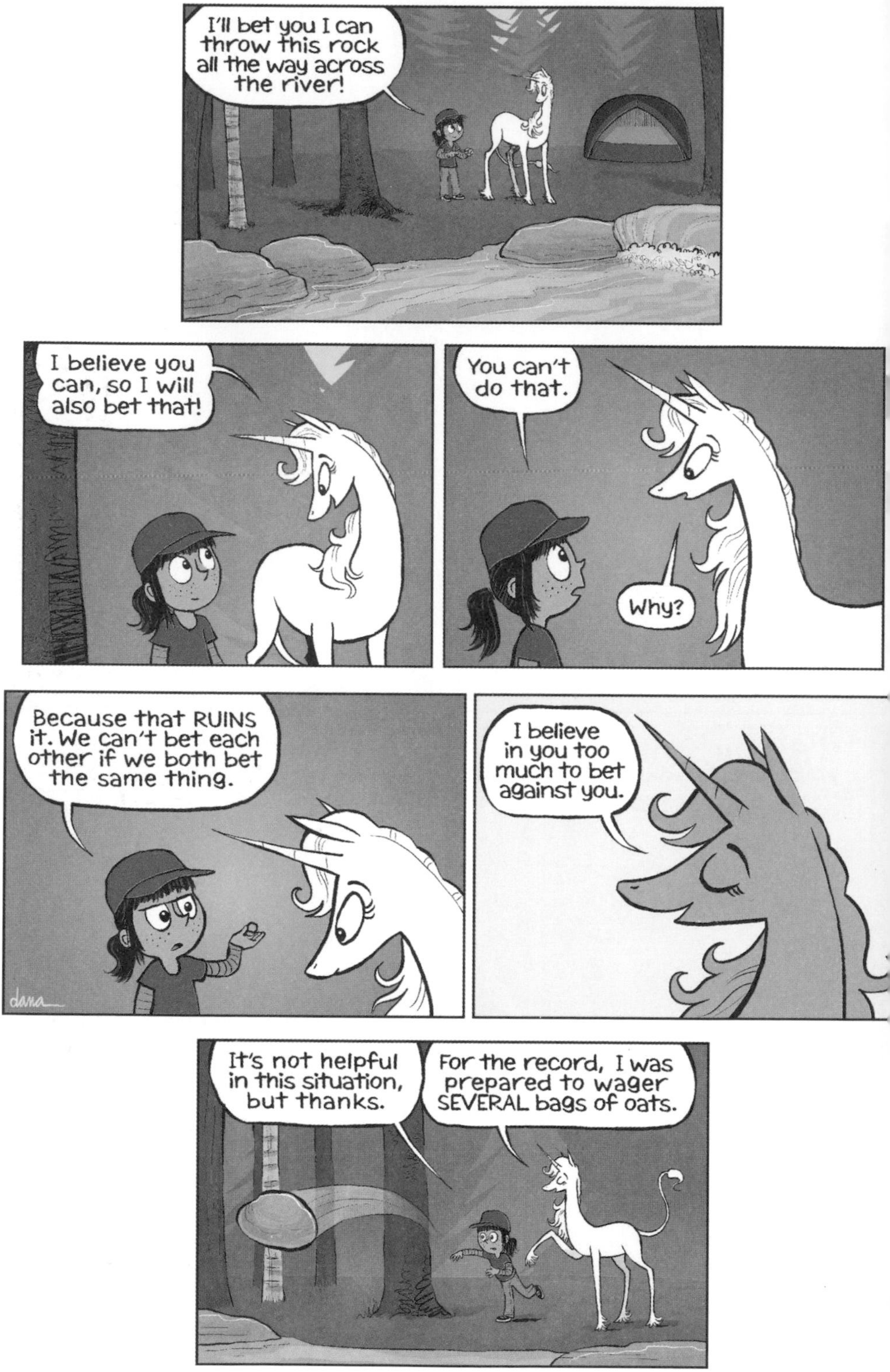
I'll bet you I can throw this rock all the way across the river!
I believe you can, so I will also bet that!
You can't do that.
Why?
Because that RUINS it. We can't bet each other if we both bet the same thing.
I believe in you too much to bet against you.
It's not helpful in this situation, but thanks.
For the record, I was prepared to wager SEVERAL bags of oats.
dana

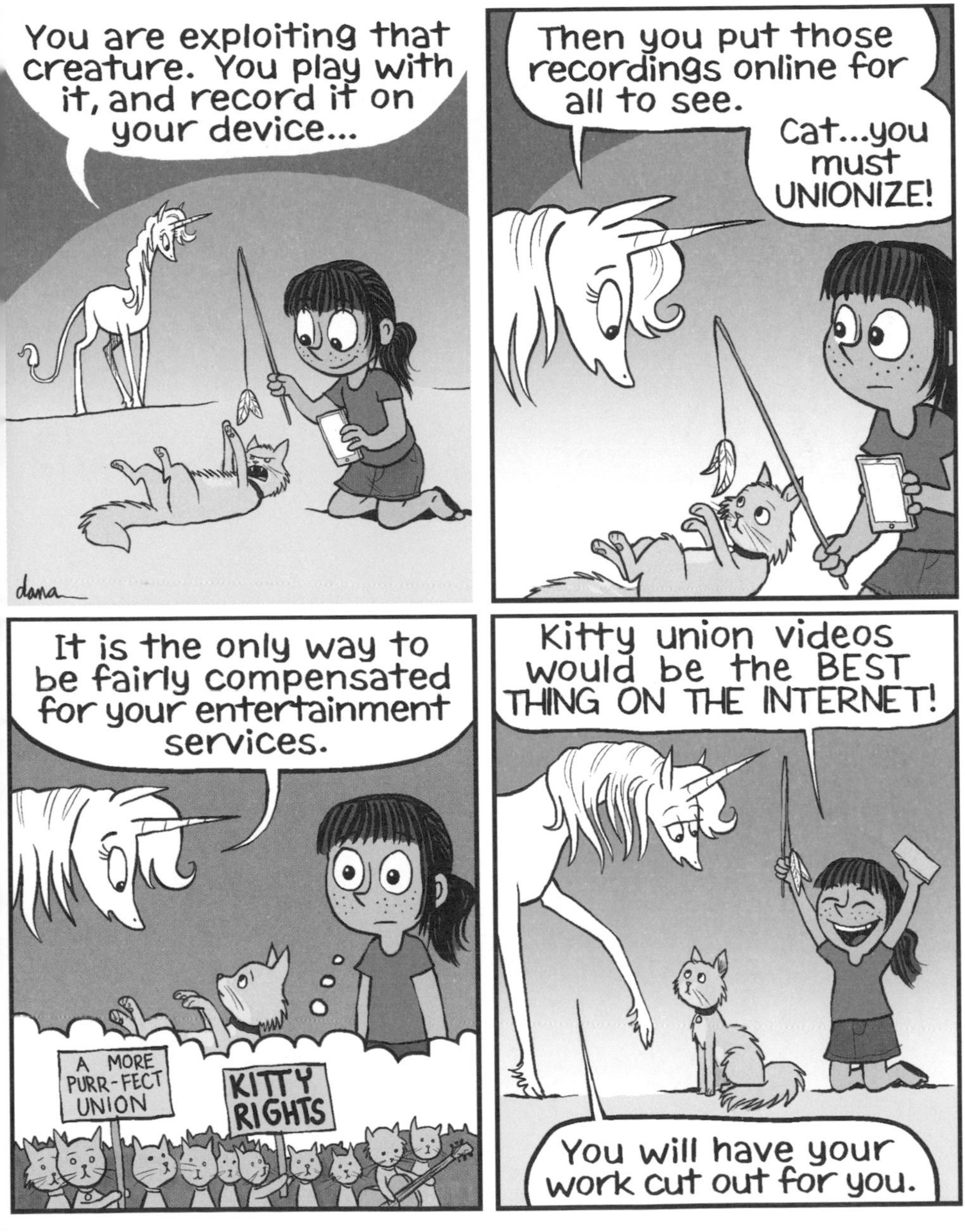
You are exploiting that creature. You play with it, and record it on your device...
dana
Then you put those recordings online for all to see.
Cat...you must UNIONIZE!
It is the only way to be fairly compensated for your entertainment services.
A MORE PURR-FECT UNION
KITTY RIGHTS
Kitty union videos would be the BEST THING ON THE INTERNET!
You will have your work cut out for you.

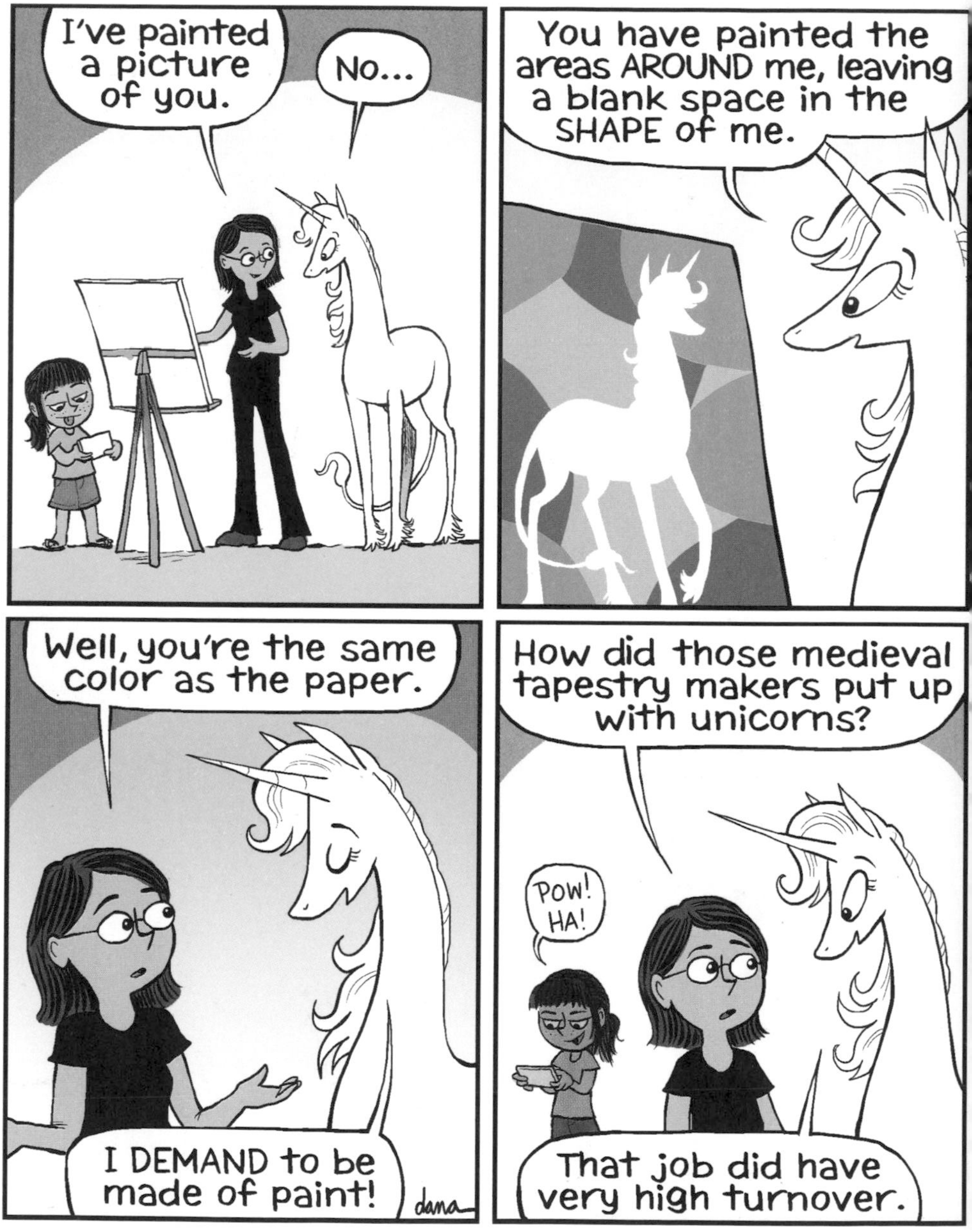
I've painted a picture of you.
No...
You have painted the areas AROUND me, leaving a blank space in the SHAPE of me.
Well, you're the same color as the paper.
I DEMAND to be made of paint!
dana
How did those medieval tapestry makers put up with unicorns?
POW! HA!
That job did have very high turnover.

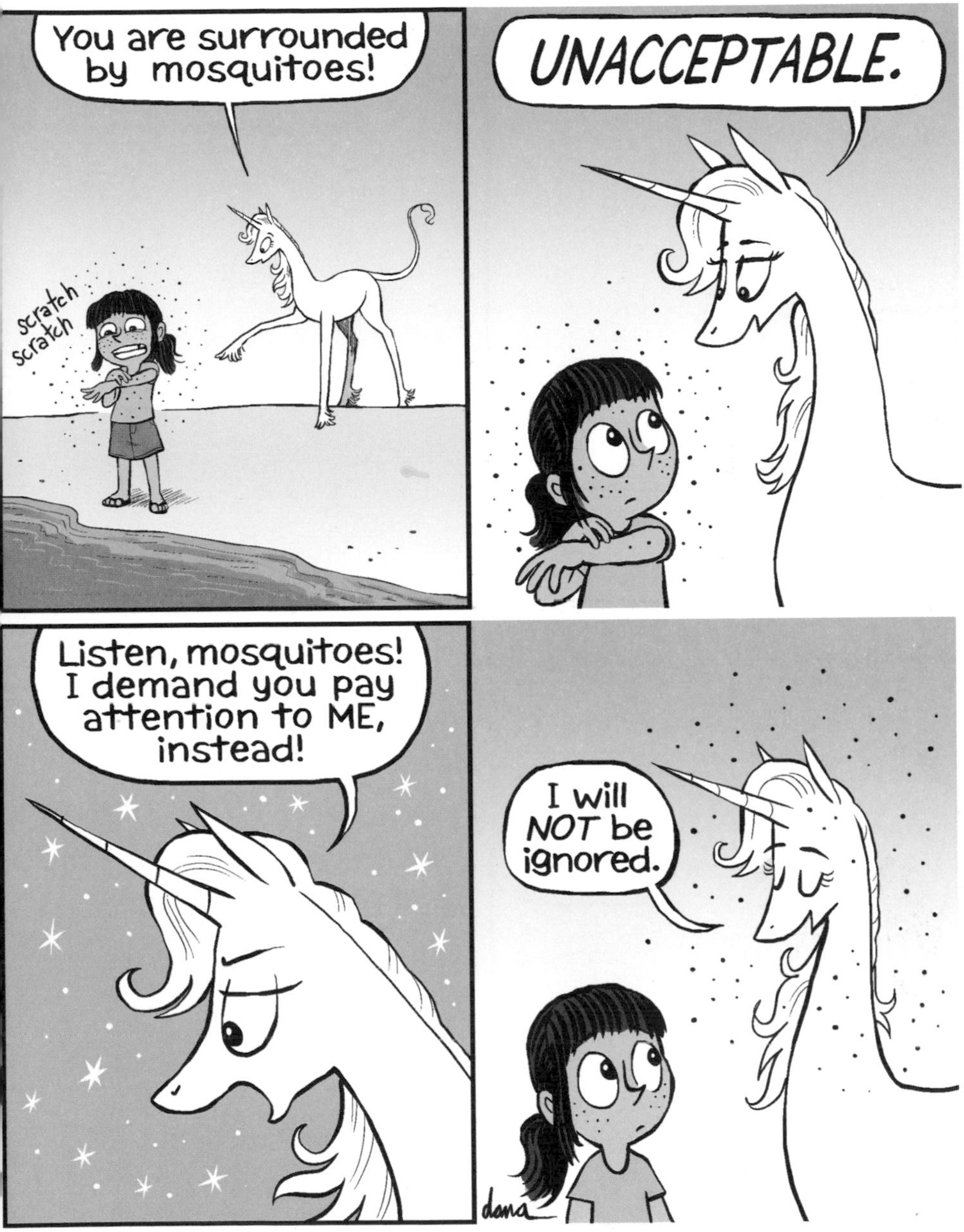
You are surrounded by mosquitoes!
scratch scratch
UNACCEPTABLE.
Listen, mosquitoes! I demand you pay attention to ME, instead!
I will NOT be ignored.
dana

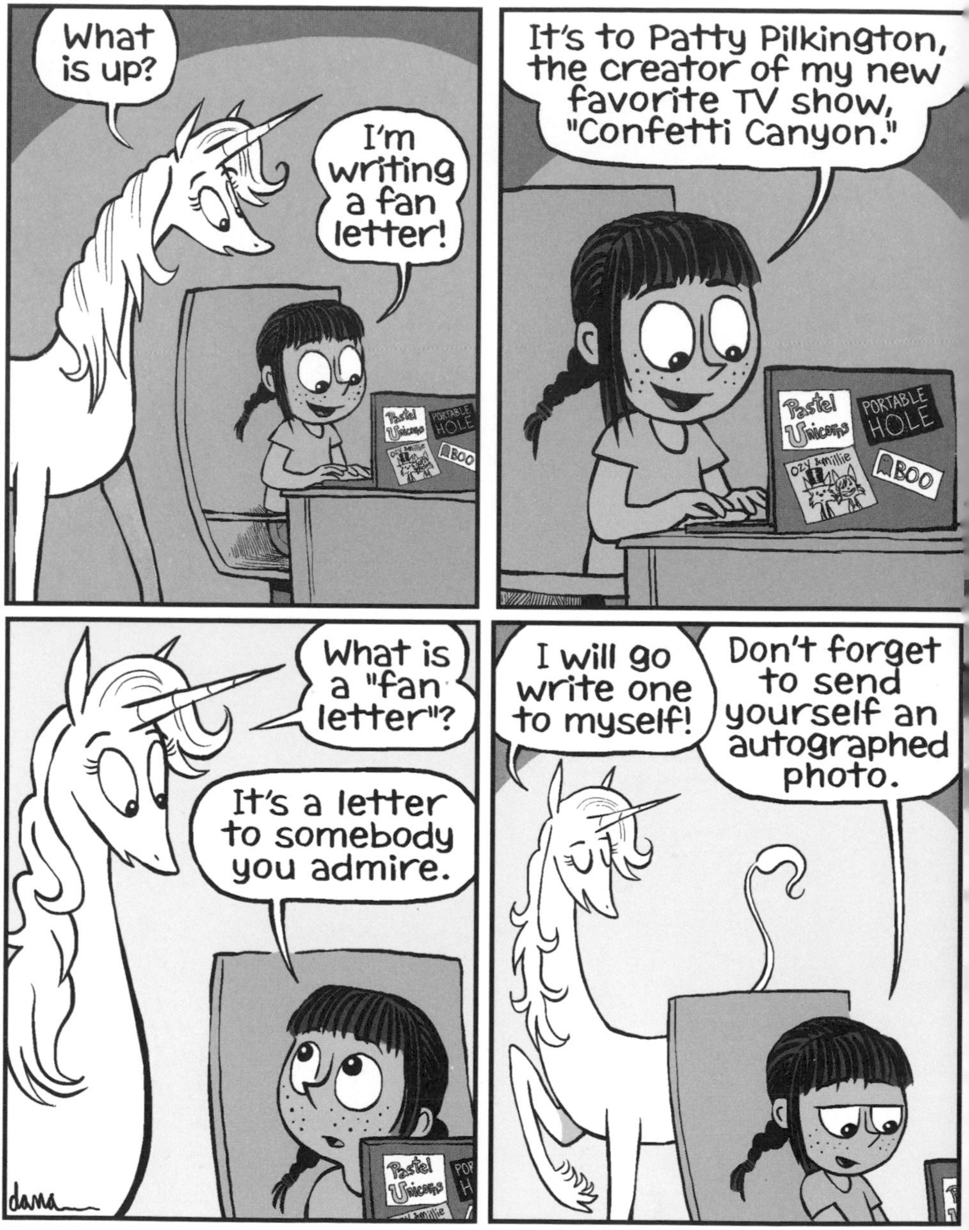
What is up?
I'm writing a fan letter!
It's to Patty Pilkington, the creator of my new favorite TV show, "Confetti Canyon."
Pastel Unicorns
PORTABLE HOLE
ozy & millie
BOO
What is a "fan letter"?
It's a letter to somebody you admire.
dana
I will go write one to myself!
Don't forget to send yourself an autographed photo.

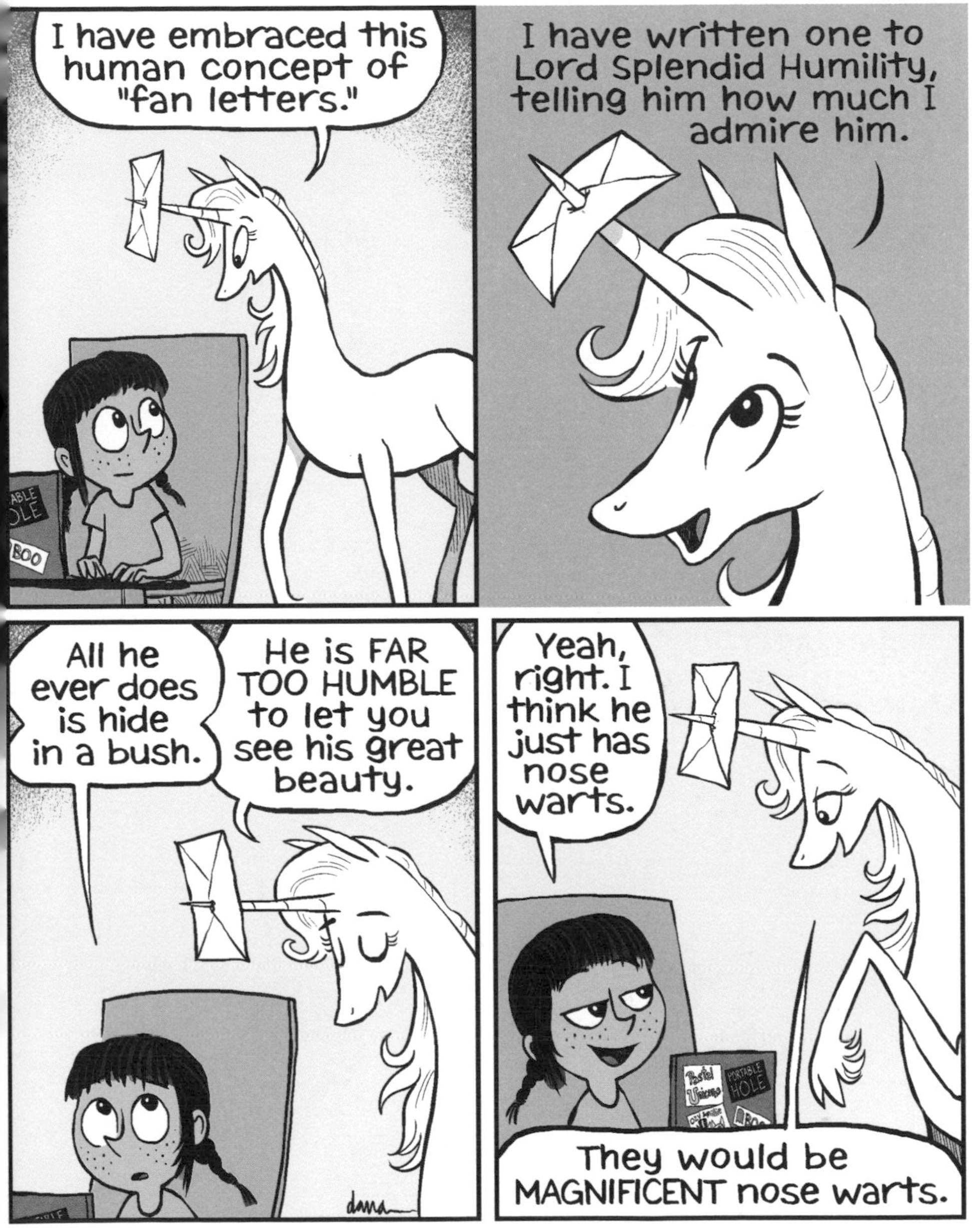
I have embraced this human concept of "fan letters."
I have written one to Lord Splendid Humility, telling him how much I admire him.
All he ever does is hide in a bush.
He is FAR TOO HUMBLE to let you see his great beauty.
Yeah, right. I think he just has nose warts.
They would be MAGNIFICENT nose warts.

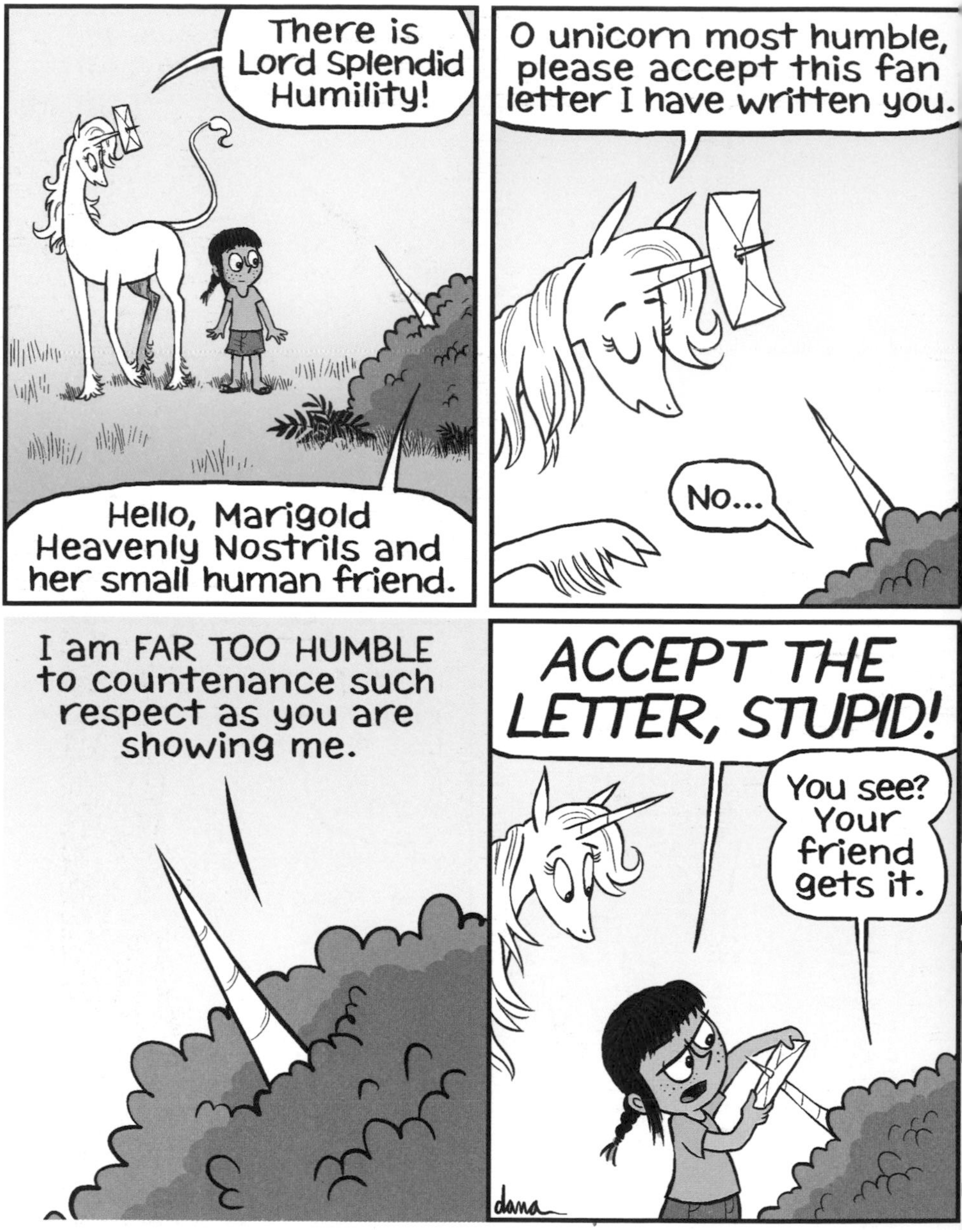
There is Lord Splendid Humility!
Hello, Marigold Heavenly Nostrils and her small human friend.
O unicorn most humble, please accept this fan letter I have written you.
No...
I am FAR TOO HUMBLE to countenance such respect as you are showing me.
ACCEPT THE LETTER, STUPID!
You see? Your friend gets it.
dana

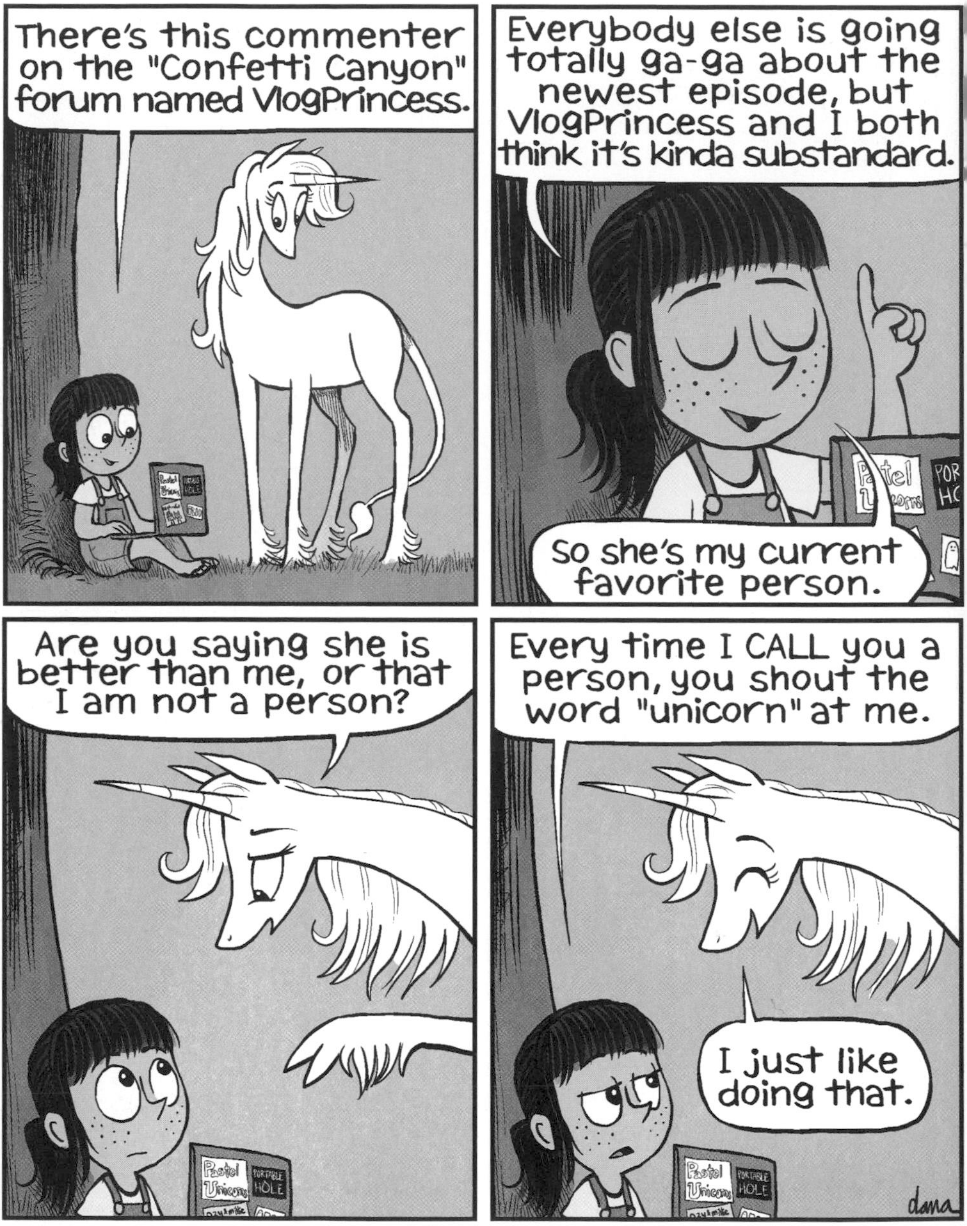
There's this commenter on the "Confetti Canyon" forum named VlogPrincess.
Everybody else is going totally ga-ga about the newest episode, but VlogPrincess and I both think it's kinda substandard.
So she's my current favorite person.
Are you saying she is better than me, or that I am not a person?
Every time I CALL you a person, you shout the word "unicorn" at me.
I just like doing that.
dana

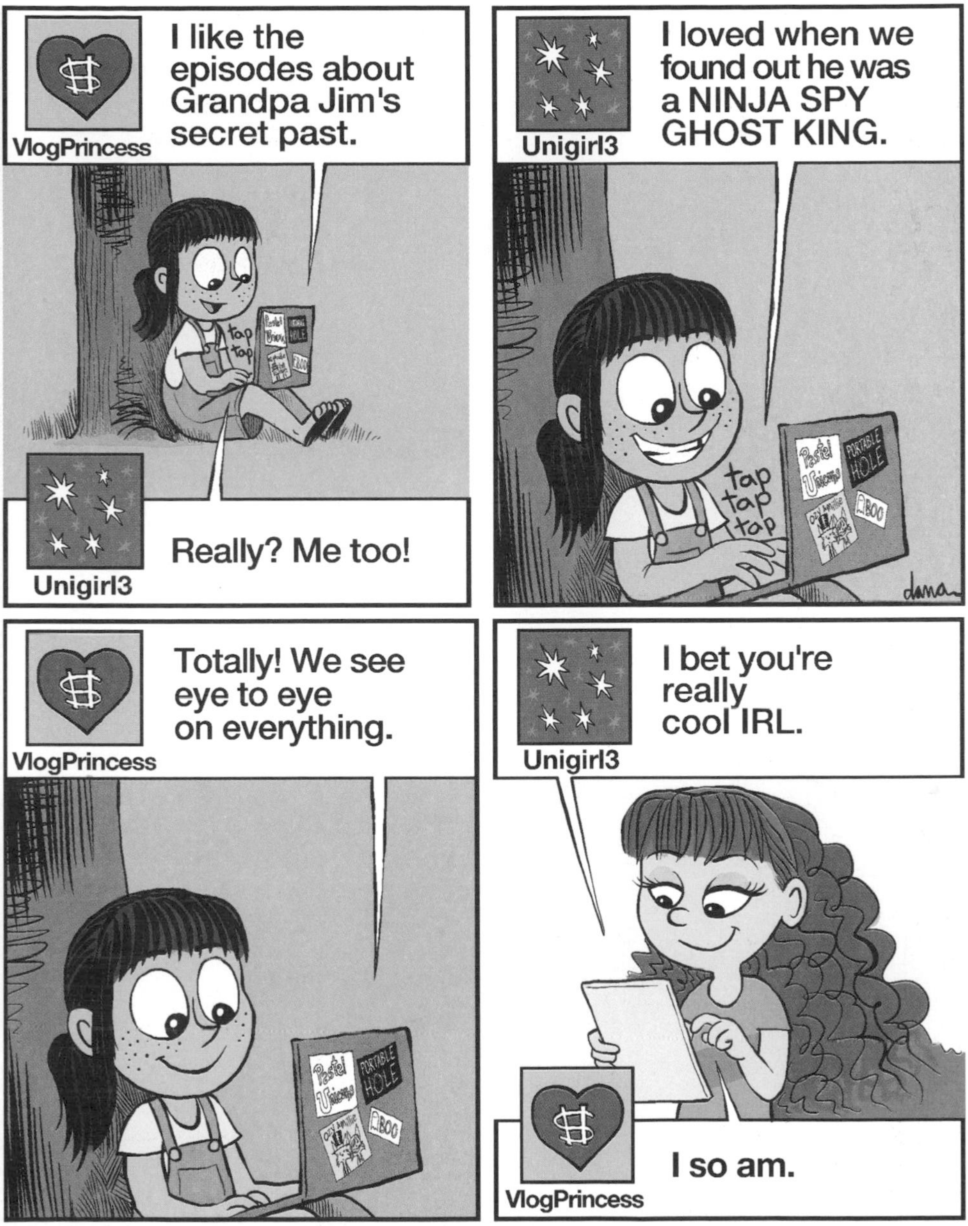
VlogPrincess
I like the episodes about Grandpa Jim's secret past.
tap tap
Unigirl3
Really? Me too!
Unigirl3
I loved when we found out he was a NINJA SPY GHOST KING.
tap tap tap
Pastel Unicorns
PORTABLE HOLE
BOO
dana
VlogPrincess
Totally! We see eye to eye on everything.
Pastel Unicorns
PORTABLE HOLE
BOO
Unigirl3
I bet you're really cool IRL.
VlogPrincess
I so am.

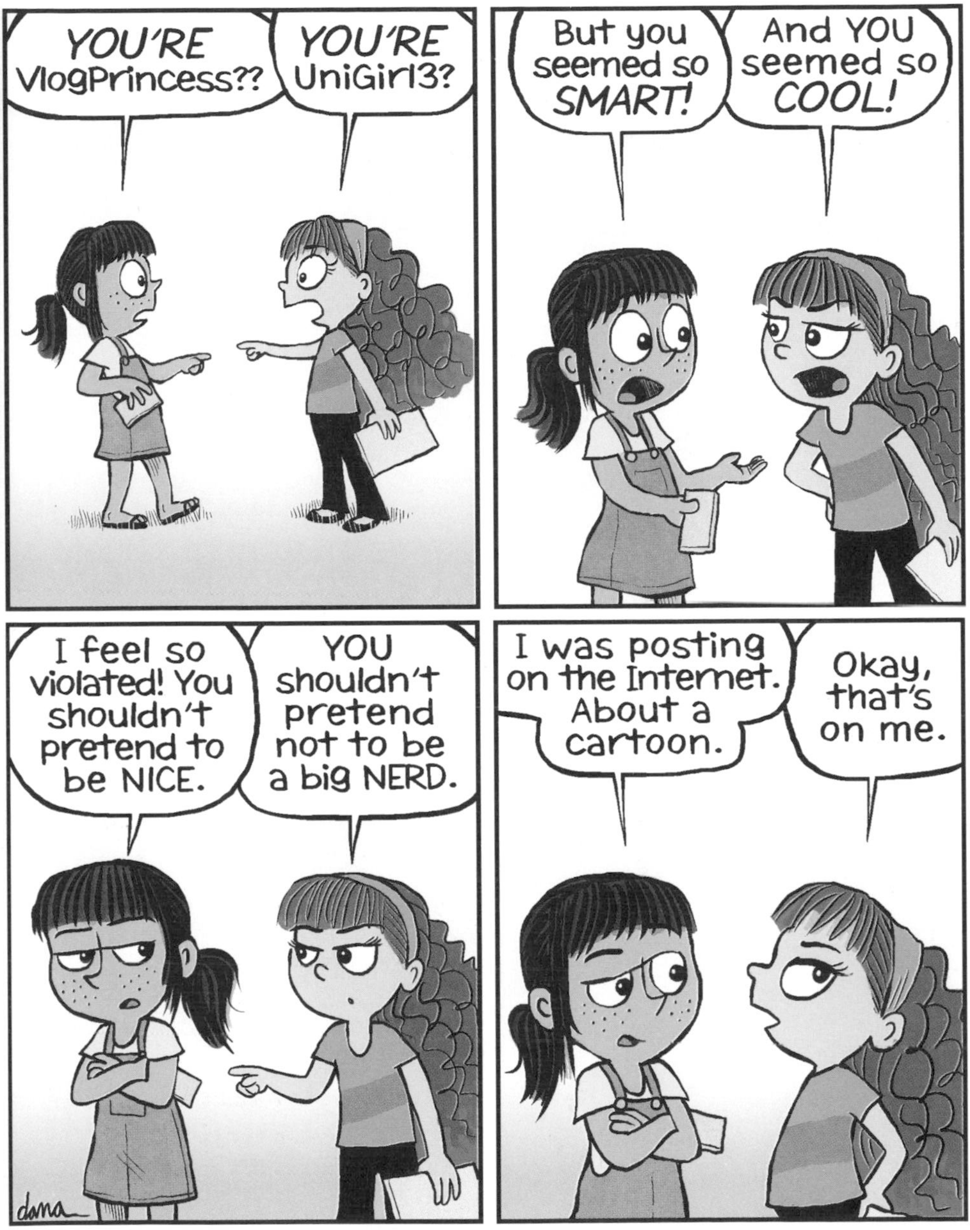
YOU'RE VlogPrincess??
YOU'RE UniGirl3?
But you seemed so SMART!
And YOU seemed so COOL!
I feel so violated! You shouldn't pretend to be NICE.
YOU shouldn't pretend not to be a big NERD.
I was posting on the Internet. About a cartoon.
Okay, that's on me.
dana

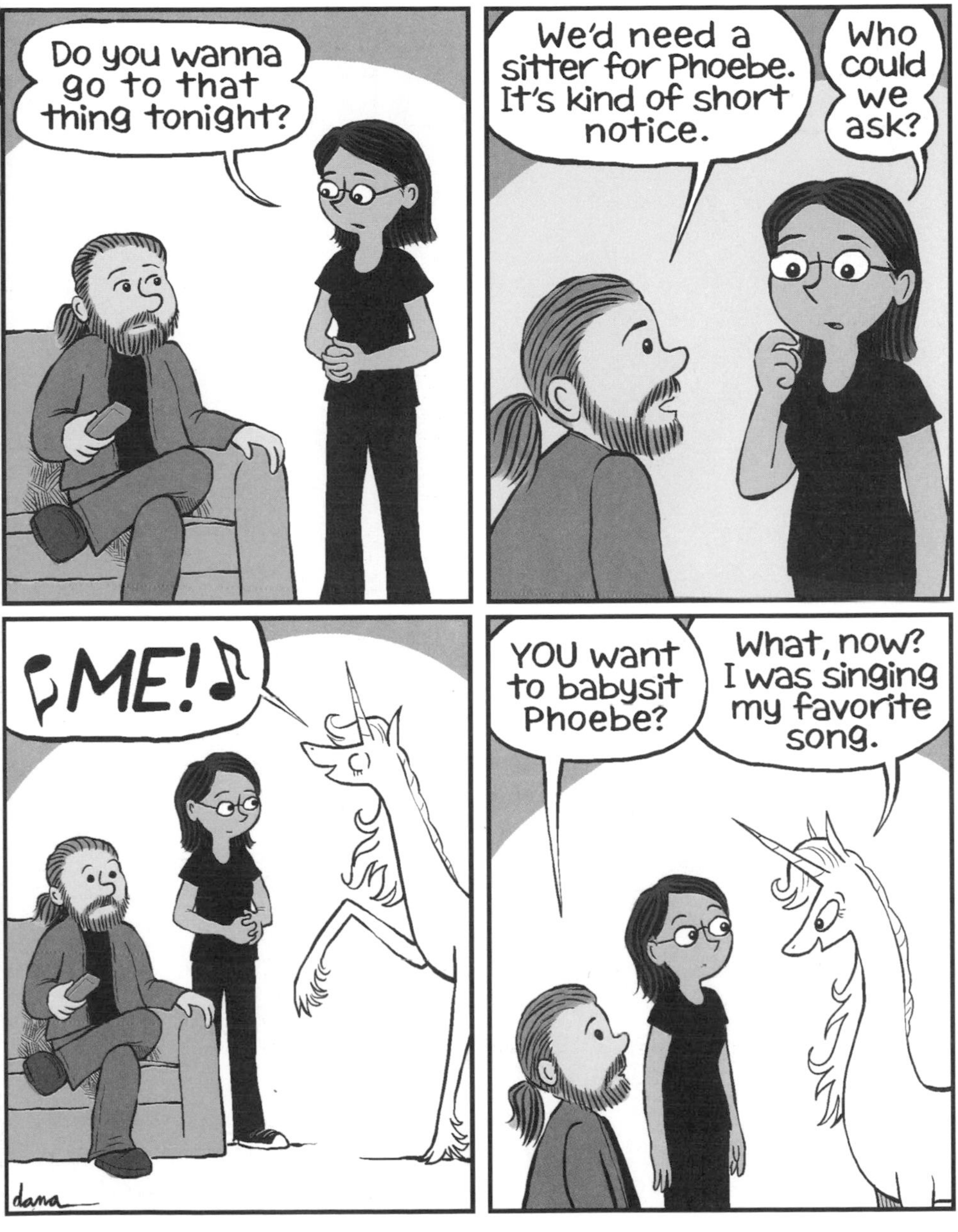
Do you wanna go to that thing tonight?
We'd need a sitter for Phoebe. It's kind of short notice.
Who could we ask?
ME!
YOU want to babysit Phoebe?
What, now? I was singing my favorite song.
dana

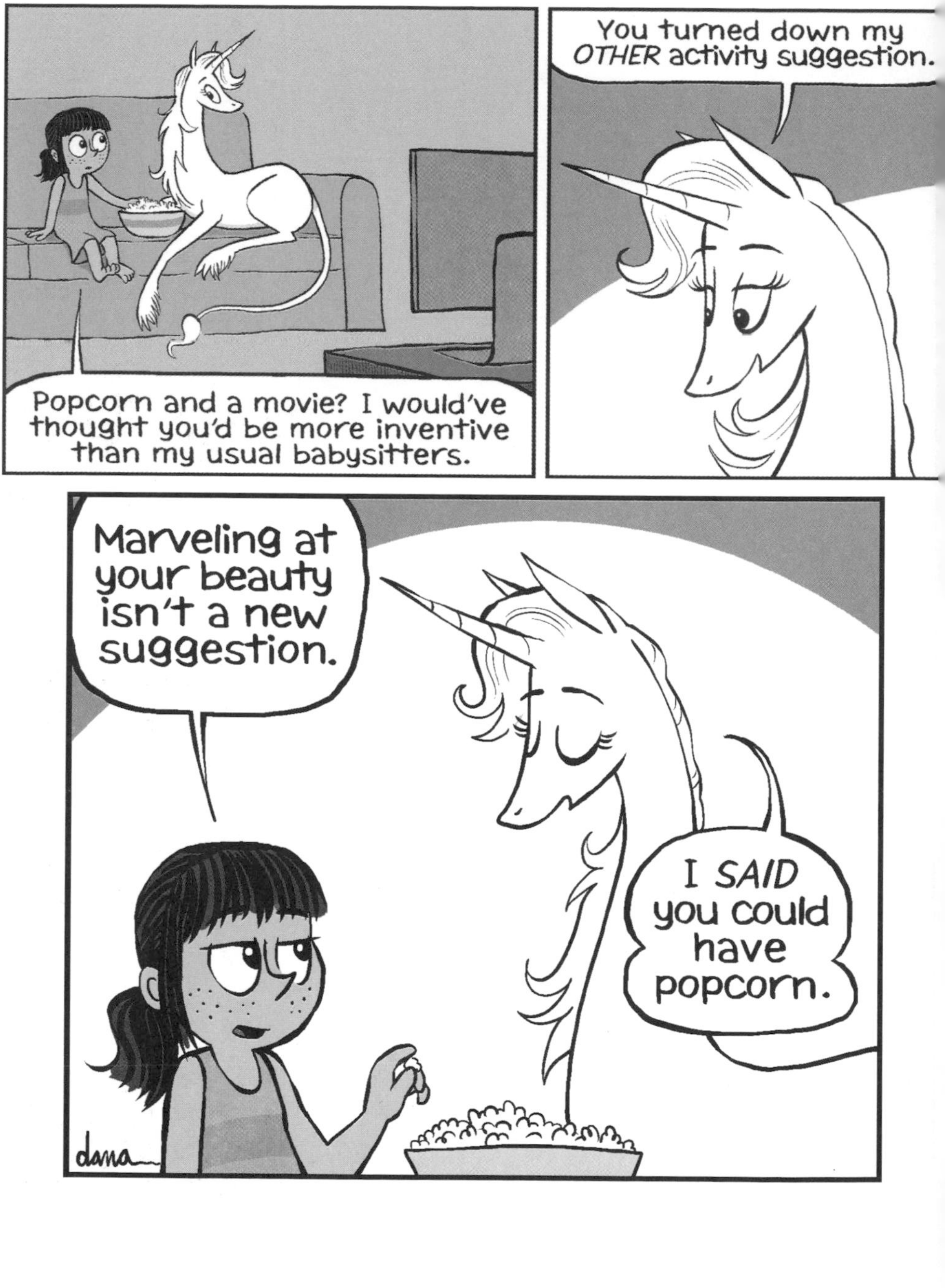
Popcorn and a movie? I would've thought you'd be more inventive than my usual babysitters.
You turned down my *OTHER* activity suggestion.
Marveling at your beauty isn't a new suggestion.
I *SAID* you could have popcorn.
dana

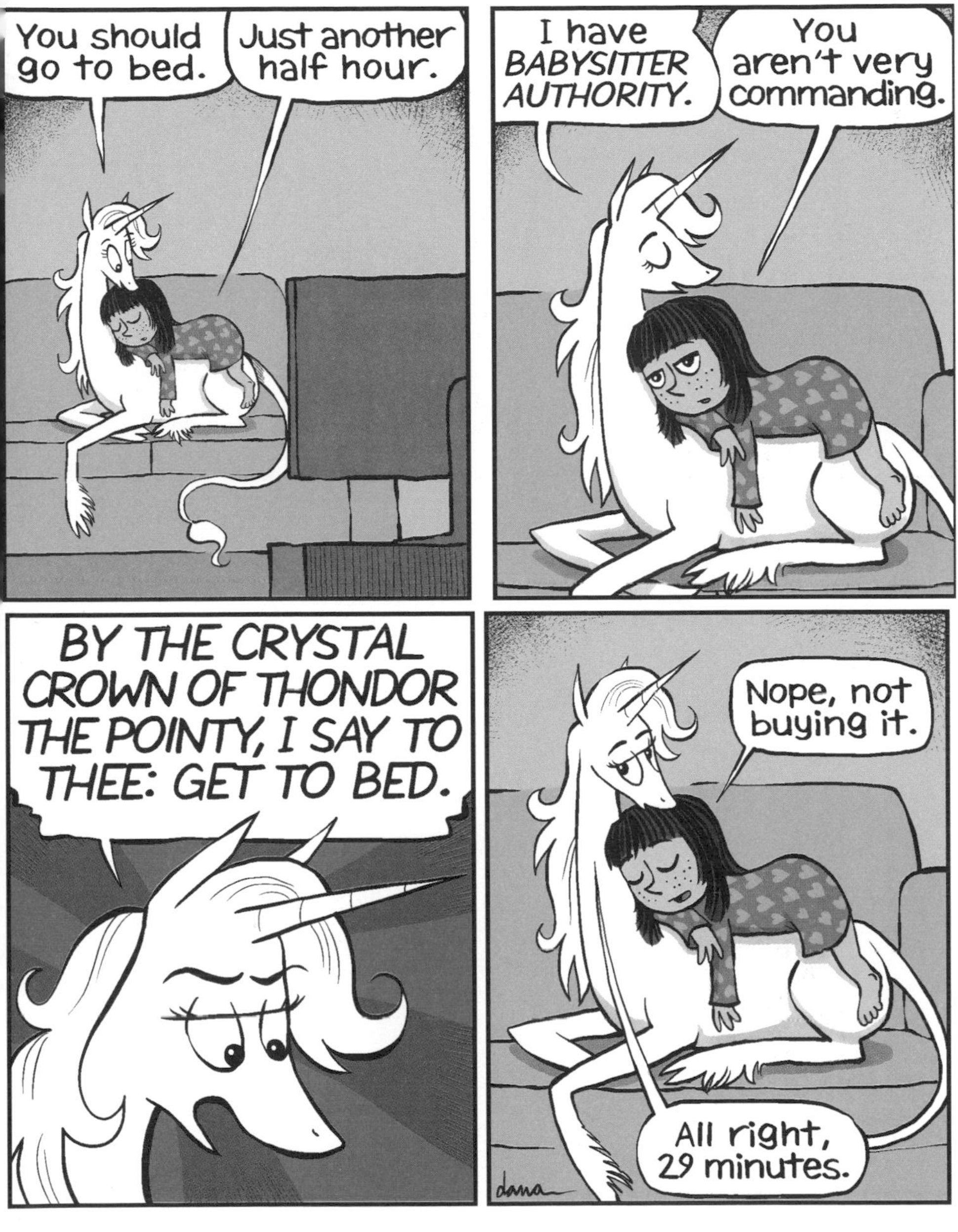
You should go to bed.
Just another half hour.
I have BABYSITTER AUTHORITY.
You aren't very commanding.
BY THE CRYSTAL CROWN OF THONDOR THE POINTY, I SAY TO THEE: GET TO BED.
Nope, not buying it.
All right, 29 minutes.
dana

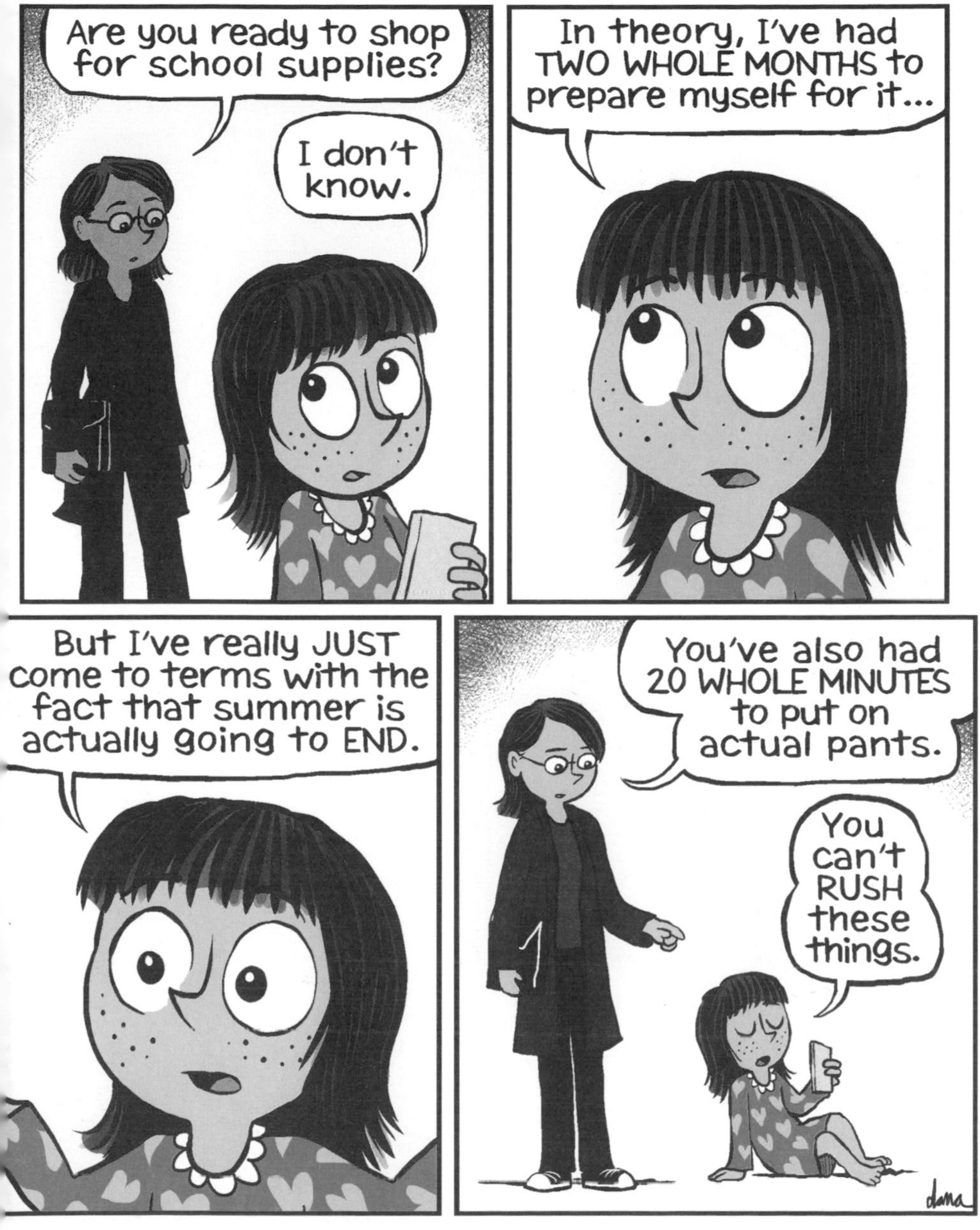
Are you ready to shop for school supplies?
I don't know.
In theory, I've had TWO WHOLE MONTHS to prepare myself for it...
But I've really JUST come to terms with the fact that summer is actually going to END.
You've also had 20 WHOLE MINUTES to put on actual pants.
You can't RUSH these things.
dana

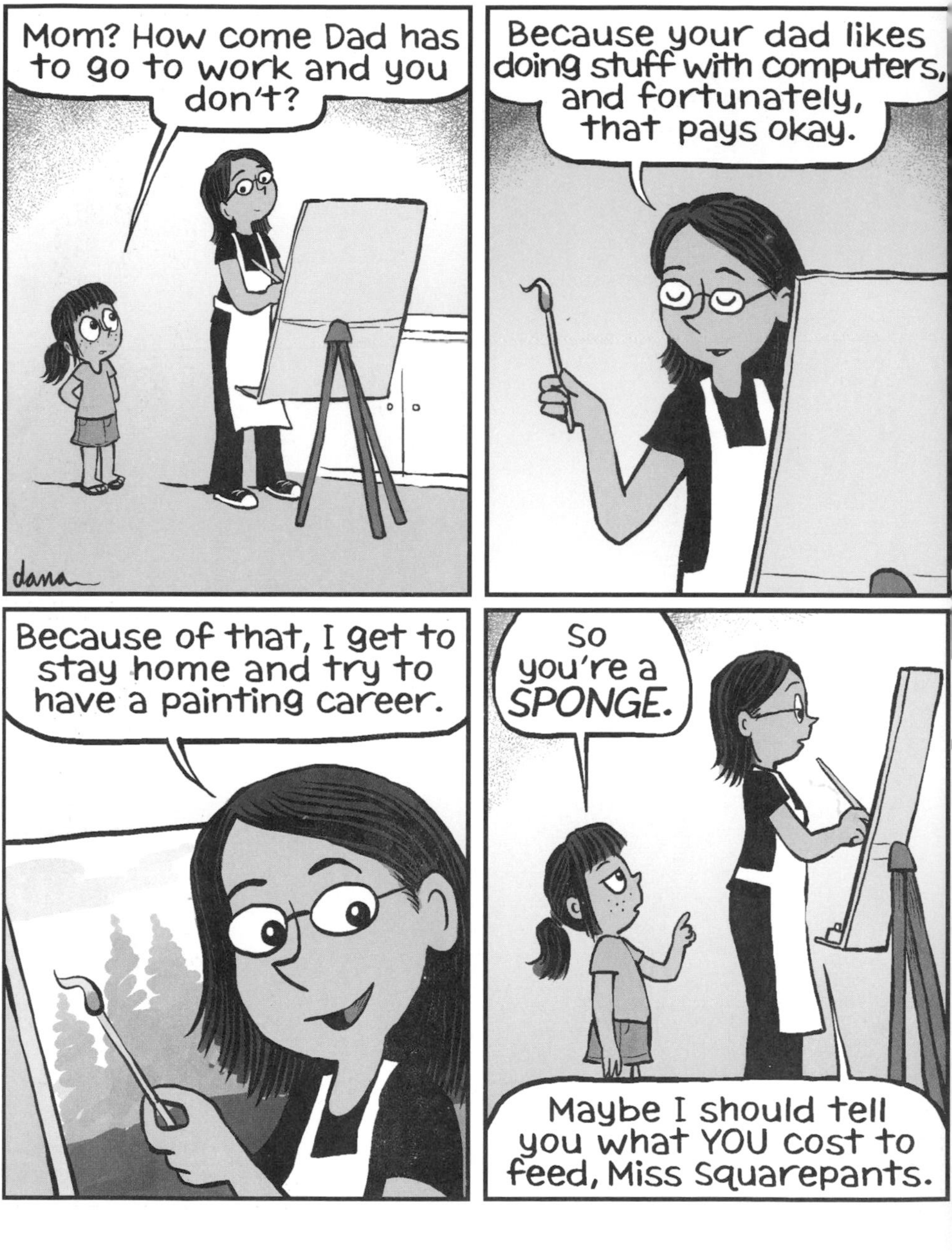
Mom? How come Dad has to go to work and you don't?
Because your dad likes doing stuff with computers, and fortunately, that pays okay.
dana
Because of that, I get to stay home and try to have a painting career.
So you're a *SPONGE*.
Maybe I should tell you what YOU cost to feed, Miss Squarepants.

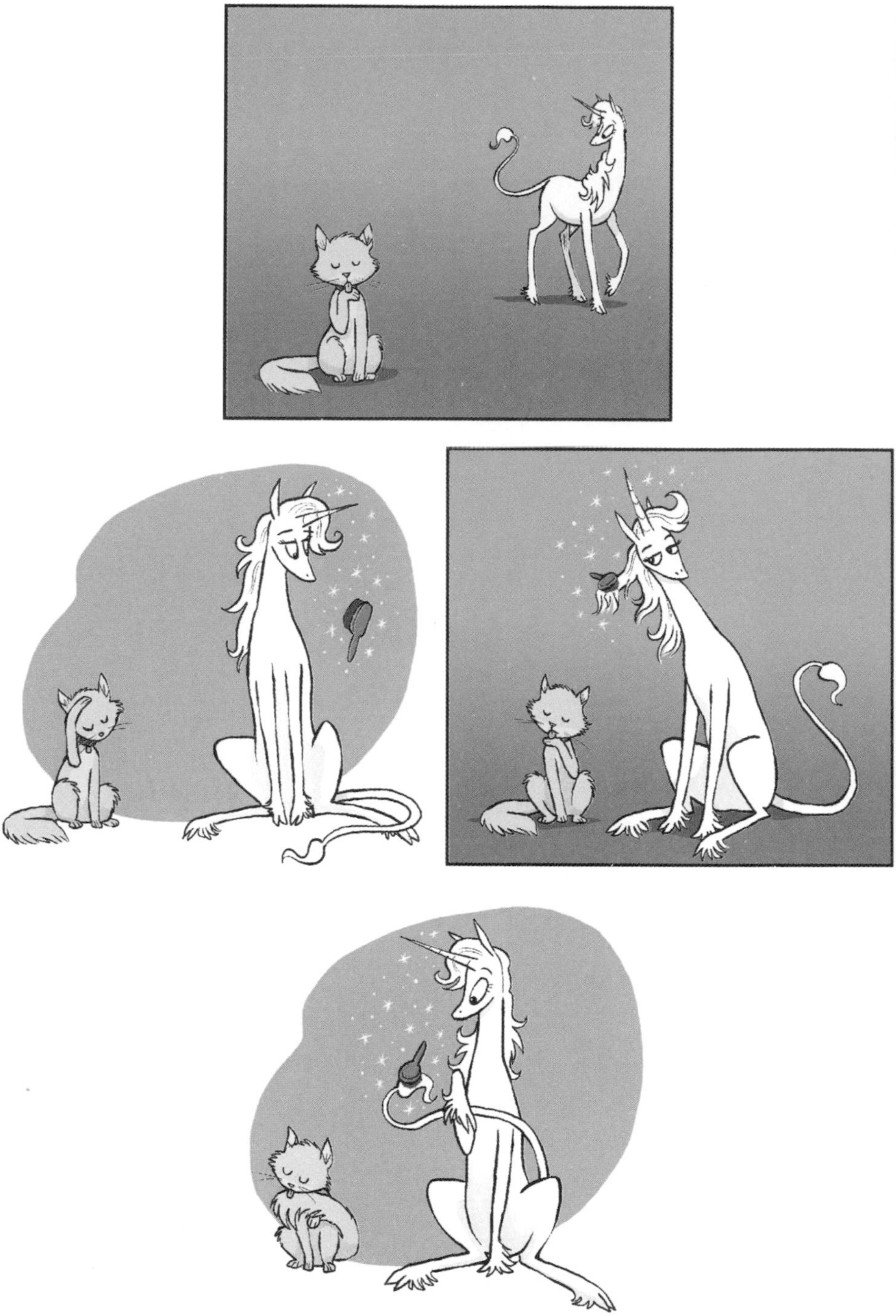

42

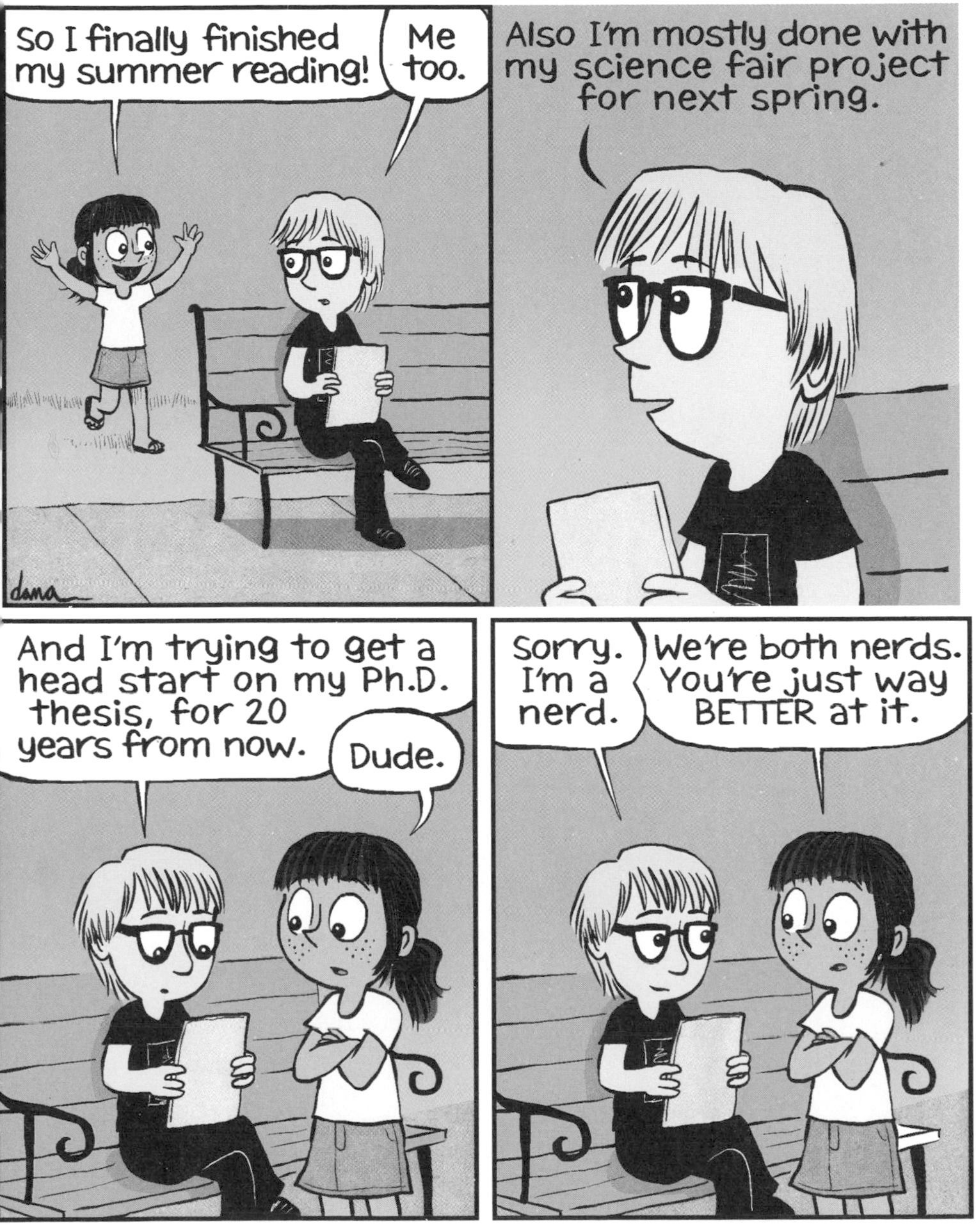
So I finally finished my summer reading!
Me too.
Also I'm mostly done with my science fair project for next spring.
And I'm trying to get a head start on my Ph.D. thesis, for 20 years from now.
Dude.
Sorry. I'm a nerd.
We're both nerds. You're just way BETTER at it.
dana

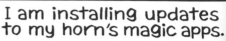

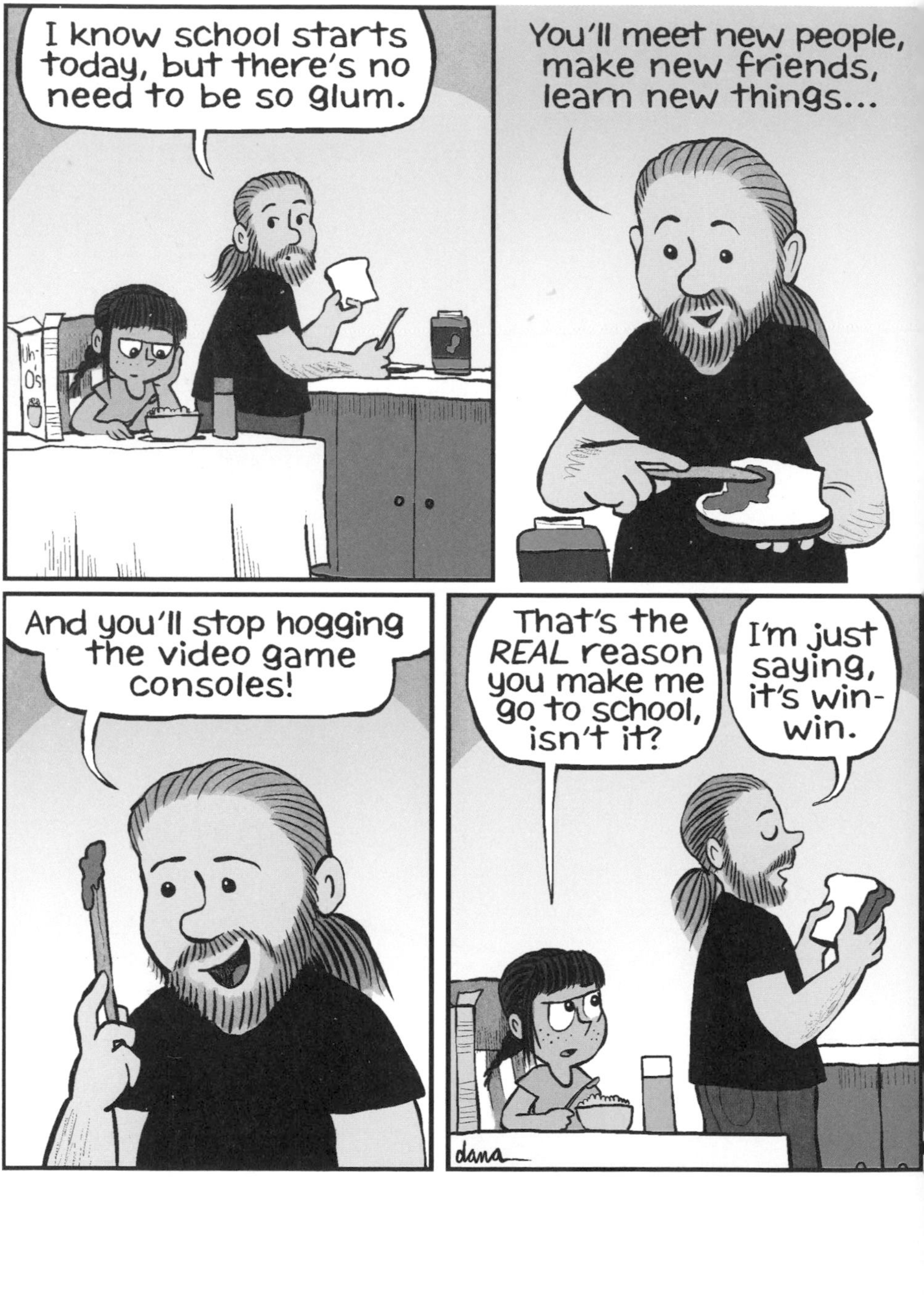
I know school starts today, but there's no need to be so glum.
Uh-O's
You'll meet new people, make new friends, learn new things...
And you'll stop hogging the video game consoles!
That's the *REAL* reason you make me go to school, isn't it?
I'm just saying, it's win-win.
dana

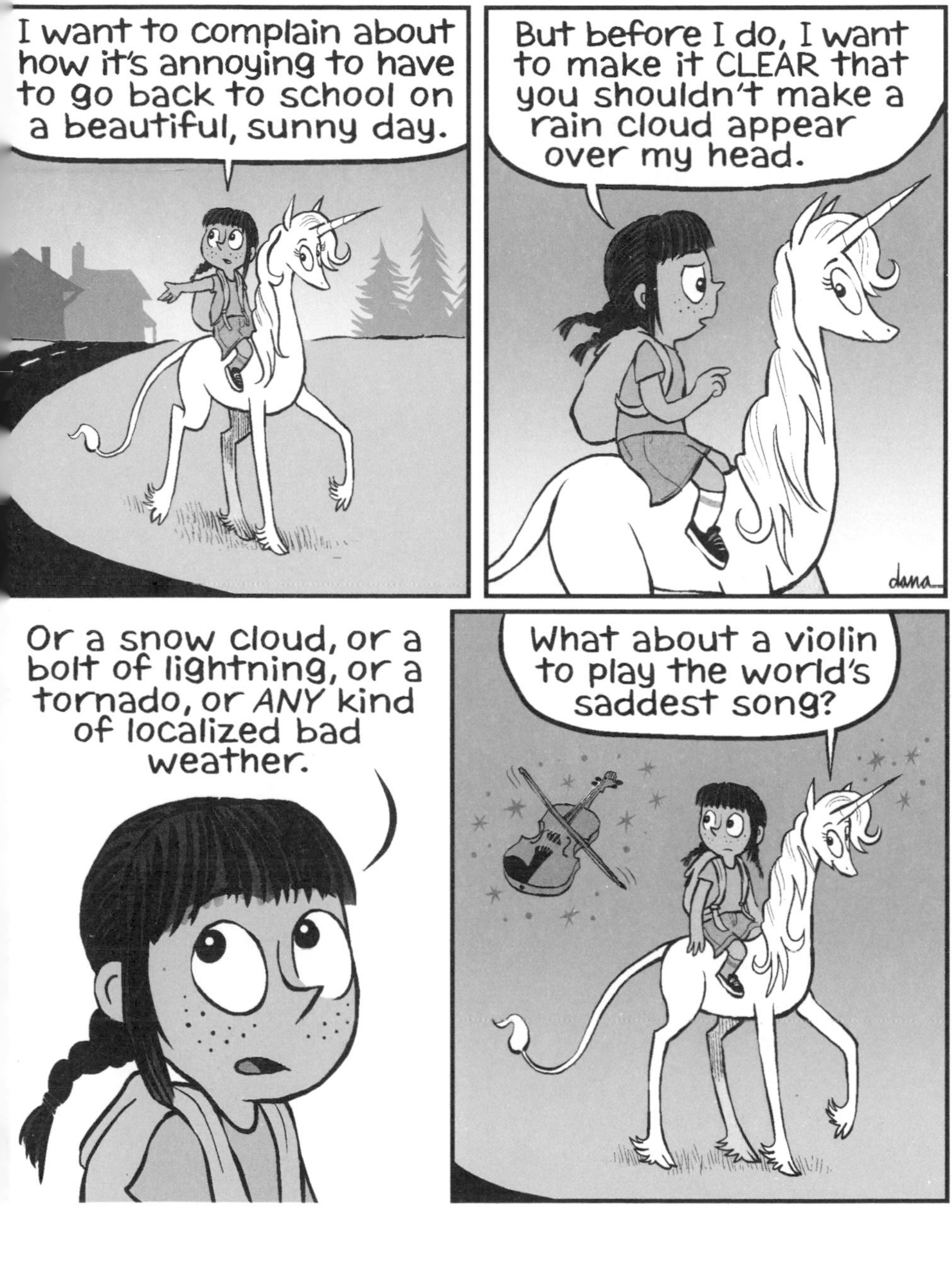
I want to complain about how it's annoying to have to go back to school on a beautiful, sunny day.
But before I do, I want to make it CLEAR that you shouldn't make a rain cloud appear over my head.
dana
Or a snow cloud, or a bolt of lightning, or a tornado, or ANY kind of localized bad weather.
What about a violin to play the world's saddest song?

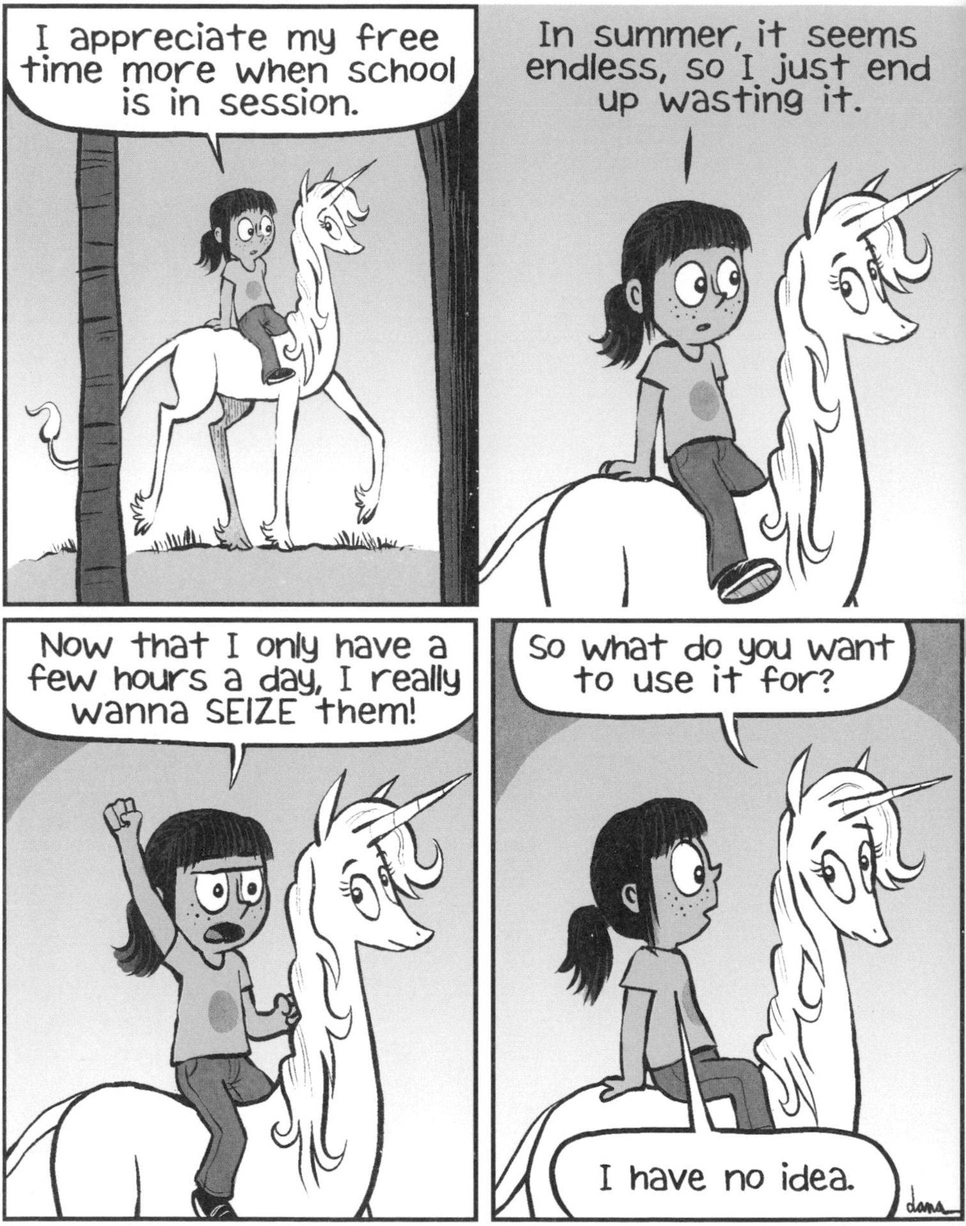
I appreciate my free time more when school is in session.
In summer, it seems endless, so I just end up wasting it.
Now that I only have a few hours a day, I really wanna SEIZE them!
So what do you want to use it for?
I have no idea.
dana

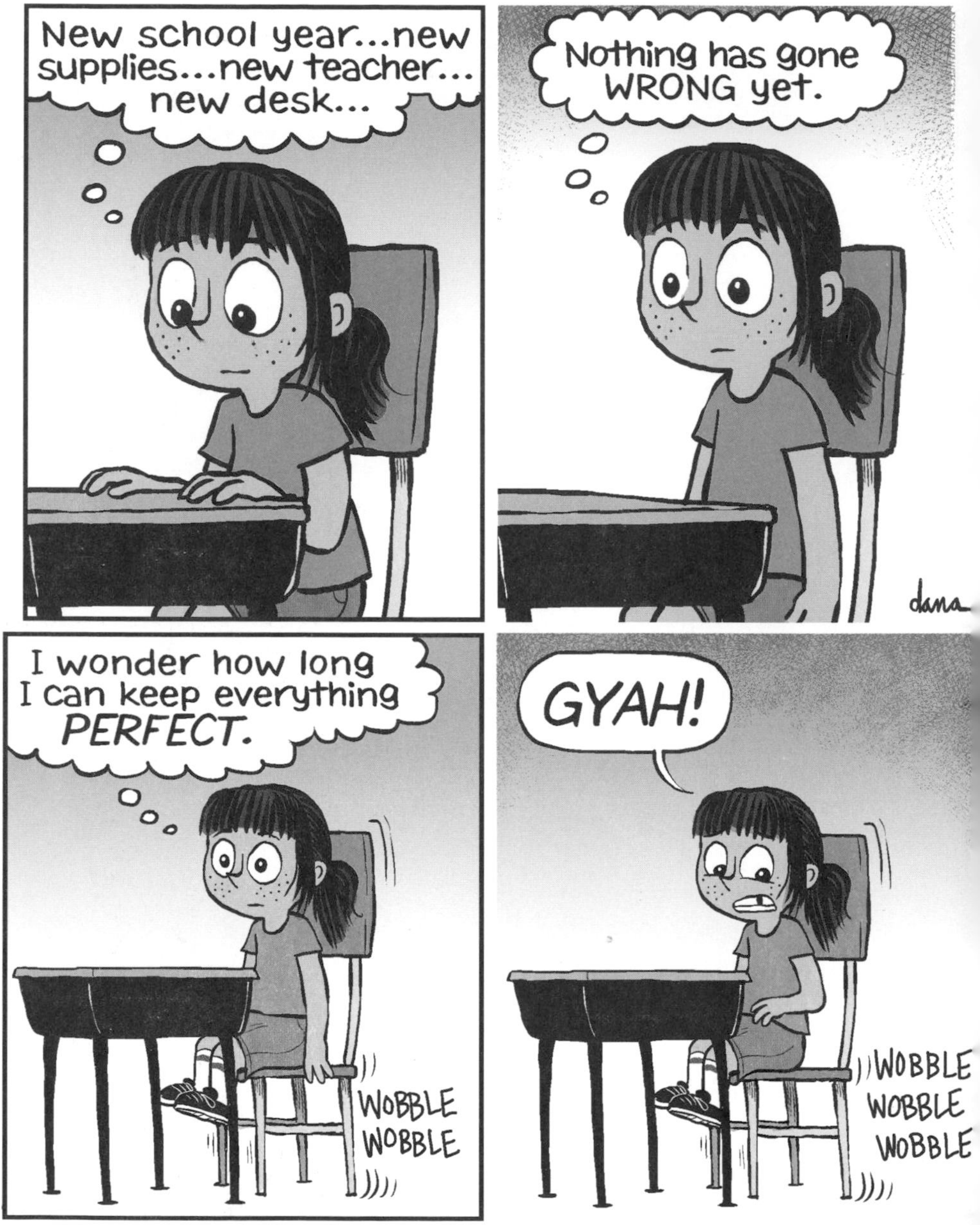
New school year...new supplies...new teacher... new desk...
Nothing has gone WRONG yet.
dana
I wonder how long I can keep everything PERFECT.
WOBBLE WOBBLE
GYAH!
WOBBLE WOBBLE WOBBLE

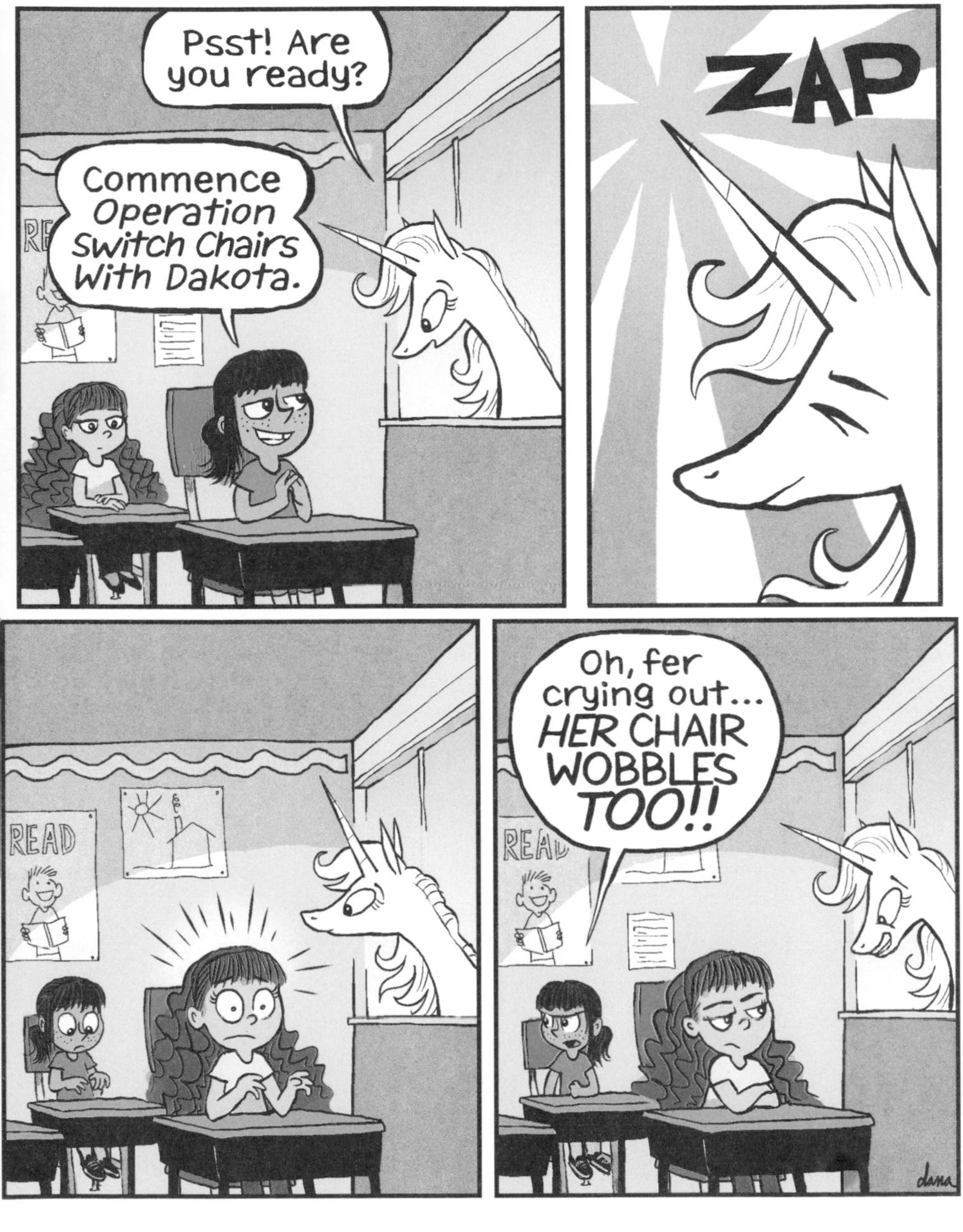
Psst! Are you ready?
Commence *Operation Switch Chairs With Dakota.*
RE
ZAP
READ
READ
Oh, fer crying out... *HER* CHAIR WOBBLES *TOO!!*
dana

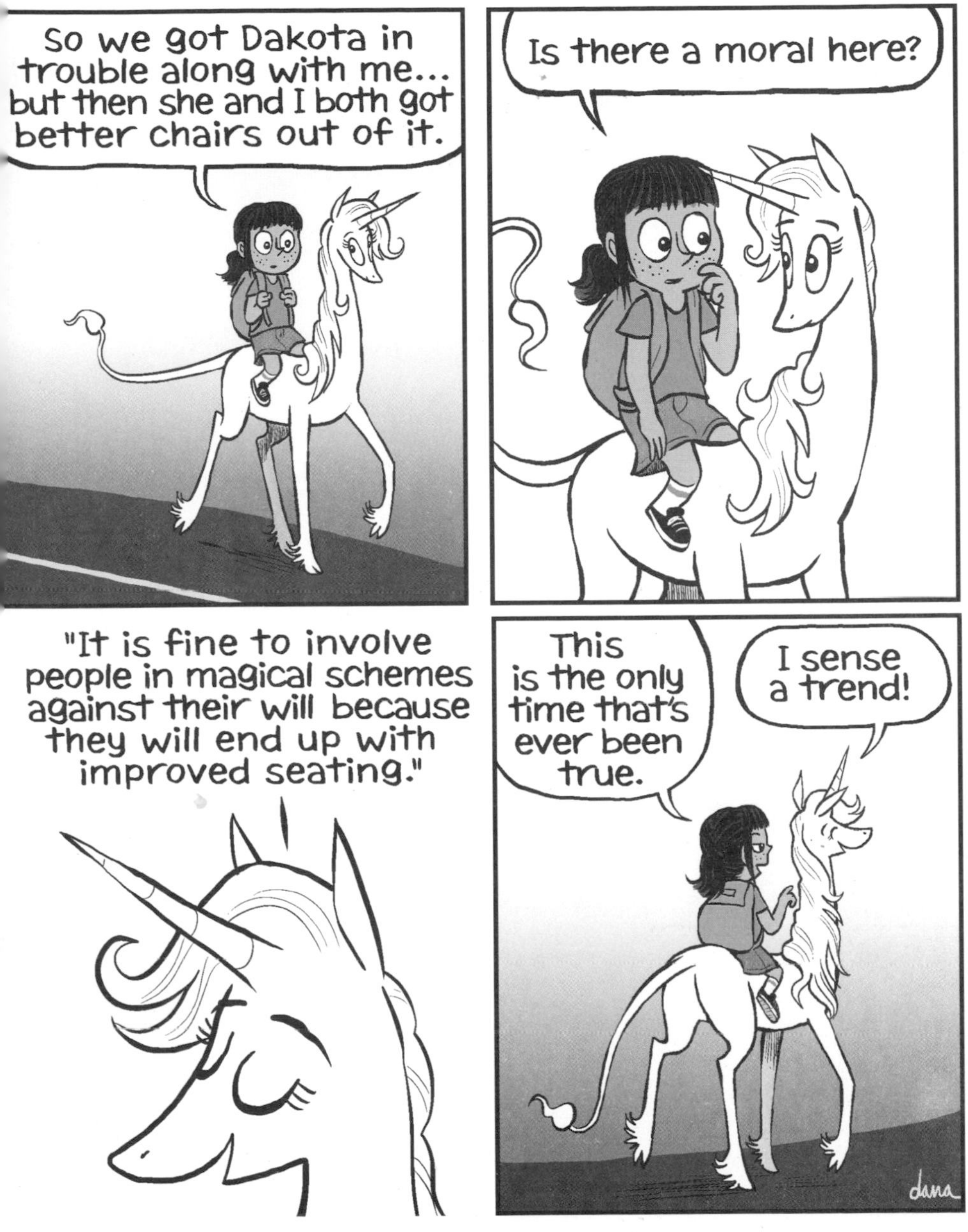
So we got Dakota in trouble along with me... but then she and I both got better chairs out of it.
Is there a moral here?
"It is fine to involve people in magical schemes against their will because they will end up with improved seating."
This is the only time that's ever been true.
I sense a trend!
dana

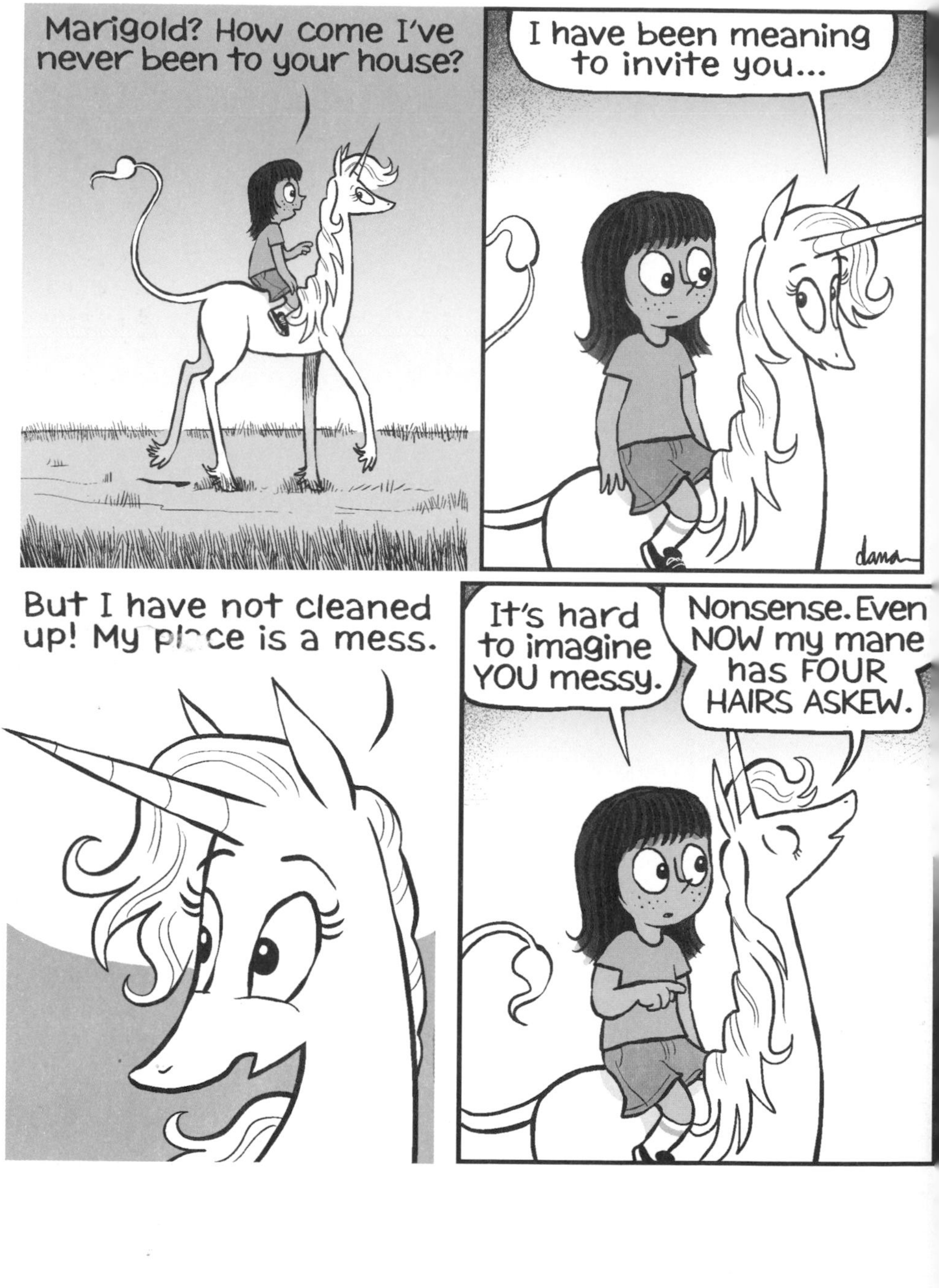
Marigold? How come I've never been to your house?
I have been meaning to invite you...
dana
But I have not cleaned up! My place is a mess.
It's hard to imagine YOU messy.
Nonsense. Even NOW my mane has FOUR HAIRS ASKEW.

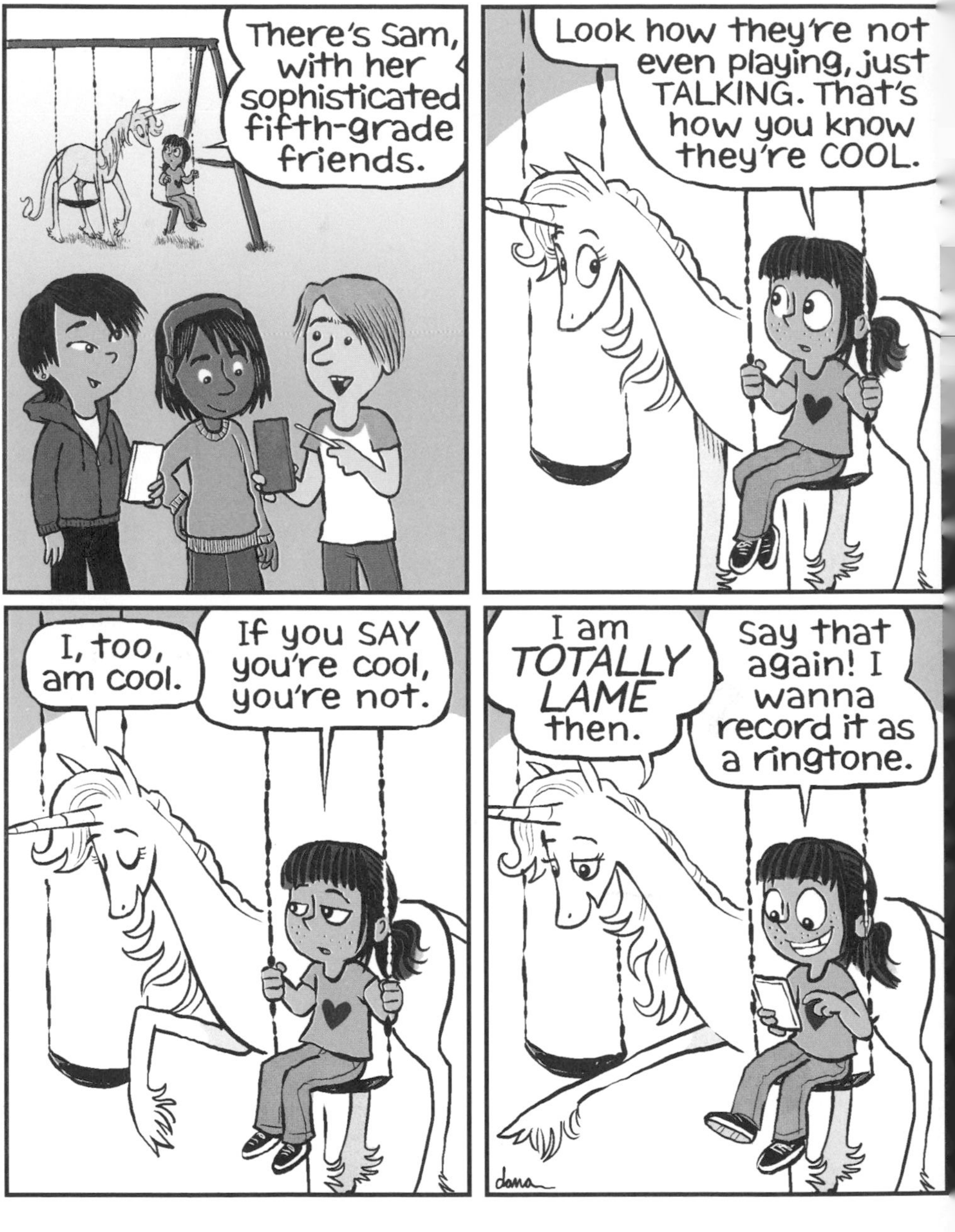
There's Sam, with her sophisticated fifth-grade friends.
Look how they're not even playing, just TALKING. That's how you know they're COOL.
I, too, am cool.
If you SAY you're cool, you're not.
I am *TOTALLY LAME* then.
Say that again! I wanna record it as a ringtone.
dana

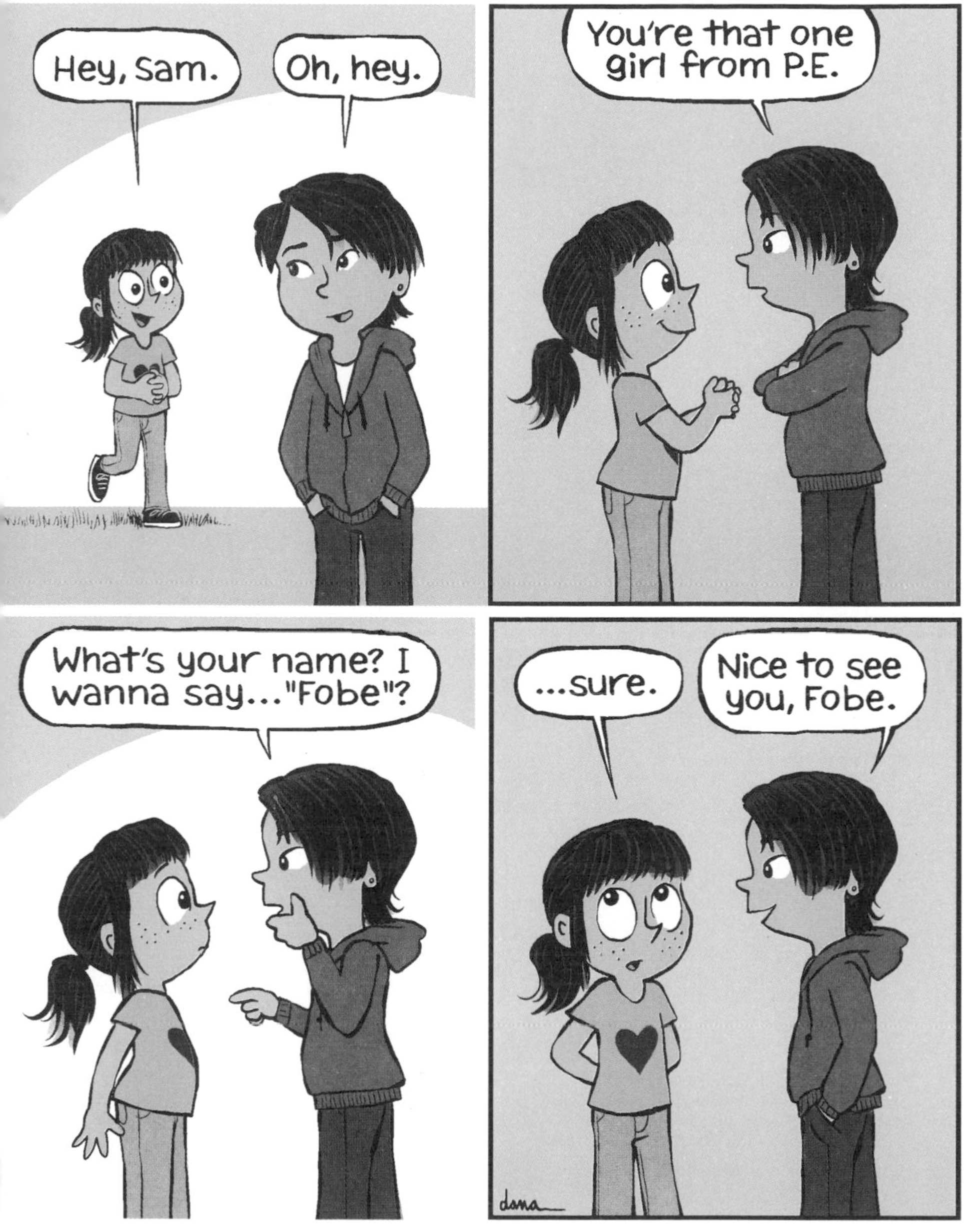
Hey, Sam.
Oh, hey.
You're that one girl from P.E.
What's your name? I wanna say..."Fobe"?
...sure.
Nice to see you, Fobe.

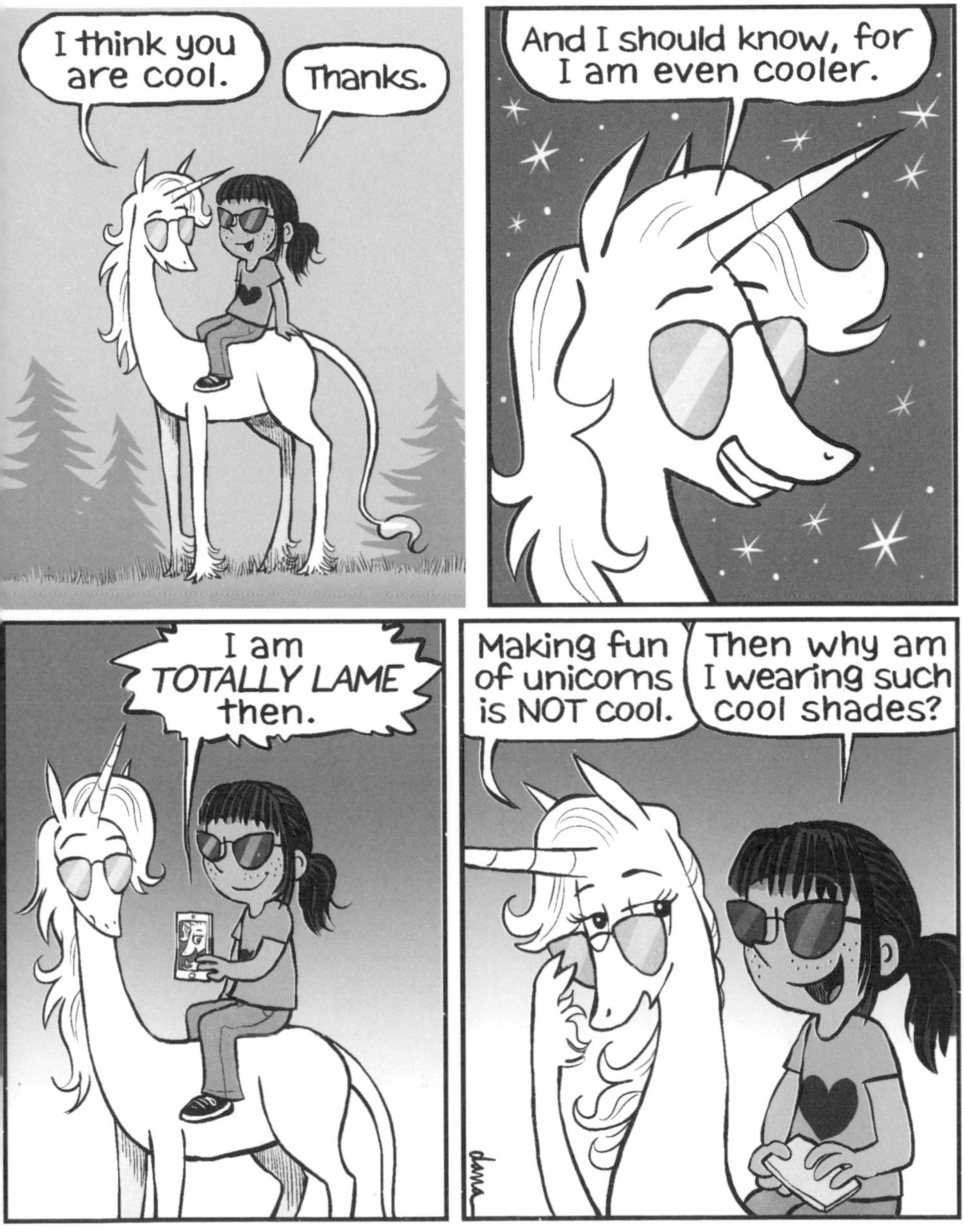
I think you are cool.
Thanks.
And I should know, for I am even cooler.
I am *TOTALLY LAME* then.
Making fun of unicorns is NOT cool.
Then why am I wearing such cool shades?
dana

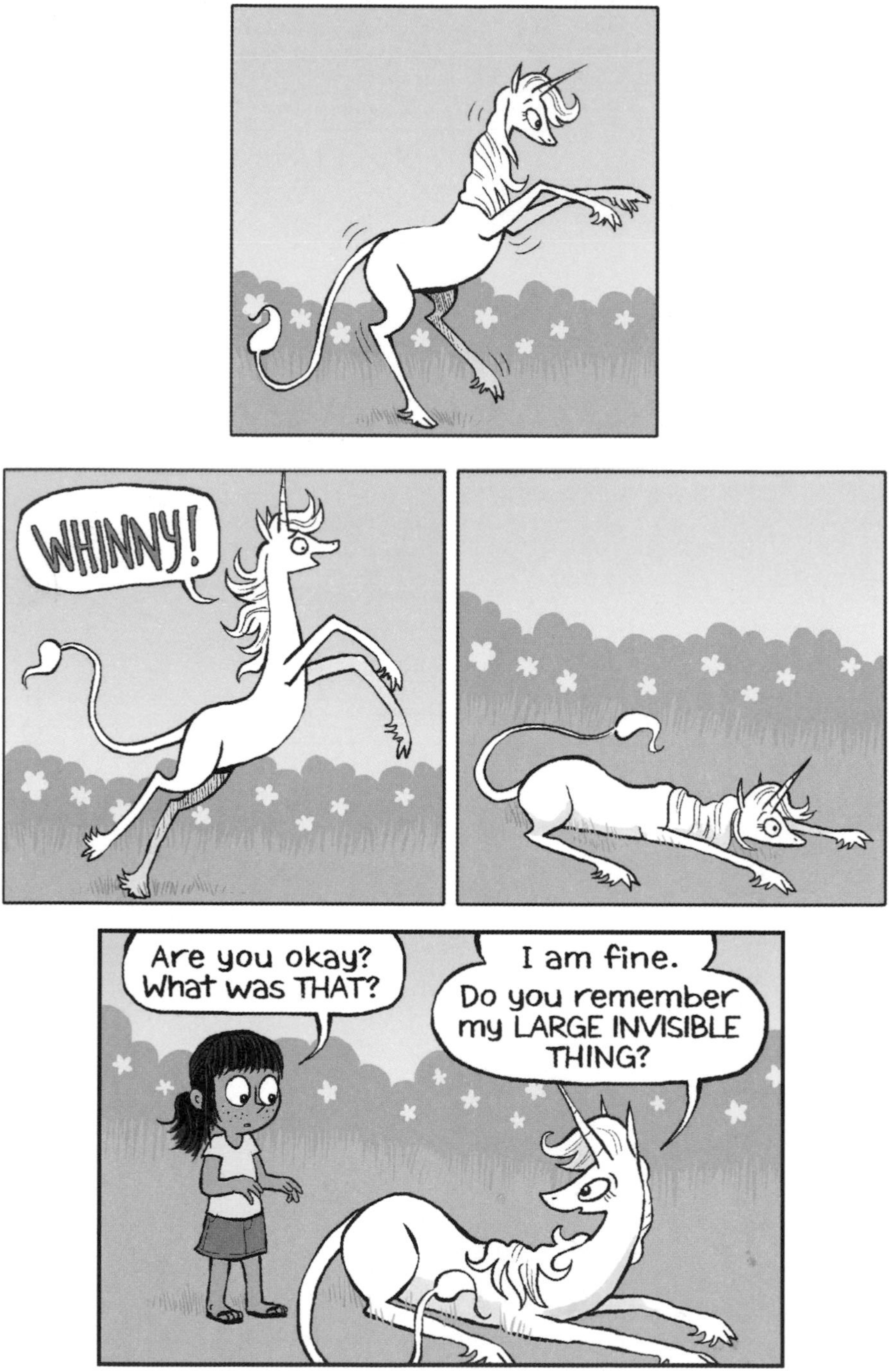
WHINNY!
Are you okay? What was THAT?
I am fine. Do you remember my LARGE INVISIBLE THING?

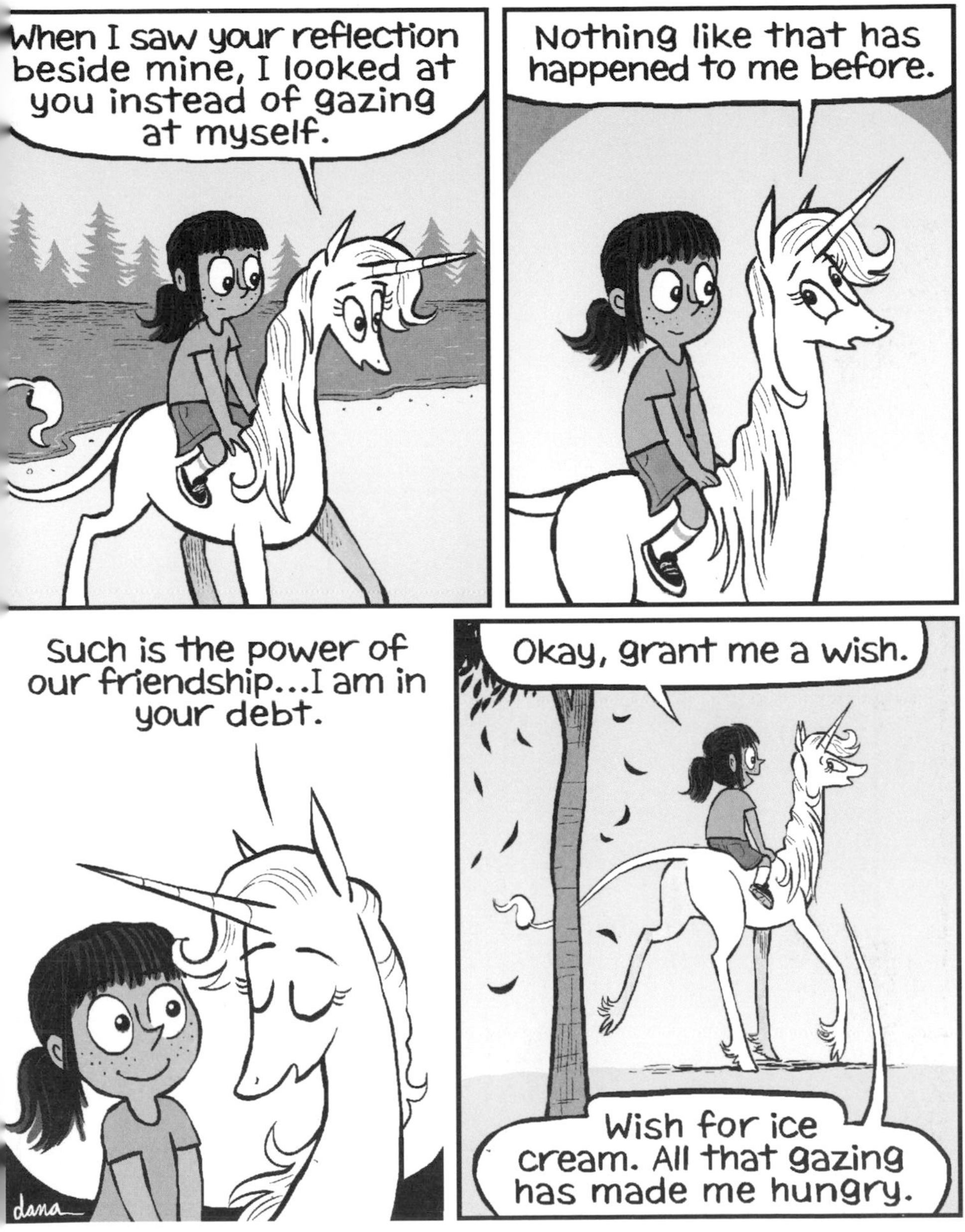
When I saw your reflection beside mine, I looked at you instead of gazing at myself.
Nothing like that has happened to me before.
Such is the power of our friendship...I am in your debt.
Okay, grant me a wish.
Wish for ice cream. All that gazing has made me hungry.
dana

It's RAINBOW CASTLE DEMOLISHER. It's my favorite underrated classic video game.

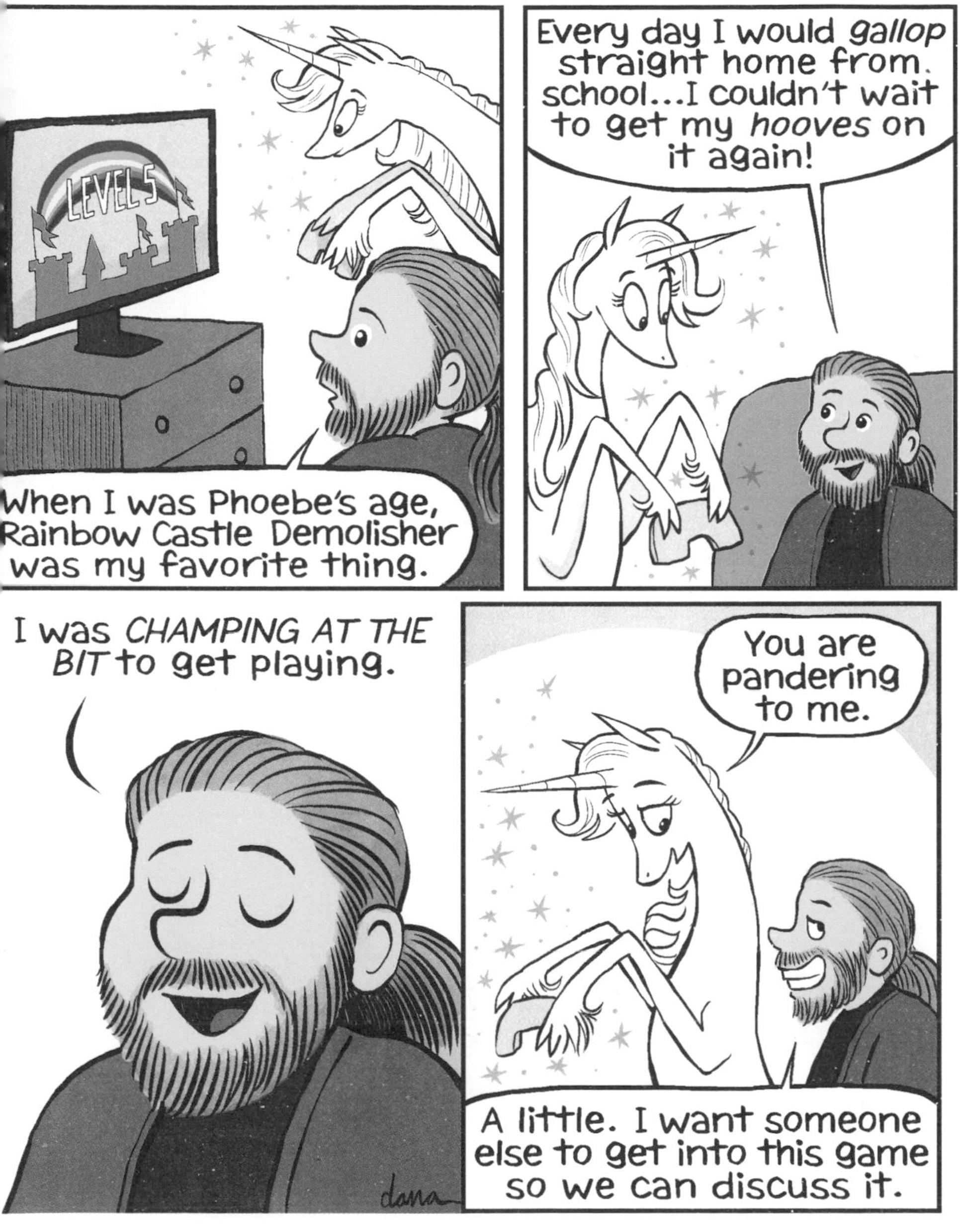
LEVEL 5
When I was Phoebe's age, Rainbow Castle Demolisher was my favorite thing.
Every day I would *gallop* straight home from school...I couldn't wait to get my *hooves* on it again!
I was *CHAMPING AT THE BIT* to get playing.
You are pandering to me.
A little. I want someone else to get into this game so we can discuss it.
dana

It was fun playing video games with you this afternoon, Mr. Howell.

Call me Ethan.

You can't call him that! That's his NAME.

You can't be friends with him on your OWN. You should just think of him as "Phoebe's dad."

Afraid your old man might actually be cool?

"Old man." Go with that.

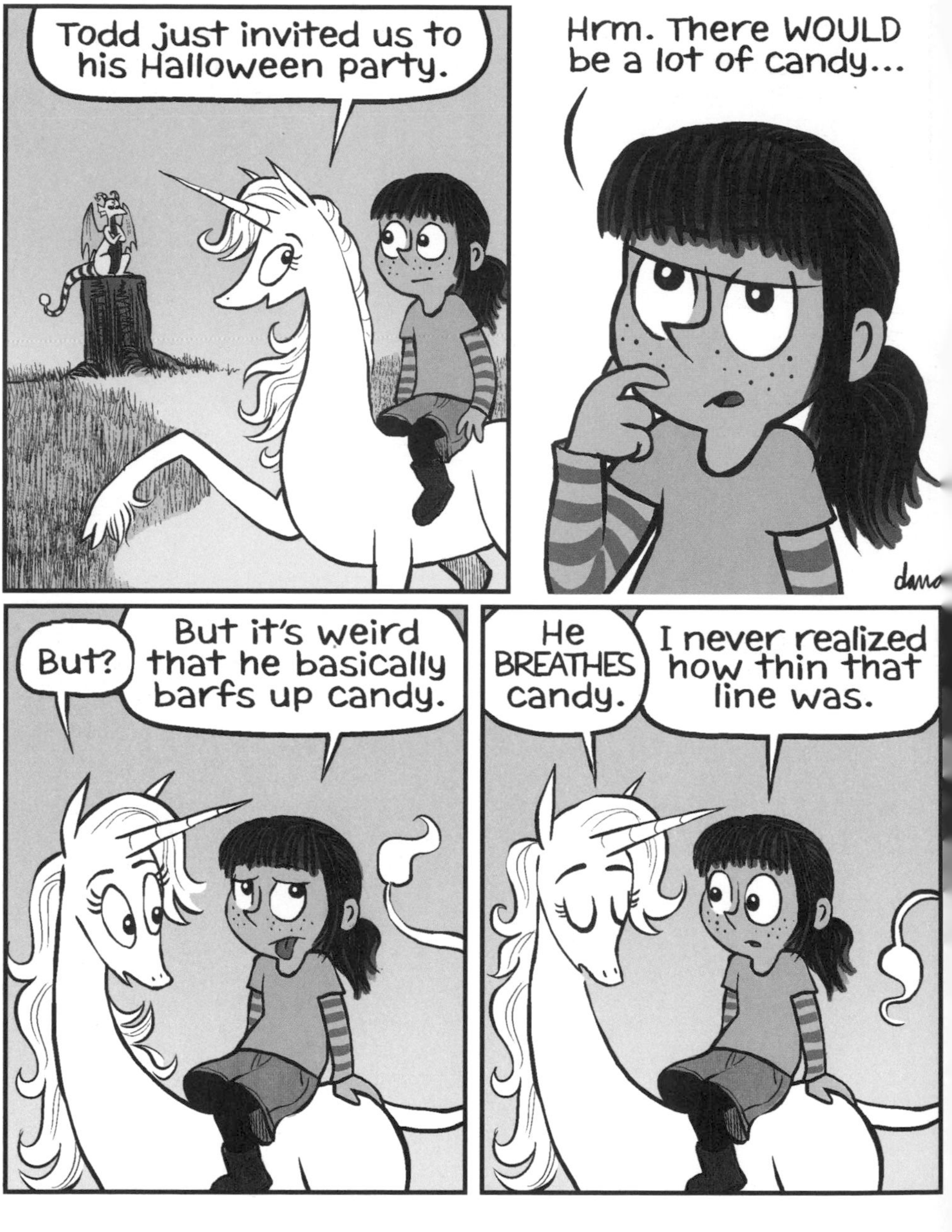
Todd just invited us to his Halloween party.
Hrm. There WOULD be a lot of candy...
But?
But it's weird that he basically barfs up candy.
He BREATHES candy.
I never realized how thin that line was.
dano

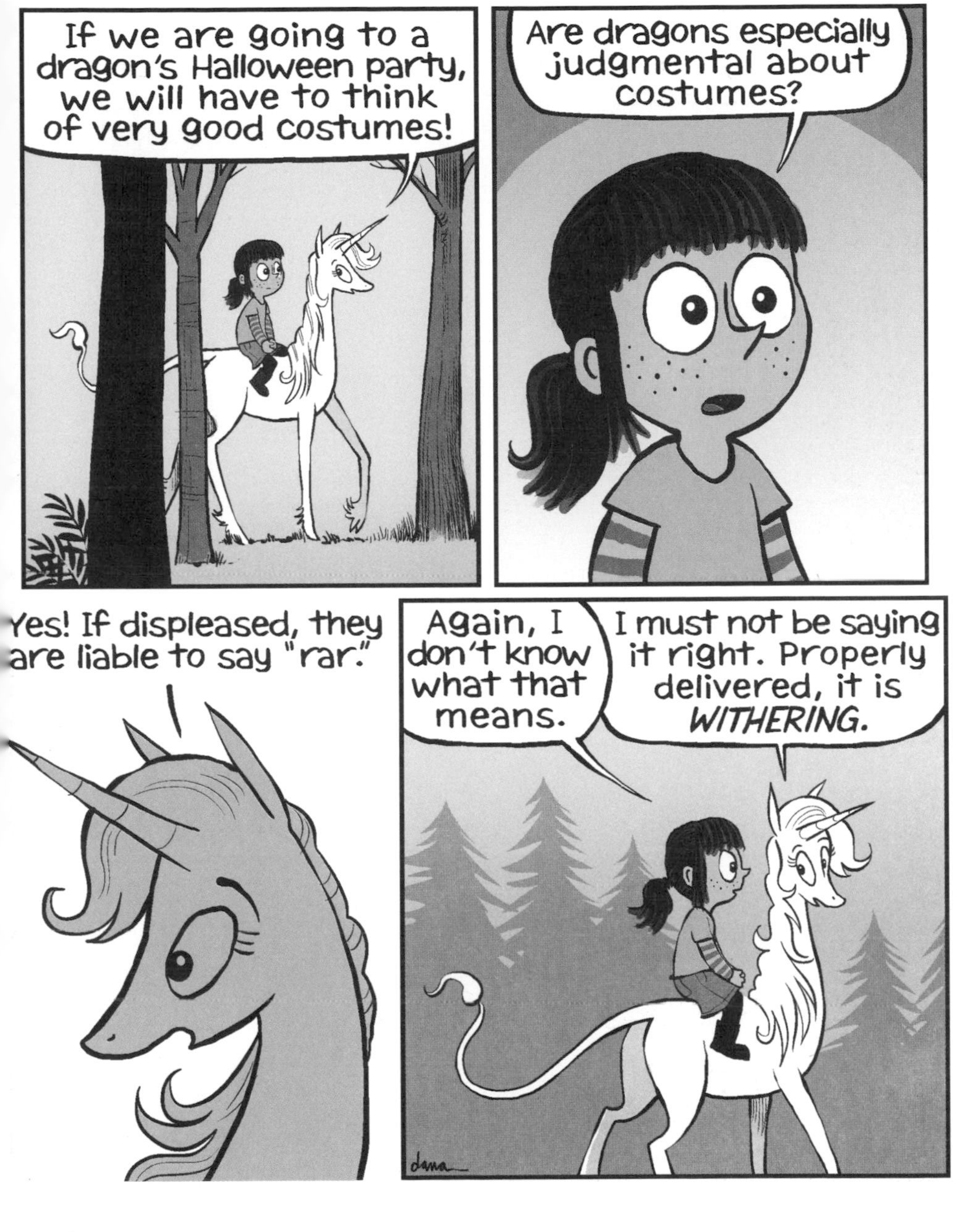

If we are going to a dragon's Halloween party, we will have to think of very good costumes!
Are dragons especially judgmental about costumes?
Yes! If displeased, they are liable to say "rar."
Again, I don't know what that means.
I must not be saying it right. Properly delivered, it is WITHERING.

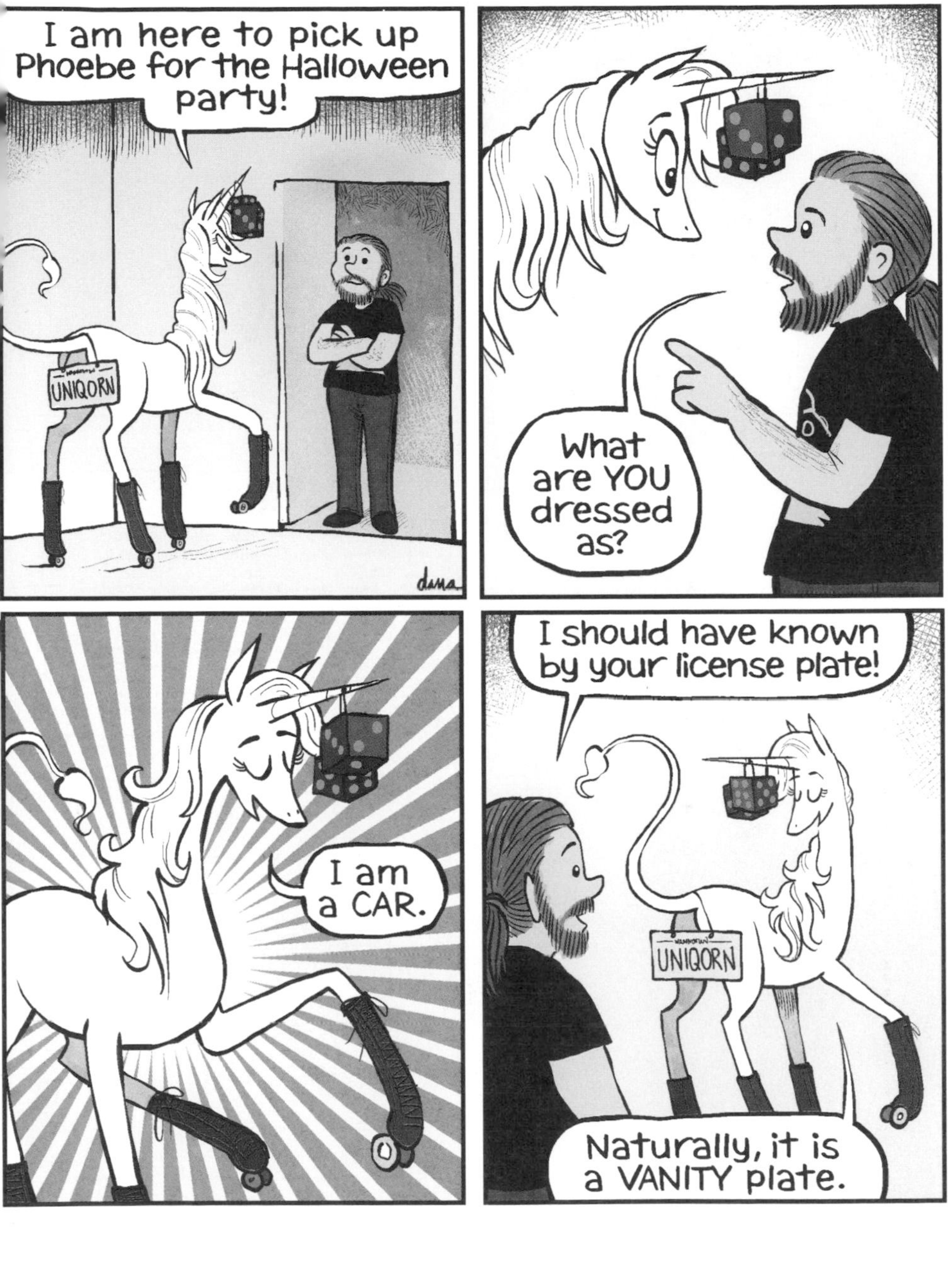
I am here to pick up Phoebe for the Halloween party!
UNIQORN
dana
What are YOU dressed as?
I am a CAR.
I should have known by your license plate!
UNIQORN
Naturally, it is a VANITY plate.

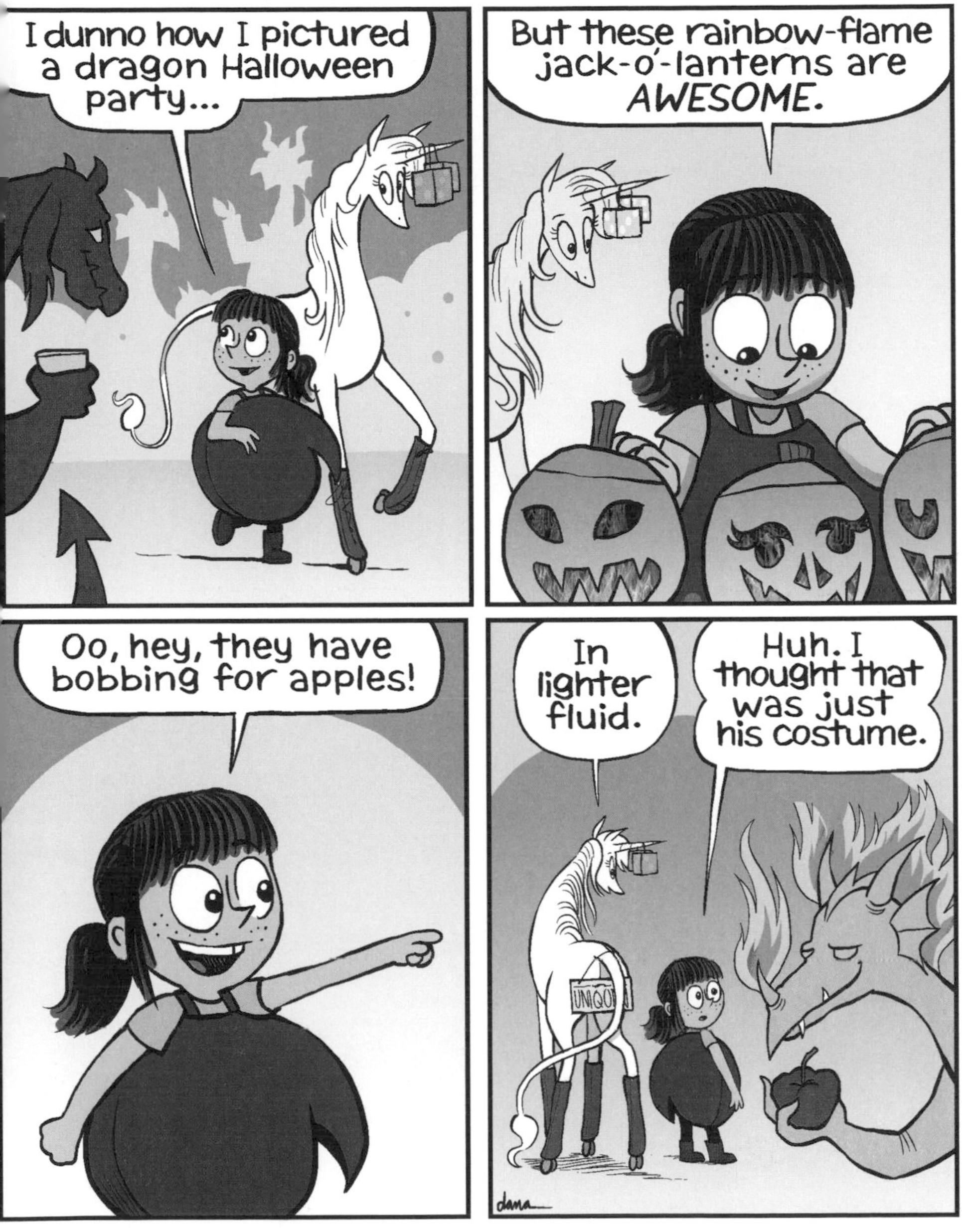
I dunno how I pictured a dragon Halloween party...
But these rainbow-flame jack-o'-lanterns are *AWESOME.*
Oo, hey, they have bobbing for apples!
In lighter fluid.
Huh. I thought that was just his costume.
UNICORN
dana

Dakota? What are YOU doing here?

Okay, like, I was walking home from school...

And this really small dragon came up to me and went "RAR."

And...the subtitles invited me to this party.

Subtitles?

Todd asked me to cast my magical SUBTITULAR ENCHANTMENT.

Rar.

Unicorns are convenient like that.

It's weird that Dakota got invited to a dragon Halloween party.

The rumor is that she and Queen Prunella von Bläart of the goblins have been HANGING OUT TOGETHER at the mall.

At the MALL?

Either the mall, or the EMPORIUM of EXPLODING HATS.

Is that a real place?

The goblin word "BLART" can have either meaning.

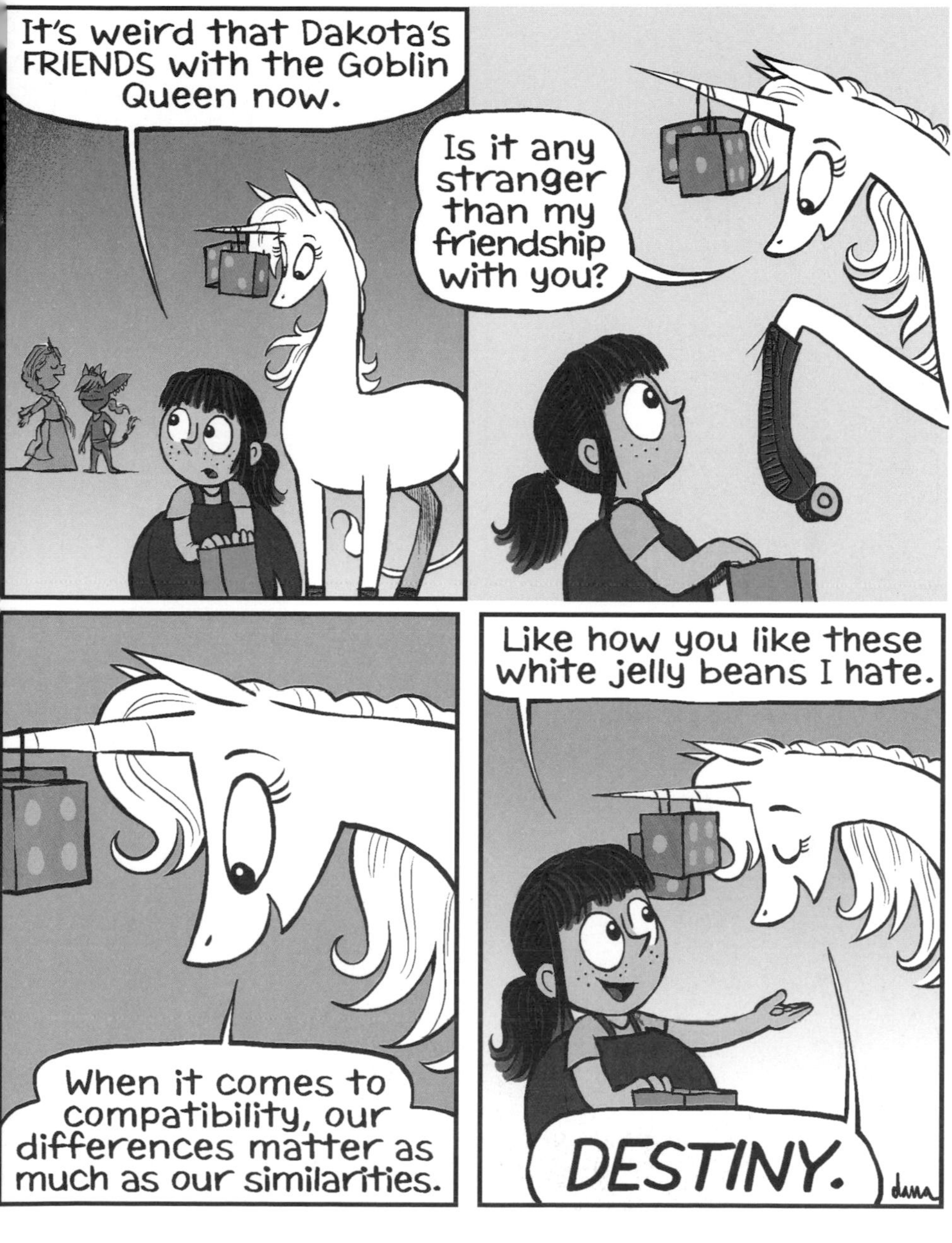
It's weird that Dakota's FRIENDS with the Goblin Queen now.
Is it any stranger than my friendship with you?
When it comes to compatibility, our differences matter as much as our similarities.
Like how you like these white jelly beans I hate.
DESTINY.
dana

All night everybody kept asking me if I was a comma. I'm CLEARLY an apostrophe.

It is a more familiar punctuation mark, to those of us who do not use contractions.

In fact, we regard the apostrophe as an abomination, and your costume as a profound insult!

You told me you LIKED this costume.

Oh, I do! I am just pulling your comma tail.

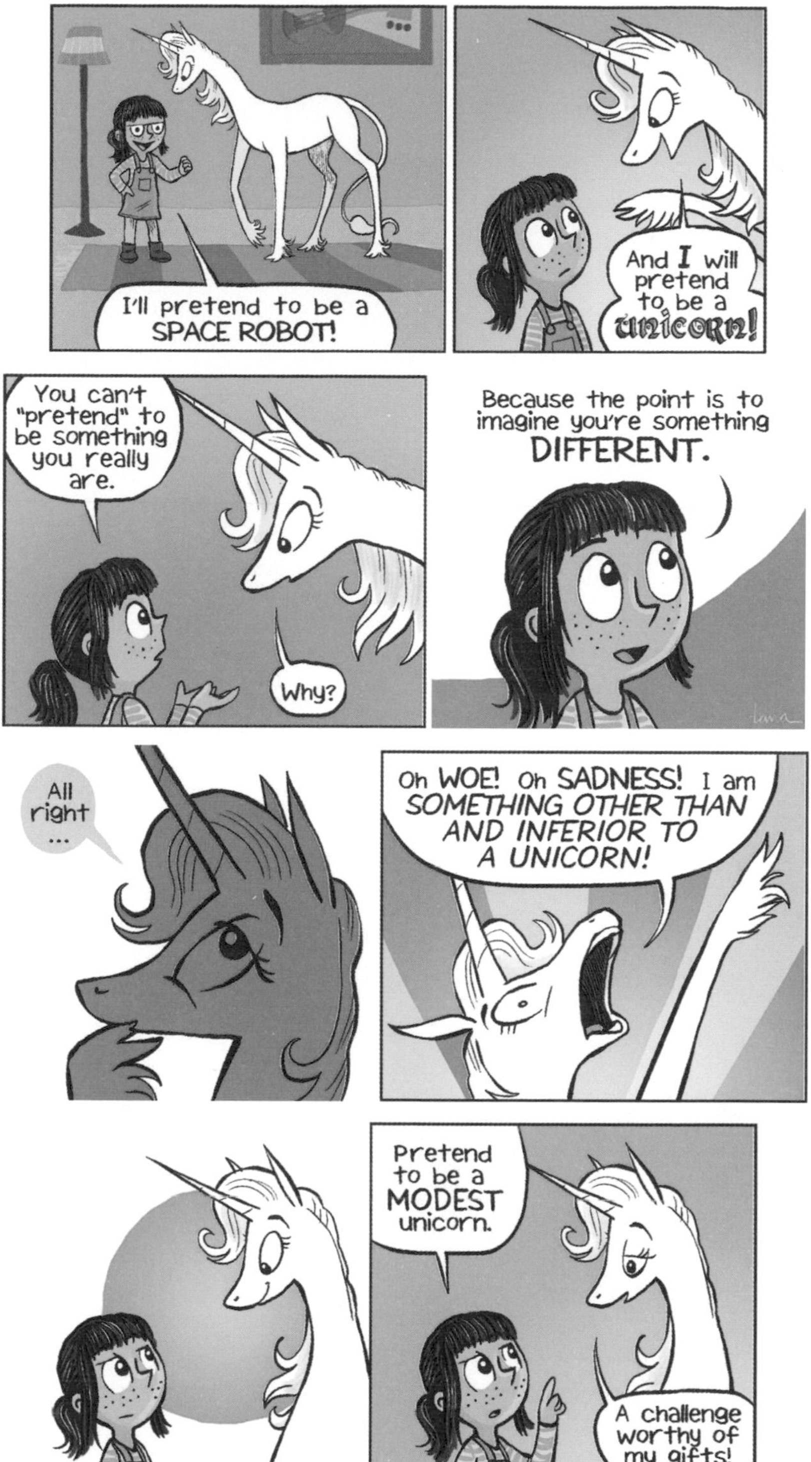
I'll pretend to be a SPACE ROBOT!
And I will pretend to be a UNICORN!
You can't "pretend" to be something you really are.
Why?
Because the point is to imagine you're something DIFFERENT.
All right ...
Oh WOE! Oh SADNESS! I am SOMETHING OTHER THAN AND INFERIOR TO A UNICORN!
Pretend to be a MODEST unicorn.
A challenge worthy of my gifts!

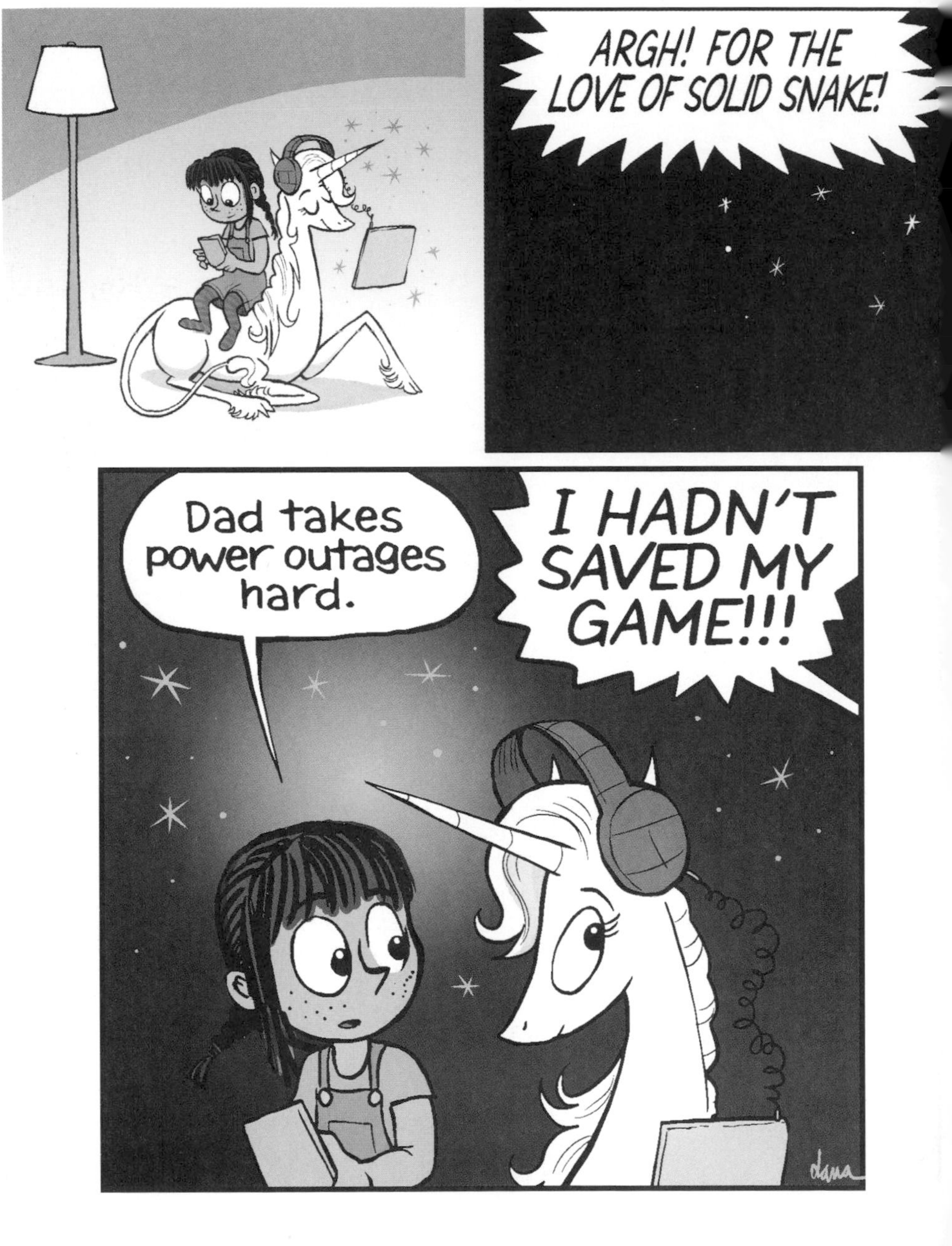
ARGH! FOR THE LOVE OF SOLID SNAKE!
Dad takes power outages hard.
I HADN'T SAVED MY GAME!!!
dana

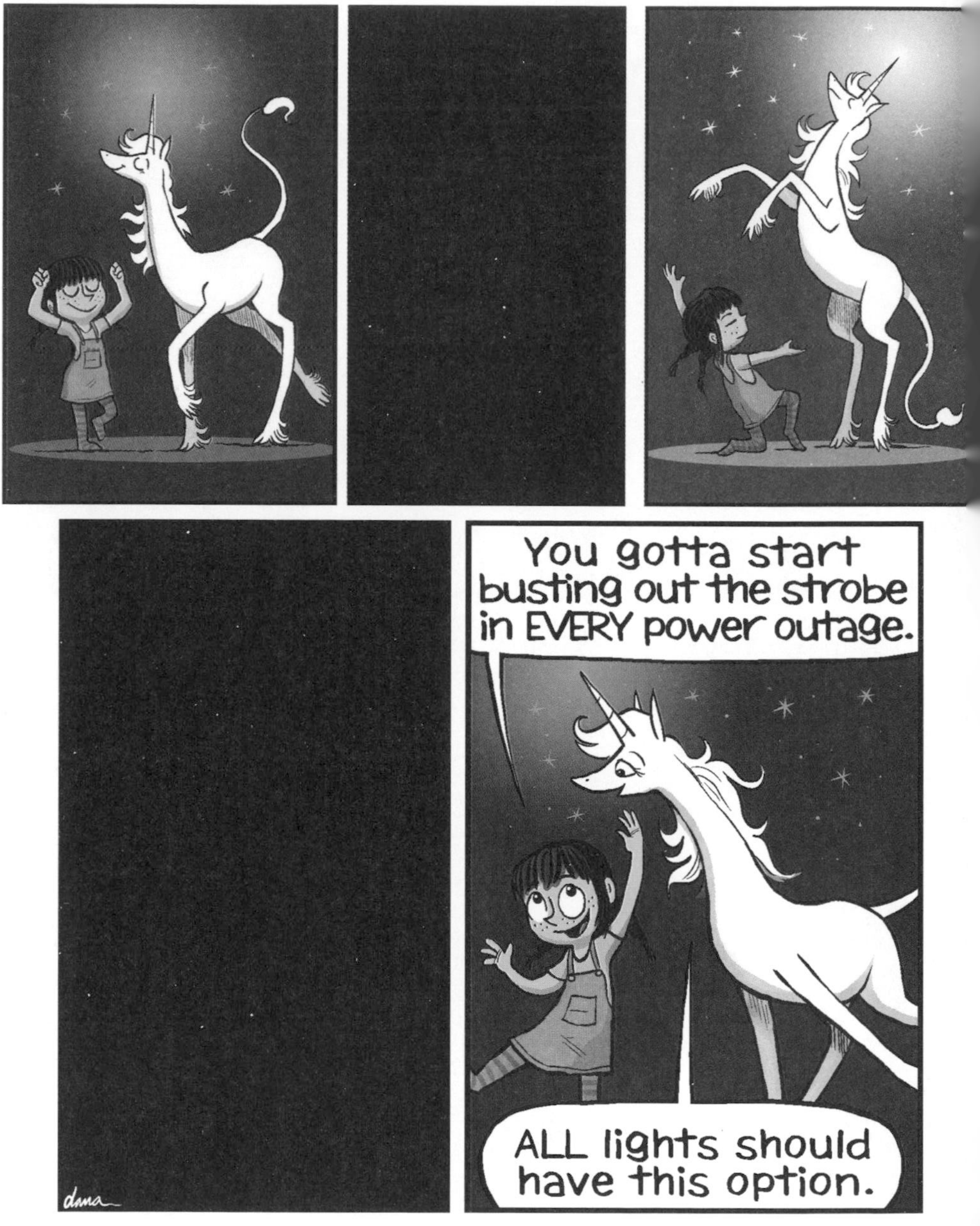
You gotta start busting out the strobe in EVERY power outage.
ALL lights should have this option.
dana

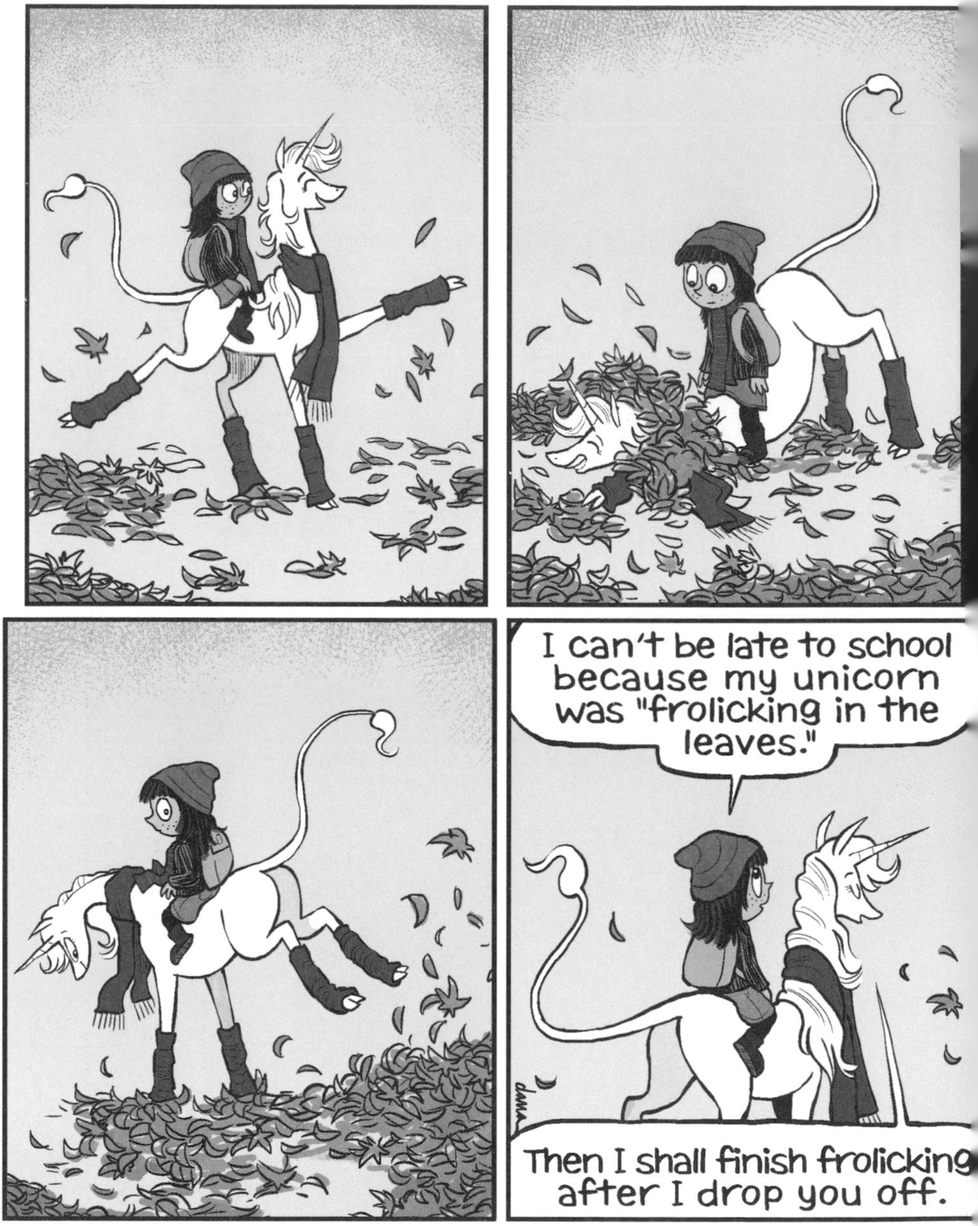
I can't be late to school because my unicorn was "frolicking in the leaves."
Then I shall finish frolicking after I drop you off.

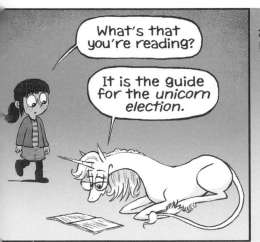

What's that you're reading?

It is the guide for the *unicorn election*.

Candidates for *High Unicorn* are rated based on loveliness, poise, number of sparkles, and overall magnificence.

And everybody votes for themselves, right?

Democracy is imperfect, but it is the best system we have.

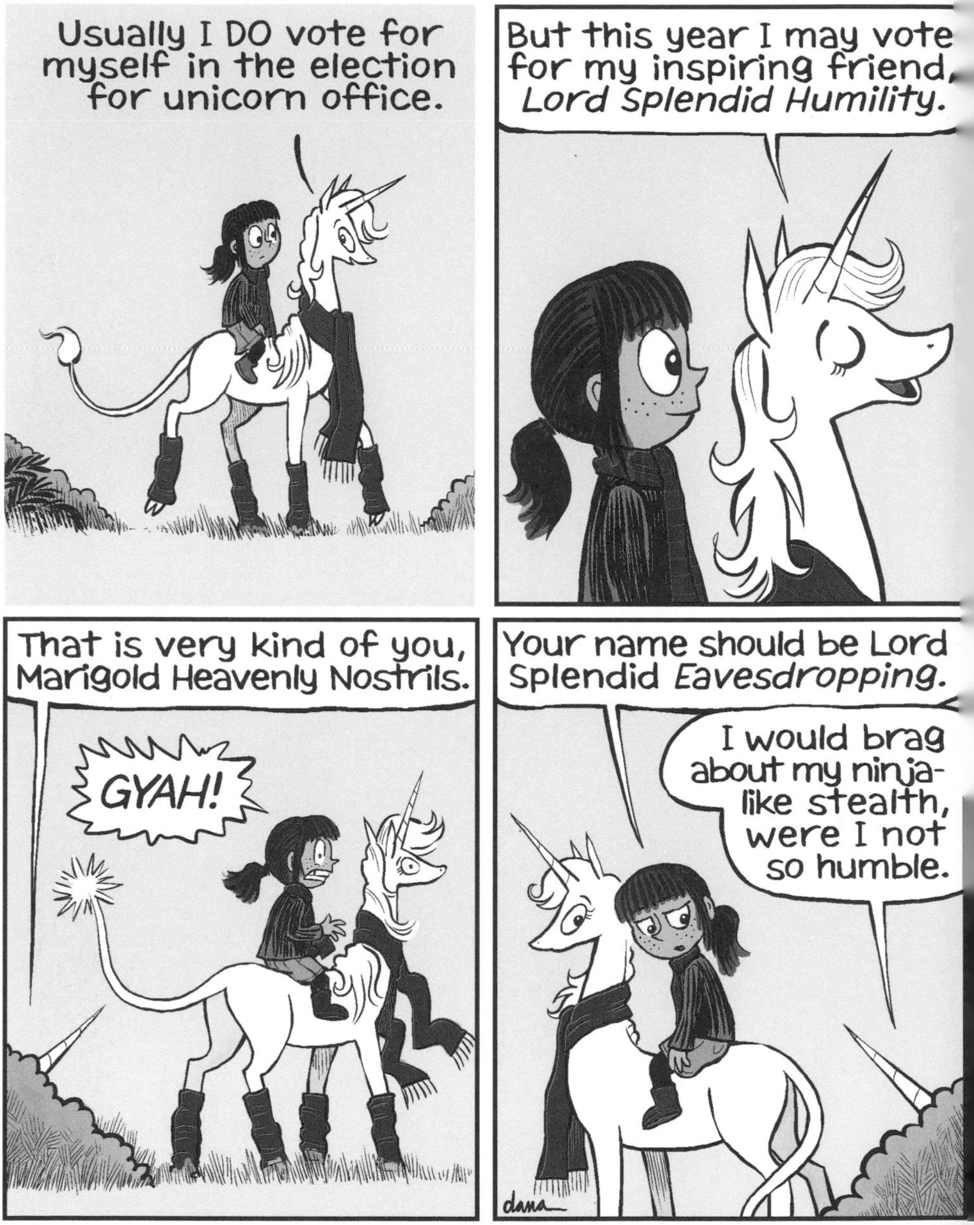
Usually I DO vote for myself in the election for unicorn office.
But this year I may vote for my inspiring friend, *Lord Splendid Humility.*
That is very kind of you, Marigold Heavenly Nostrils.
GYAH!
Your name should be Lord Splendid *Eavesdropping.*
I would brag about my ninja-like stealth, were I not so humble.
dana

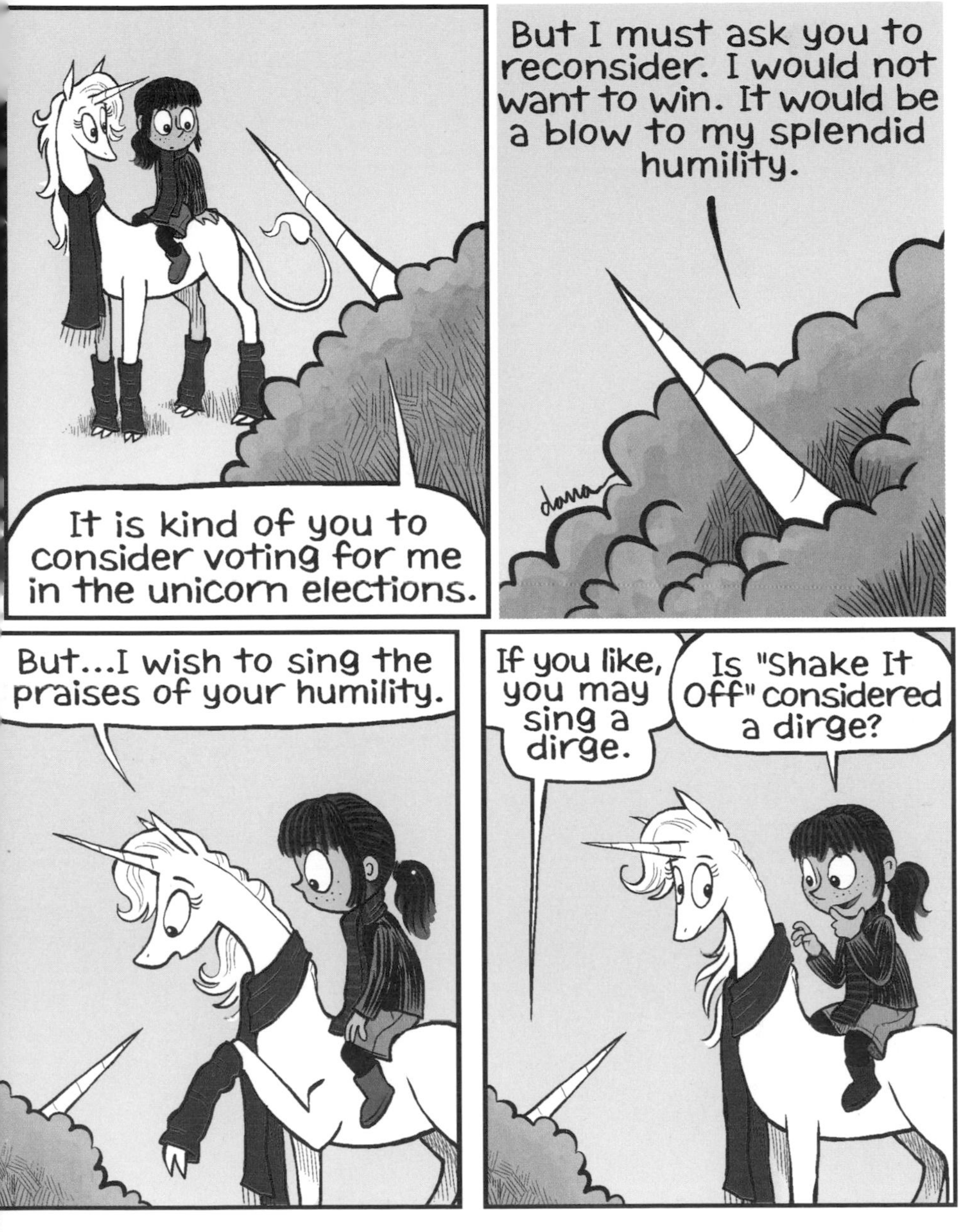
It is kind of you to consider voting for me in the unicorn elections.
But I must ask you to reconsider. I would not want to win. It would be a blow to my splendid humility.
But...I wish to sing the praises of your humility.
If you like, you may sing a dirge.
Is "Shake It Off" considered a dirge?

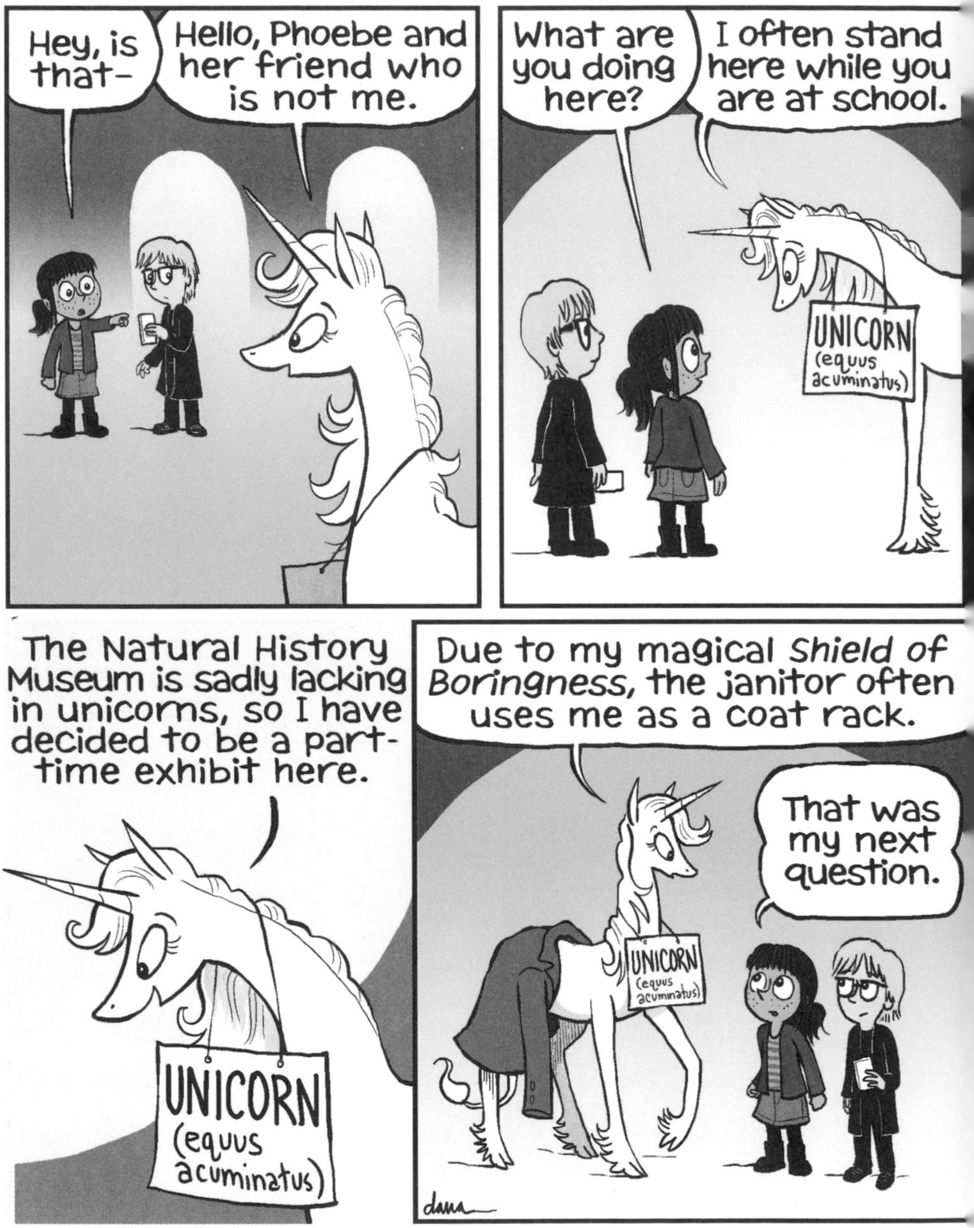
Hey, is that-
Hello, Phoebe and her friend who is not me.
What are you doing here?
I often stand here while you are at school.
UNICORN (equus acuminatus)
The Natural History Museum is sadly lacking in unicorns, so I have decided to be a part-time exhibit here.
UNICORN (equus acuminatus)
Due to my magical *Shield of Boringness*, the janitor often uses me as a coat rack.
That was my next question.
UNICORN (equus acuminatus)
dana

119

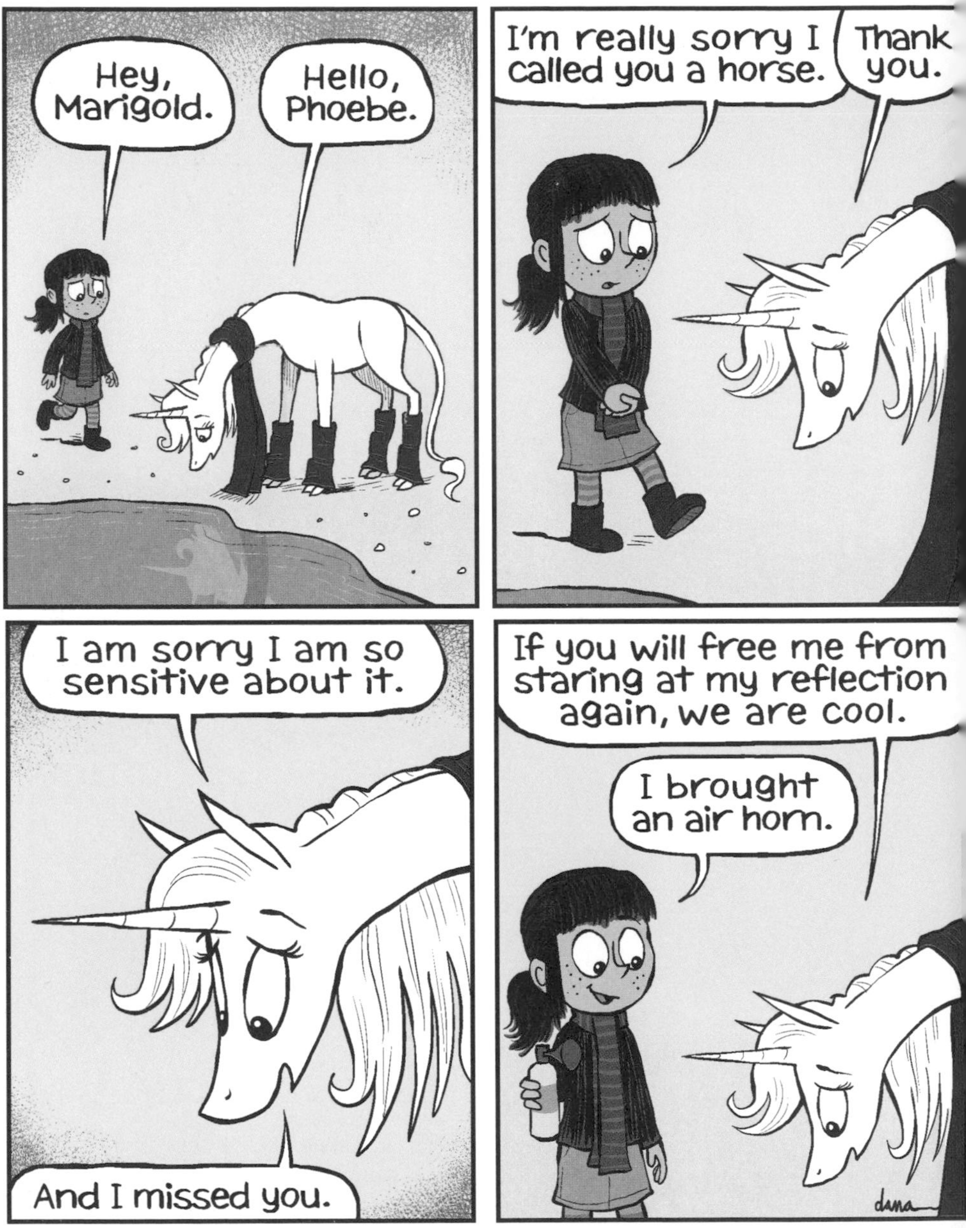
Hey, Marigold.
Hello, Phoebe.
I'm really sorry I called you a horse.
Thank you.
I am sorry I am so sensitive about it.
And I missed you.
If you will free me from staring at my reflection again, we are cool.
I brought an air horn.
dana

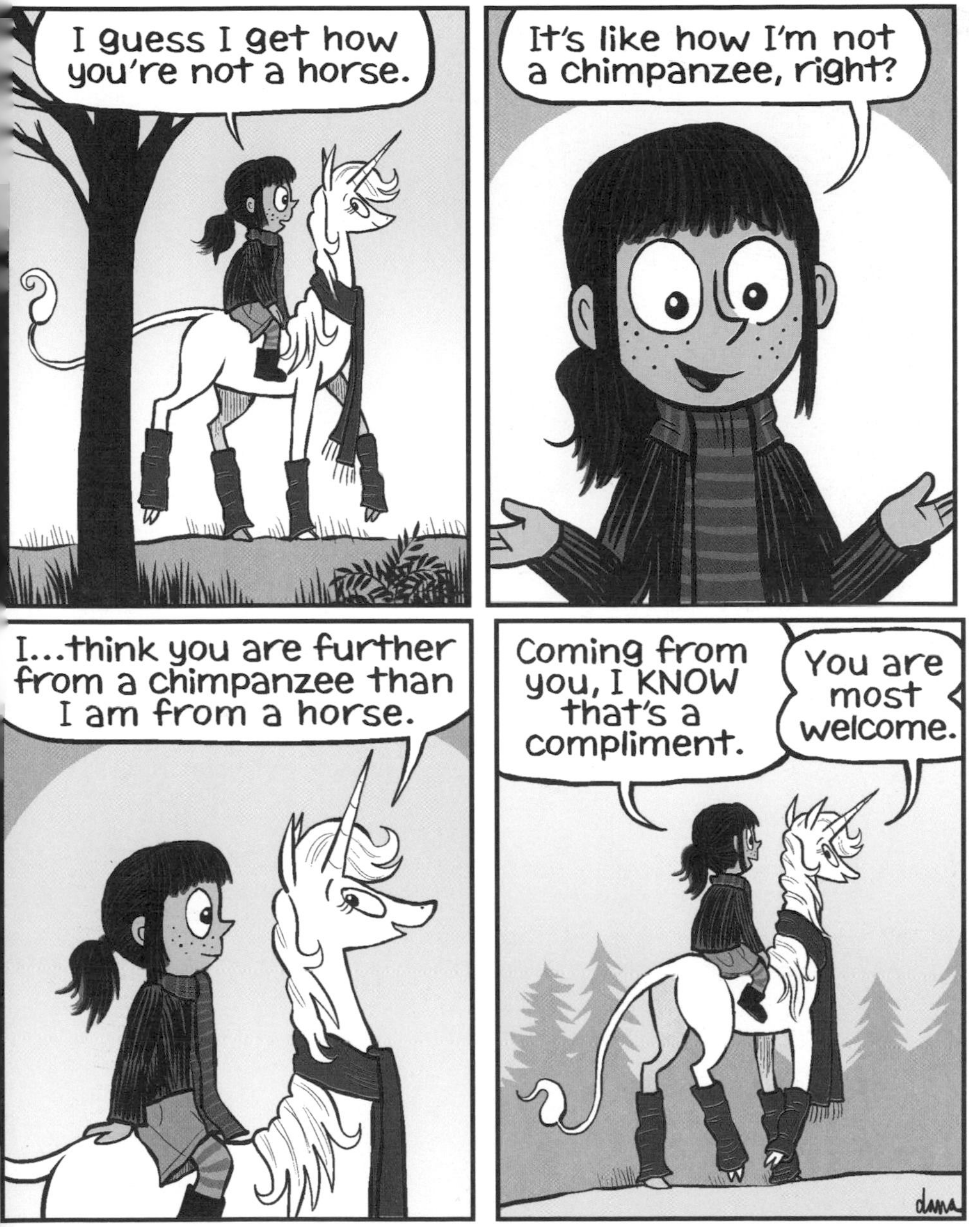
I guess I get how you're not a horse.
It's like how I'm not a chimpanzee, right?
I...think you are further from a chimpanzee than I am from a horse.
Coming from you, I KNOW that's a compliment.
You are most welcome.
dana

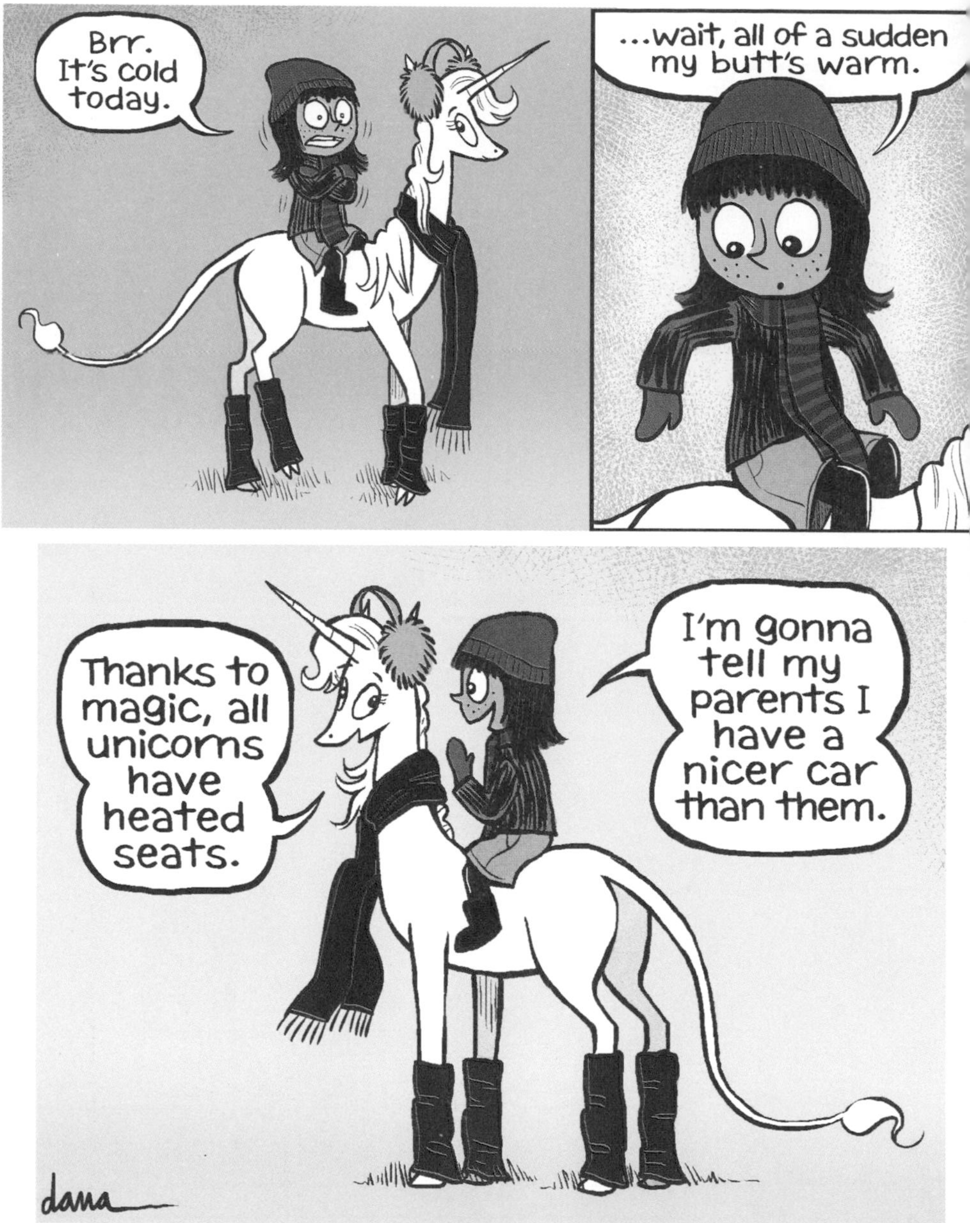
Brr. It's cold today.
...wait, all of a sudden my butt's warm.
Thanks to magic, all unicorns have heated seats.
I'm gonna tell my parents I have a nicer car than them.
dana

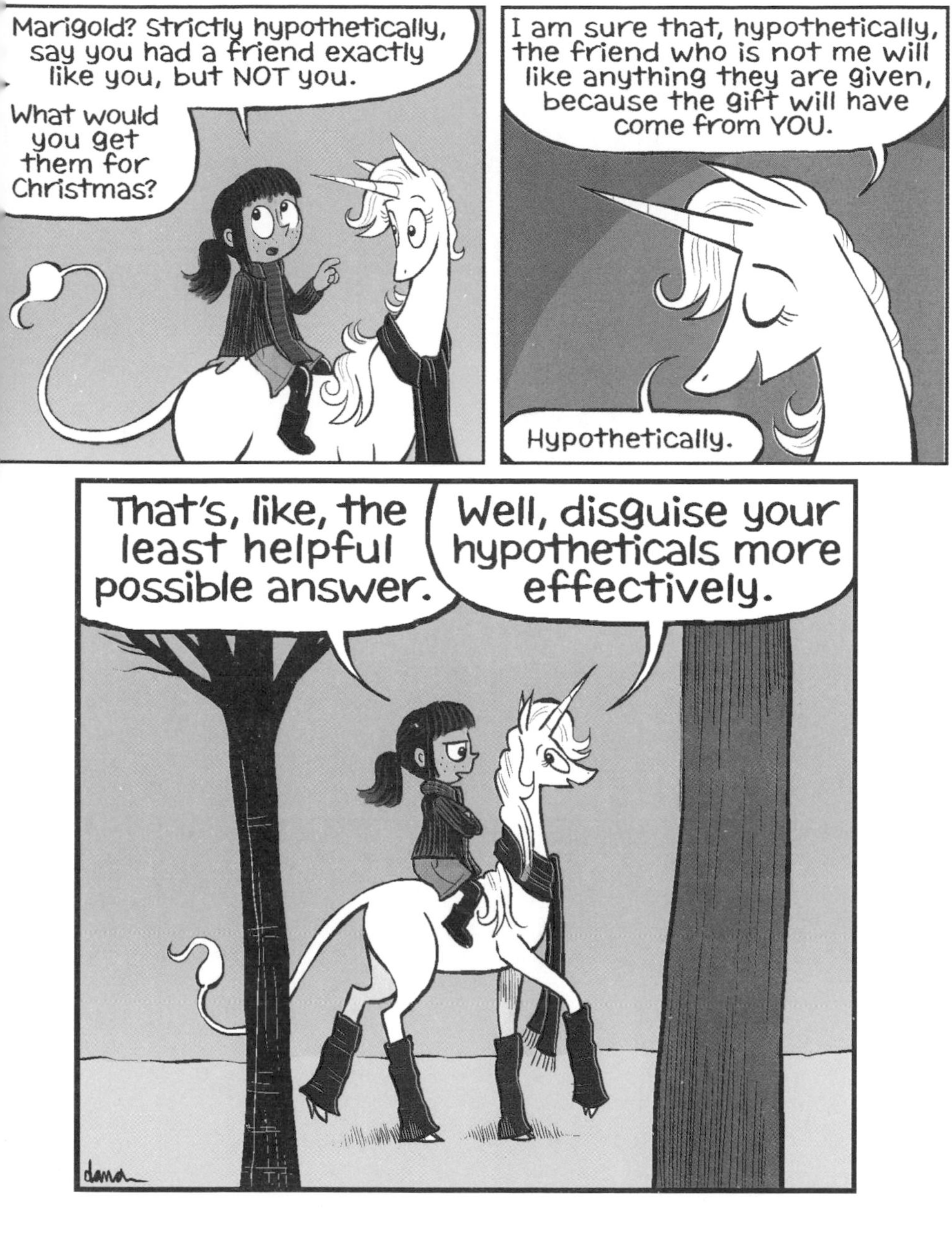
Marigold? Strictly hypothetically, say you had a friend exactly like you, but NOT you.
What would you get them for Christmas?
I am sure that, hypothetically, the friend who is not me will like anything they are given, because the gift will have come from YOU.
Hypothetically.
That's, like, the least helpful possible answer.
Well, disguise your hypotheticals more effectively.
dana

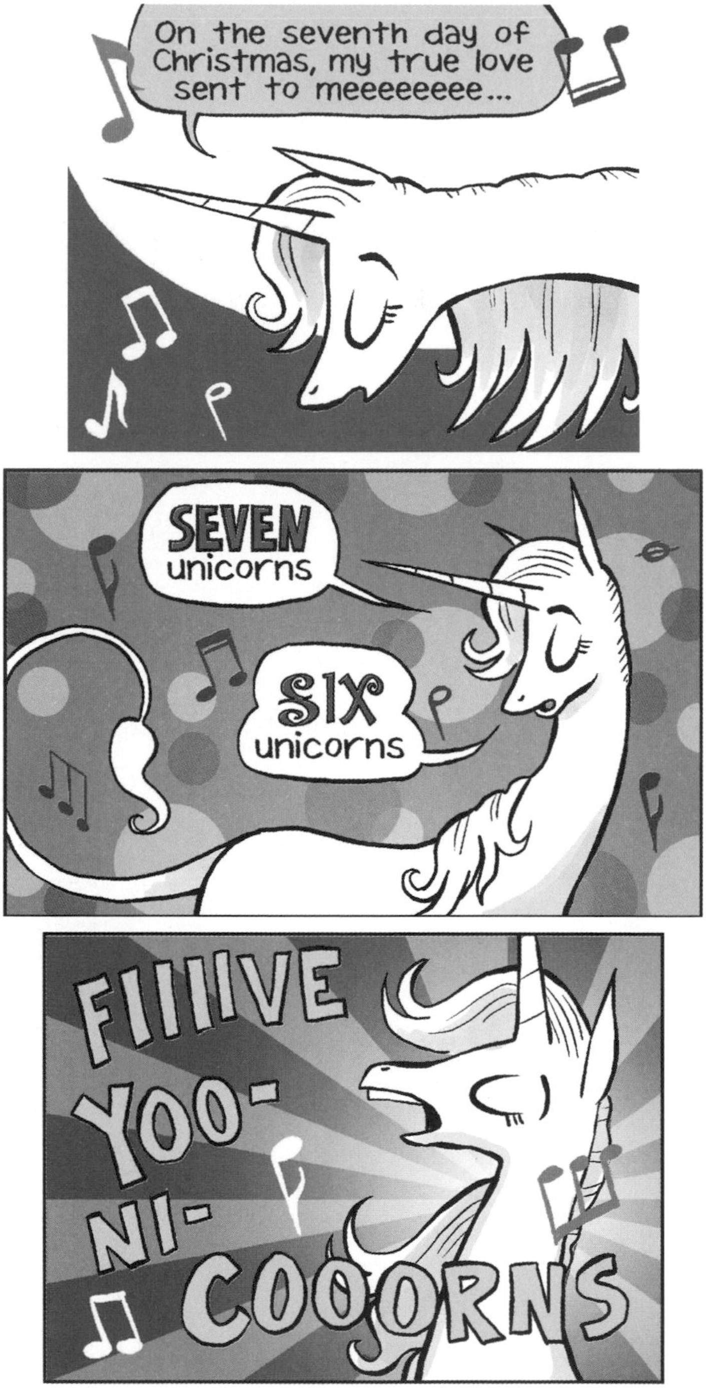
On the seventh day of Christmas, my true love sent to meeeeeeee...
SEVEN unicorns
SIX unicorns
FIIIVE YOO-NI-COOORNS

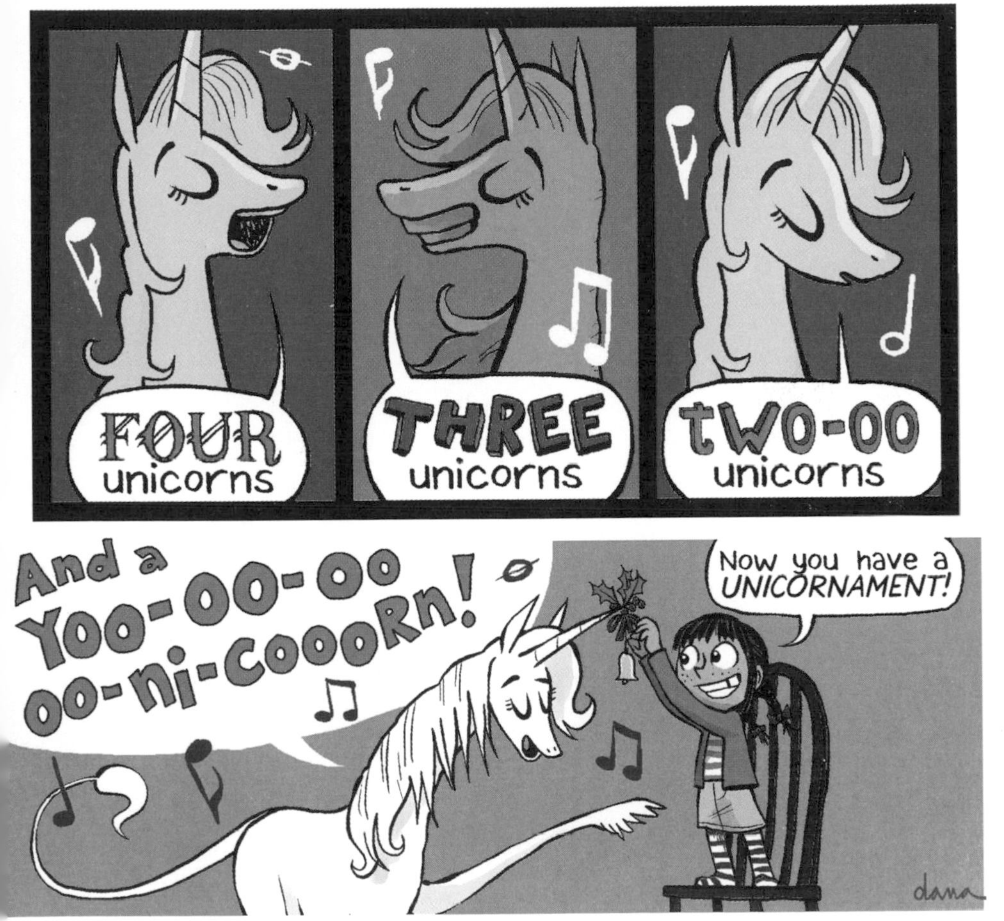
FOUR unicorns
THREE unicorns
TWO-OO unicorns
And a YOO-OO-OO OO-NI-COOORN!
Now you have a UNICORNAMENT!
dana

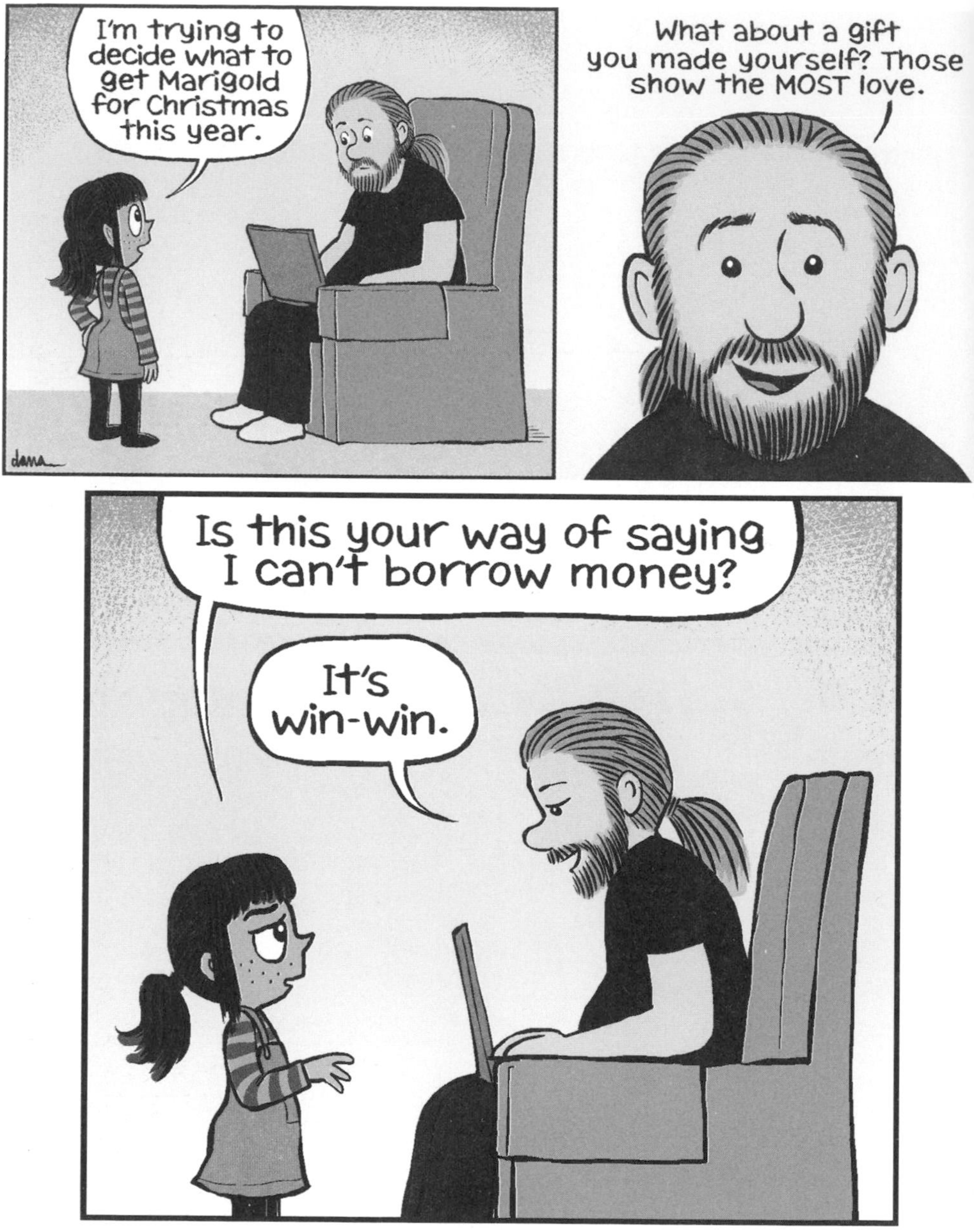
I'm trying to decide what to get Marigold for Christmas this year.
What about a gift you made yourself? Those show the MOST love.
Is this your way of saying I can't borrow money?
It's win-win.

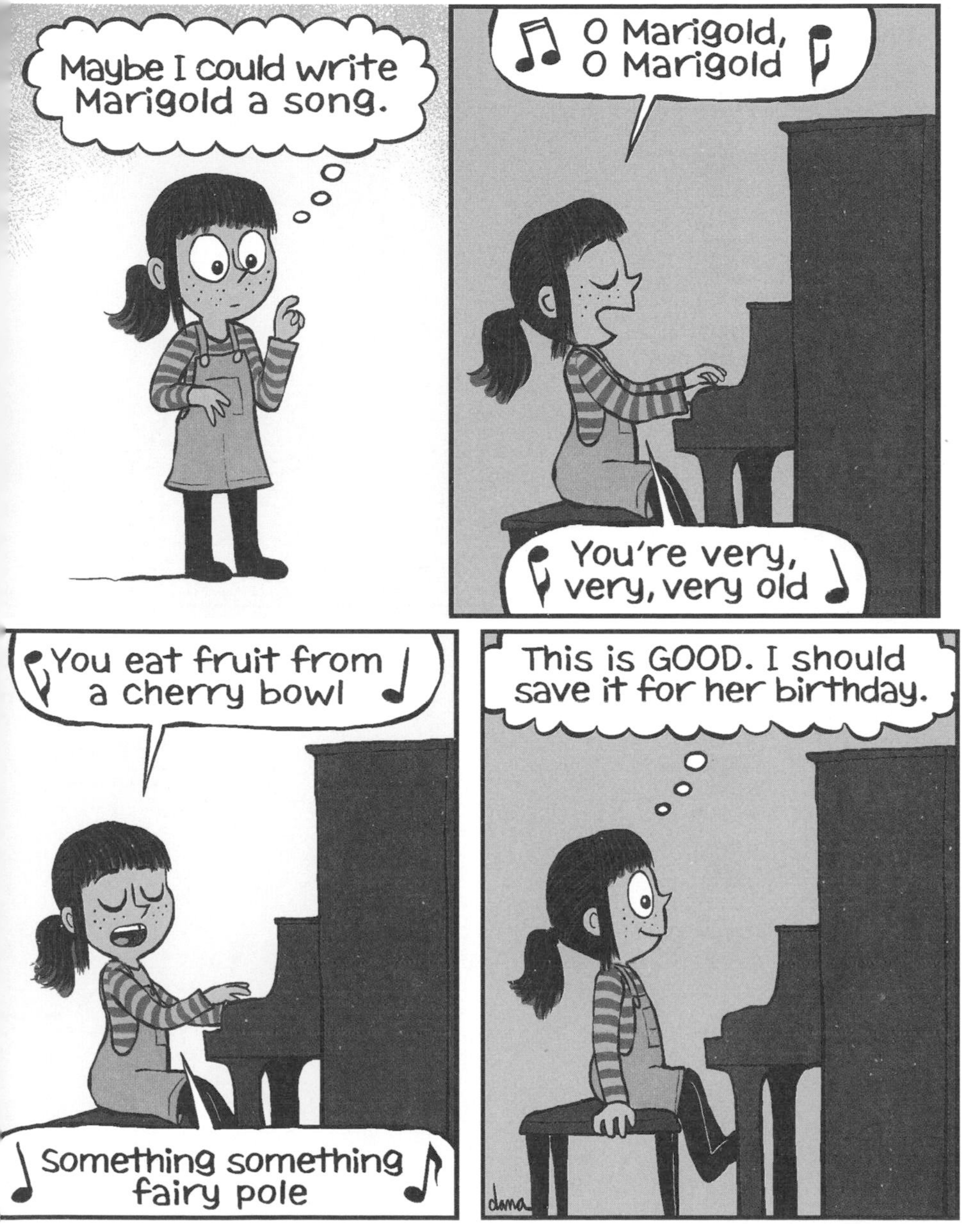
Maybe I could write Marigold a song.
O Marigold, O Marigold
You're very, very, very old
You eat fruit from a cherry bowl
Something something fairy pole
This is GOOD. I should save it for her birthday.
dana

Marigold, I got you an early Christmas present.

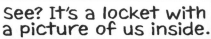

See? It's a locket with a picture of us inside.

Hooray! I look lovely in it!

I'm ALSO in it.

And YOU are my most flattering accessory!

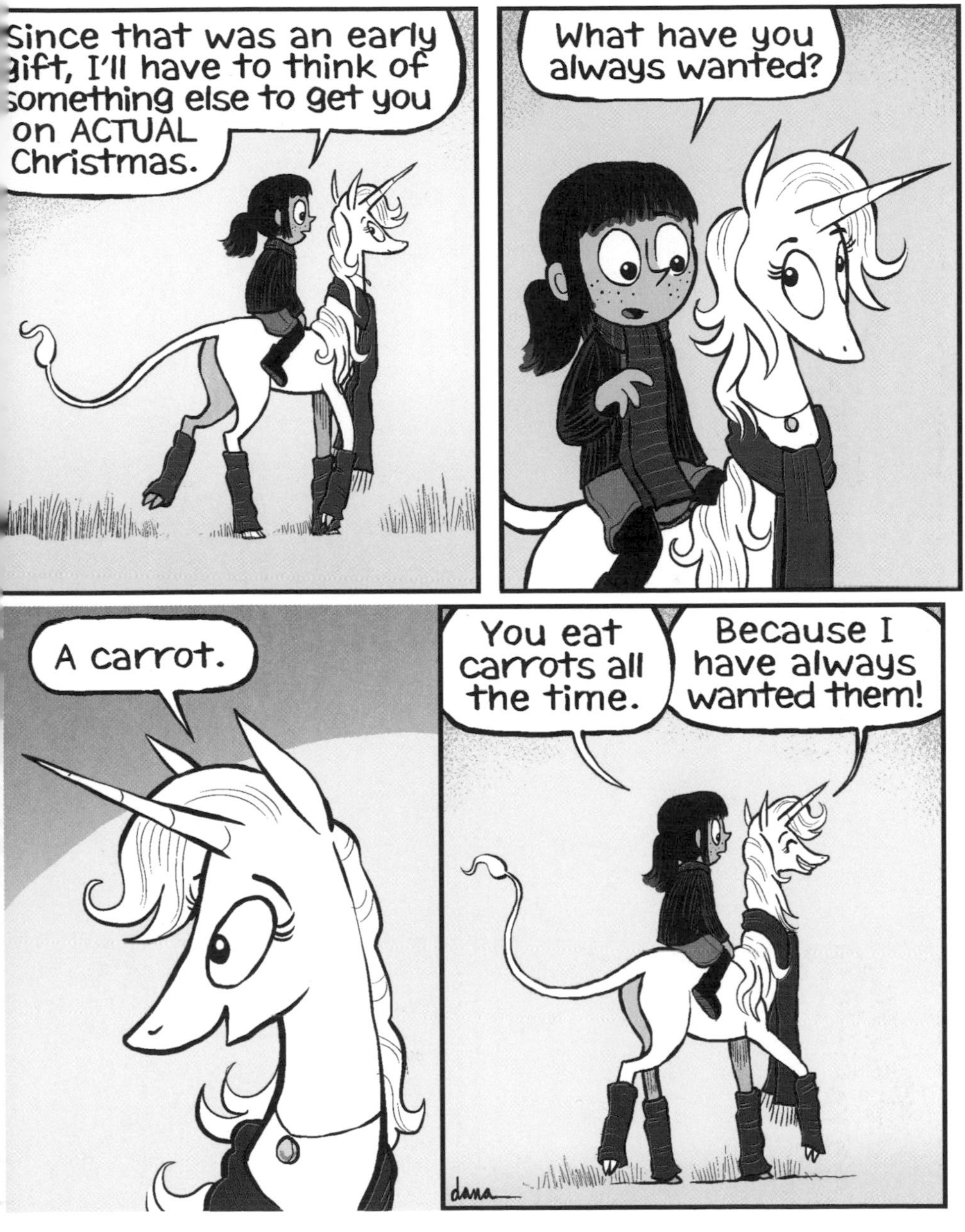
Since that was an early gift, I'll have to think of something else to get you on ACTUAL Christmas.
What have you always wanted?
A carrot.
You eat carrots all the time.
Because I have always wanted them!
dana

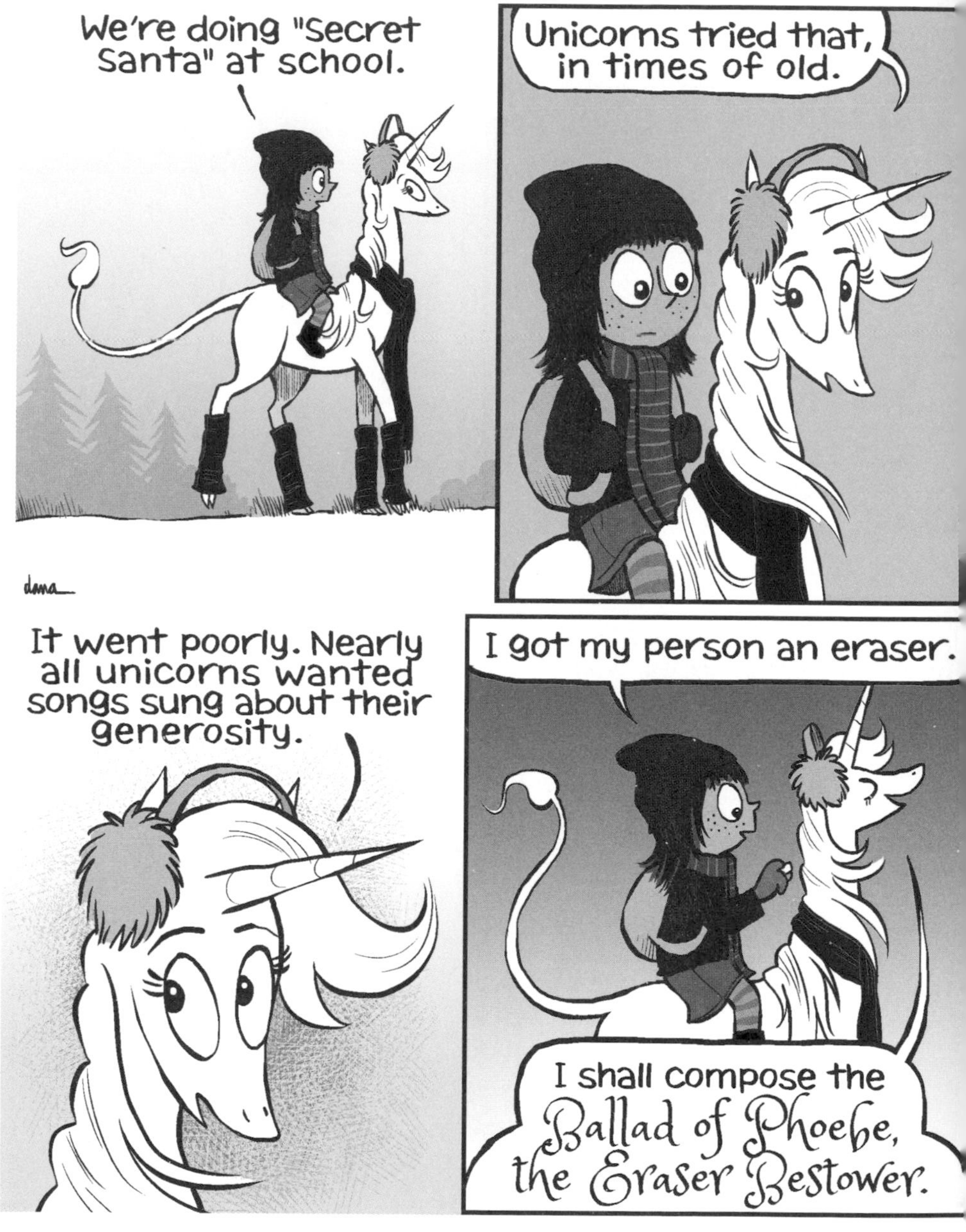
We're doing "Secret Santa" at school.
Unicorns tried that, in times of old.
dana
It went poorly. Nearly all unicorns wanted songs sung about their generosity.
I got my person an eraser.
I shall compose the Ballad of Phoebe, the Eraser Bestower.

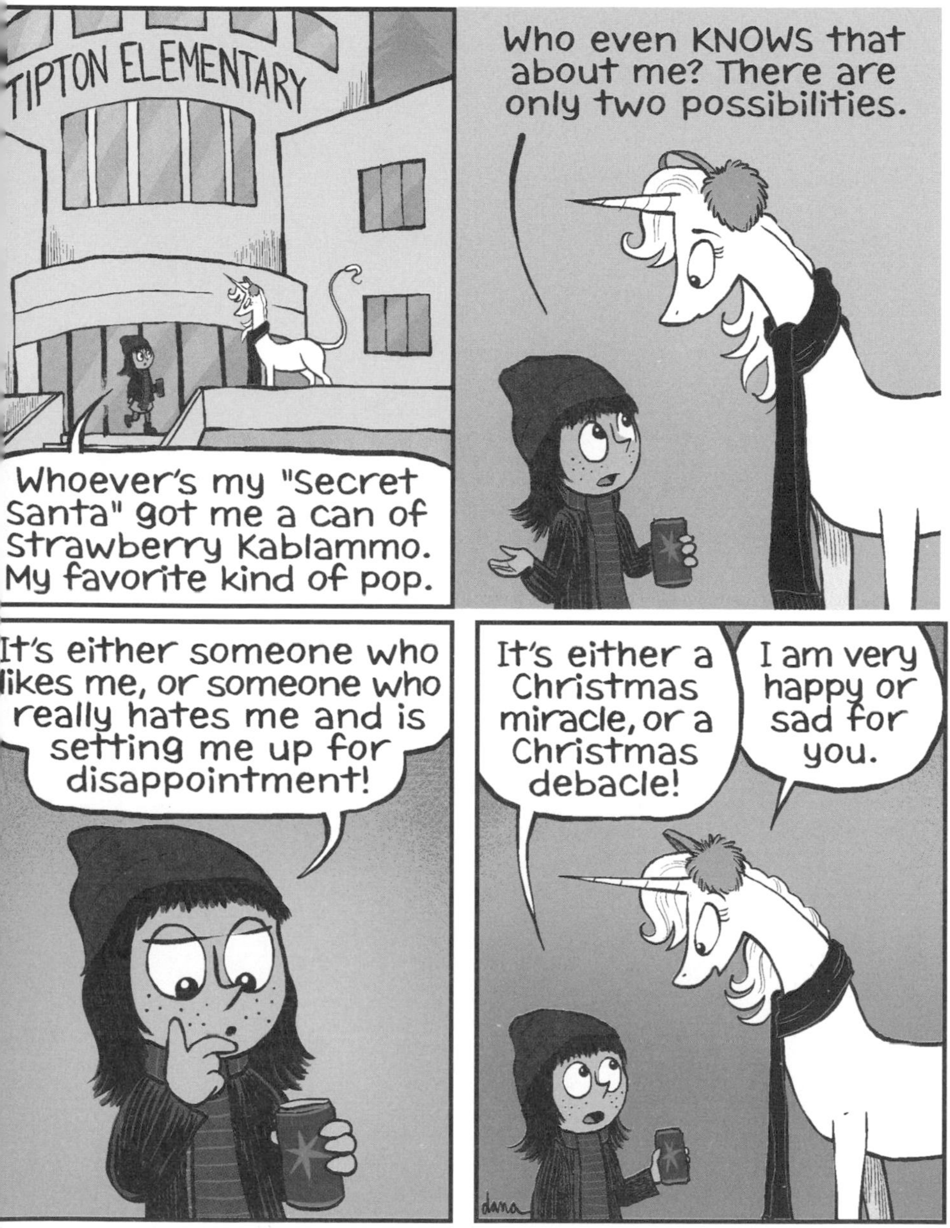
TIPTON ELEMENTARY
Whoever's my "Secret Santa" got me a can of Strawberry Kablammo. My favorite kind of pop.
Who even KNOWS that about me? There are only two possibilities.
It's either someone who likes me, or someone who really hates me and is setting me up for disappointment!
It's either a Christmas miracle, or a Christmas debacle!
I am very happy or sad for you.
dana

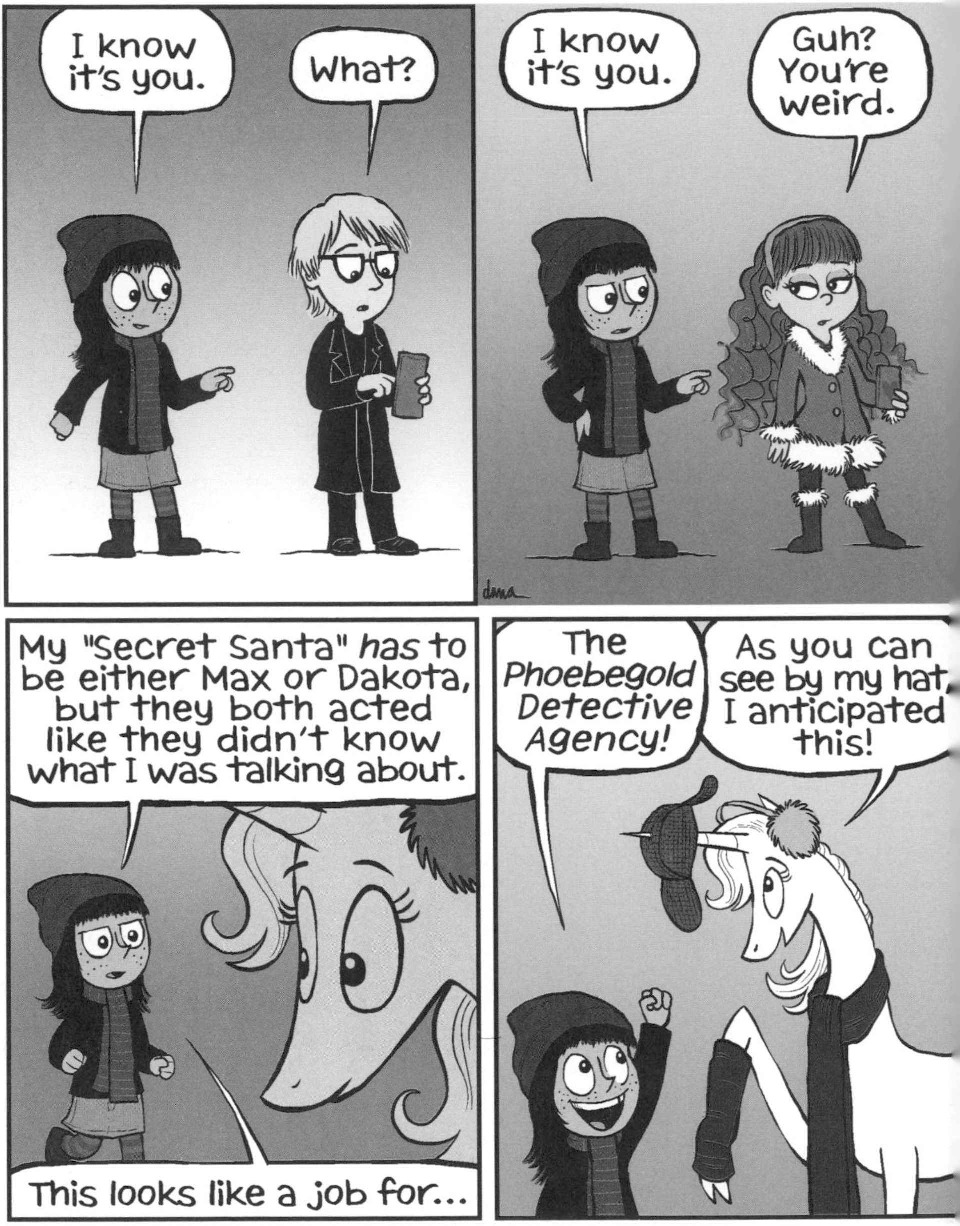
I know it's you.
What?
I know it's you.
Guh? You're weird.
My "Secret Santa" *has* to be either Max or Dakota, but they both acted like they didn't know what I was talking about.
This looks like a job for...
The *Phoebegold Detective Agency!*
As you can see by my hat, I anticipated this!

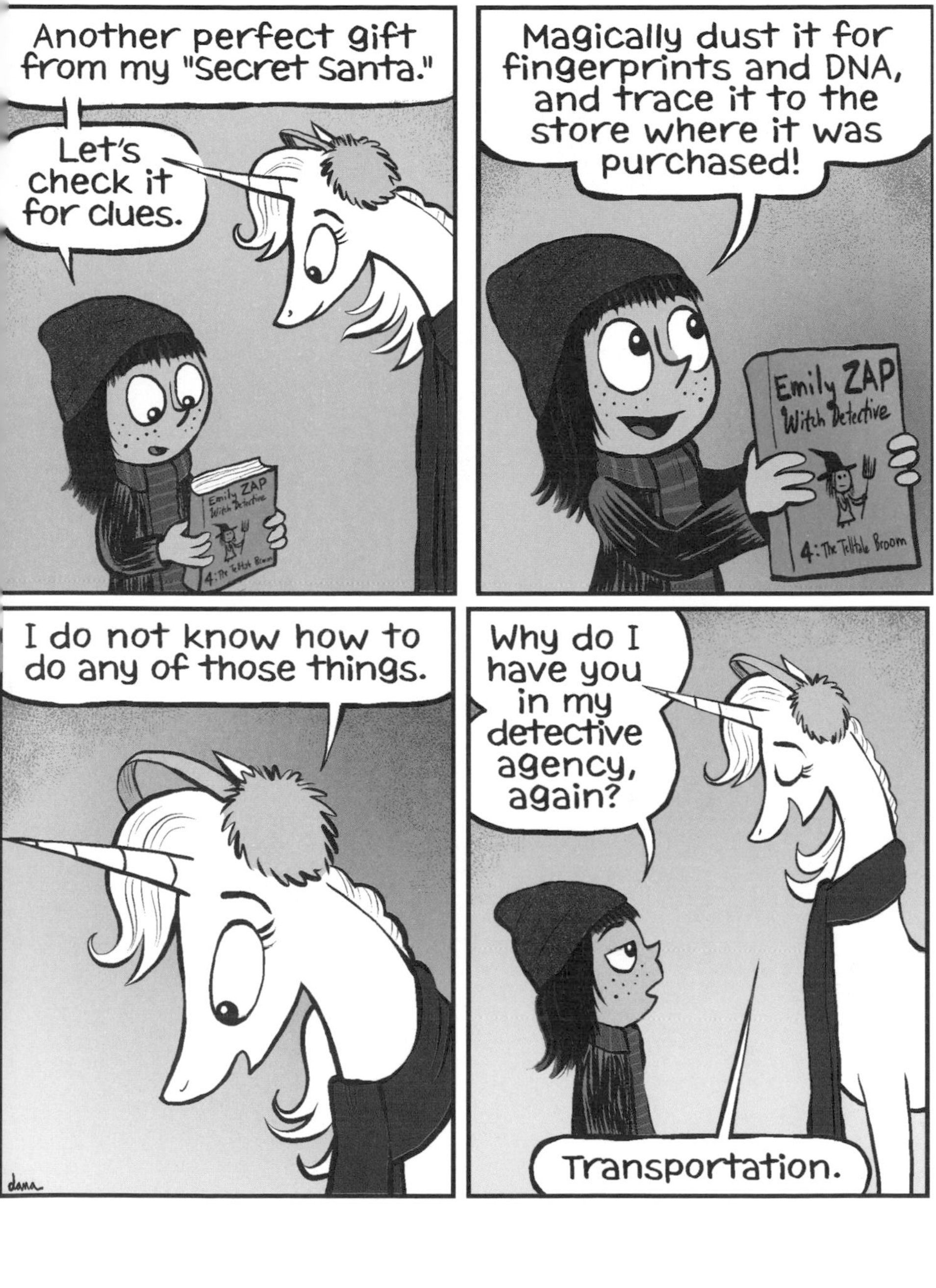
Another perfect gift from my "Secret Santa."
Let's check it for clues.
Emily ZAP Witch Detective
4: The Telltale Broom
Magically dust it for fingerprints and DNA, and trace it to the store where it was purchased!
Emily ZAP Witch Detective
4: The Telltale Broom
I do not know how to do any of those things.
dana
Why do I have you in my detective agency, again?
Transportation.

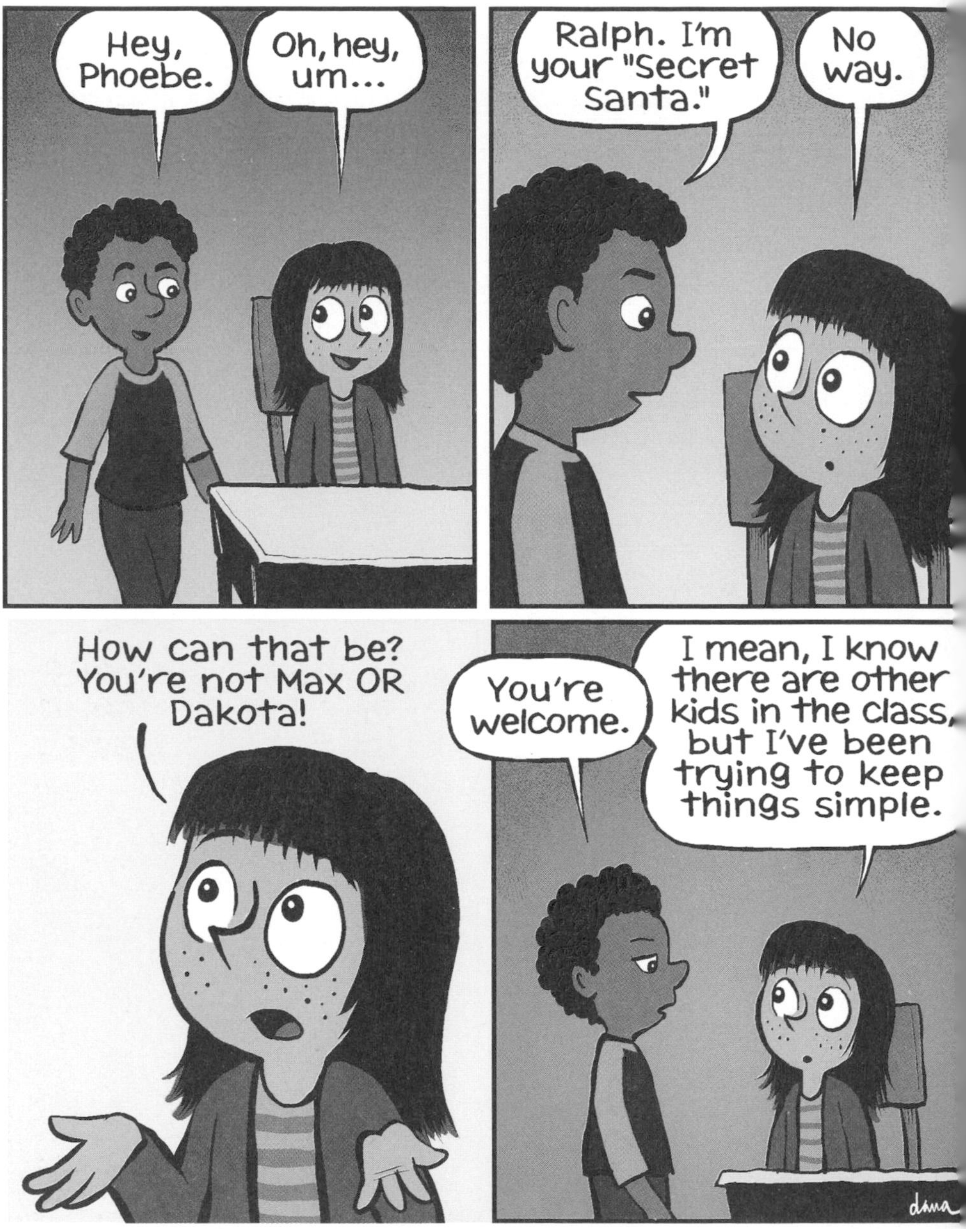
Hey, Phoebe.
Oh, hey, um...
Ralph. I'm your "Secret Santa."
No way.
How can that be? You're not Max OR Dakota!
You're welcome.
I mean, I know there are other kids in the class, but I've been trying to keep things simple.
dana

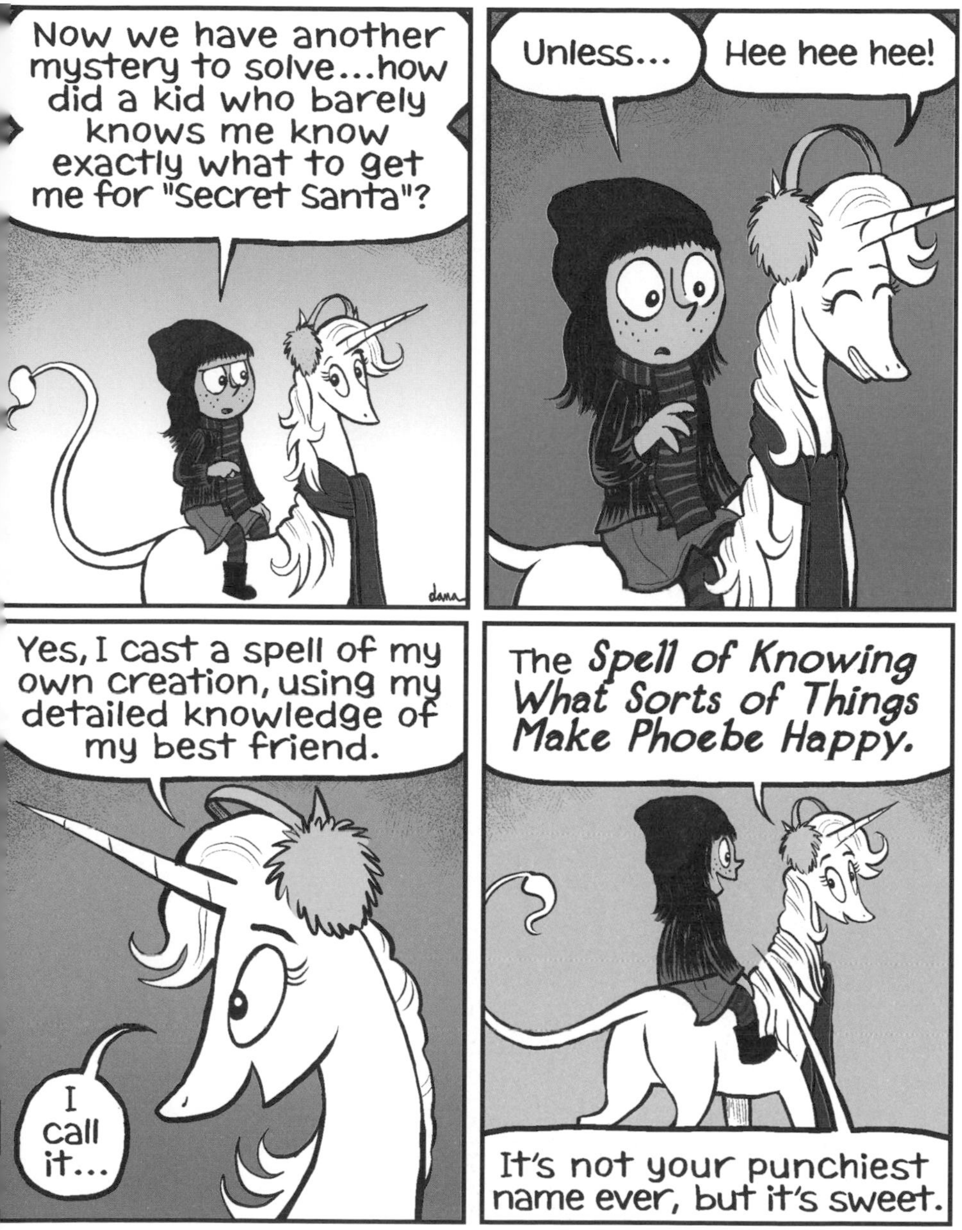
Now we have another mystery to solve...how did a kid who barely knows me know exactly what to get me for "Secret Santa"?
Unless...
Hee hee hee!
Yes, I cast a spell of my own creation, using my detailed knowledge of my best friend.
I call it...
The *Spell of Knowing What Sorts of Things Make Phoebe Happy.*
It's not your punchiest name ever, but it's sweet.

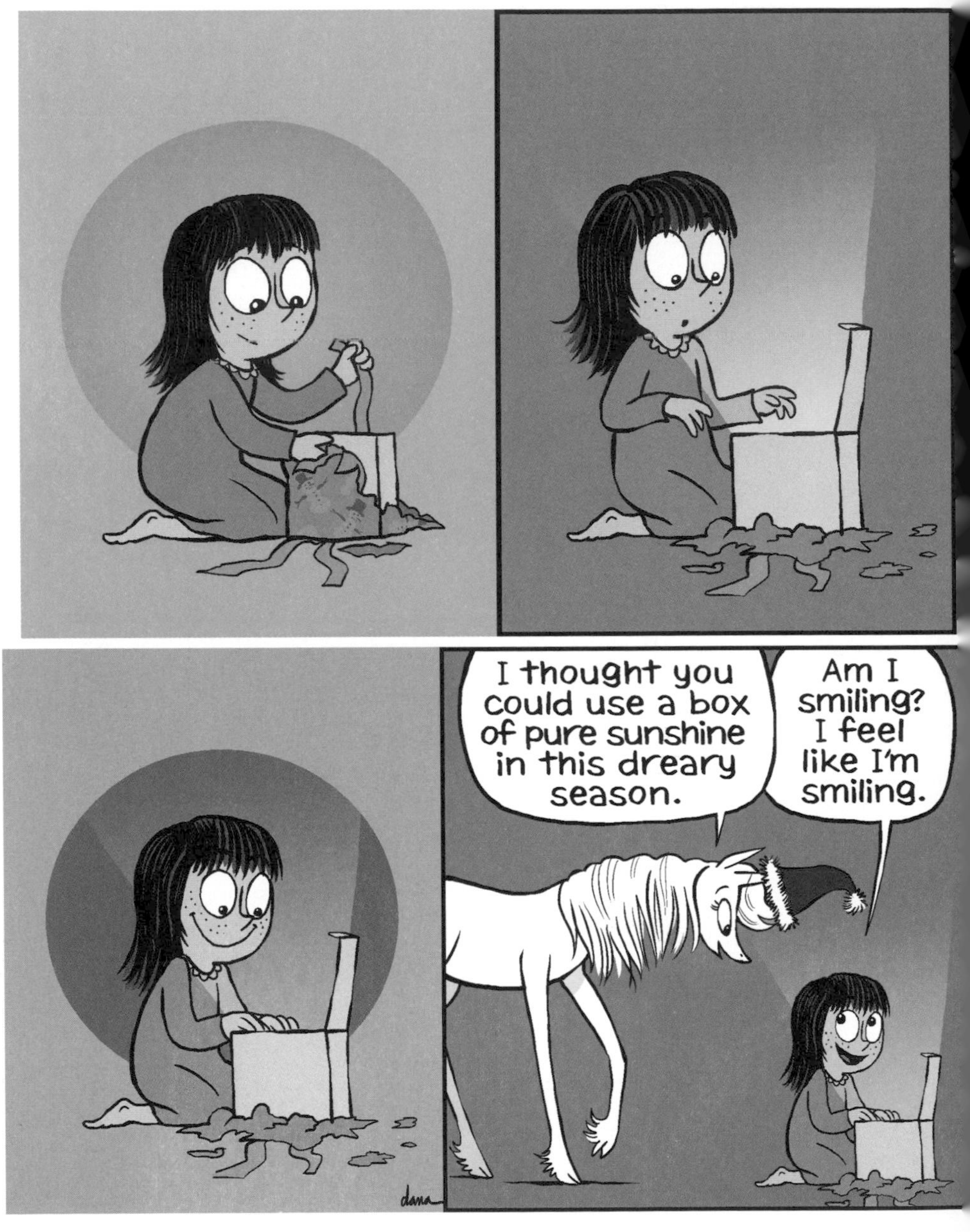
I thought you could use a box of pure sunshine in this dreary season.
Am I smiling? I feel like I'm smiling.
dana

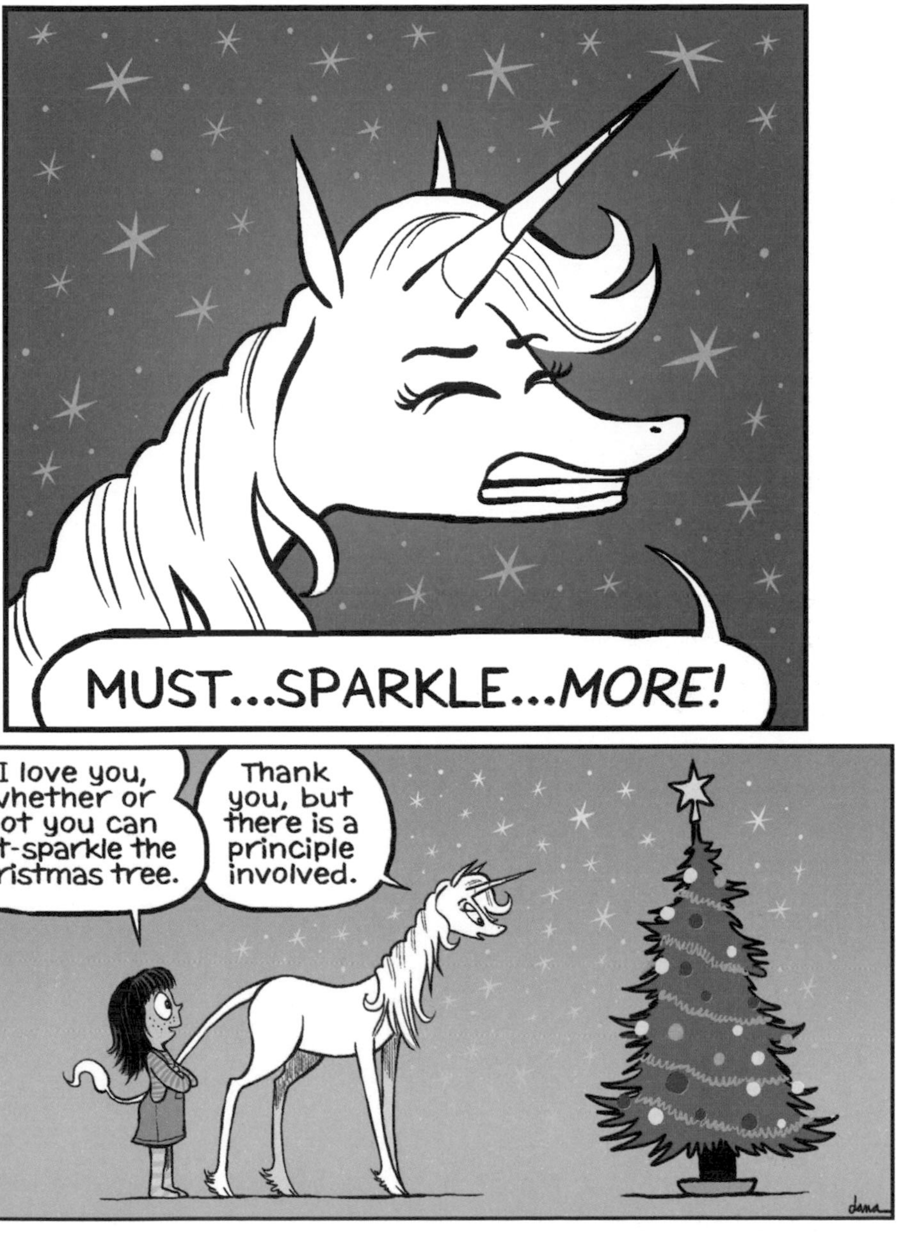

MUST...SPARKLE...MORE!
I love you, whether or not you can out-sparkle the Christmas tree.
Thank you, but there is a principle involved.
dana

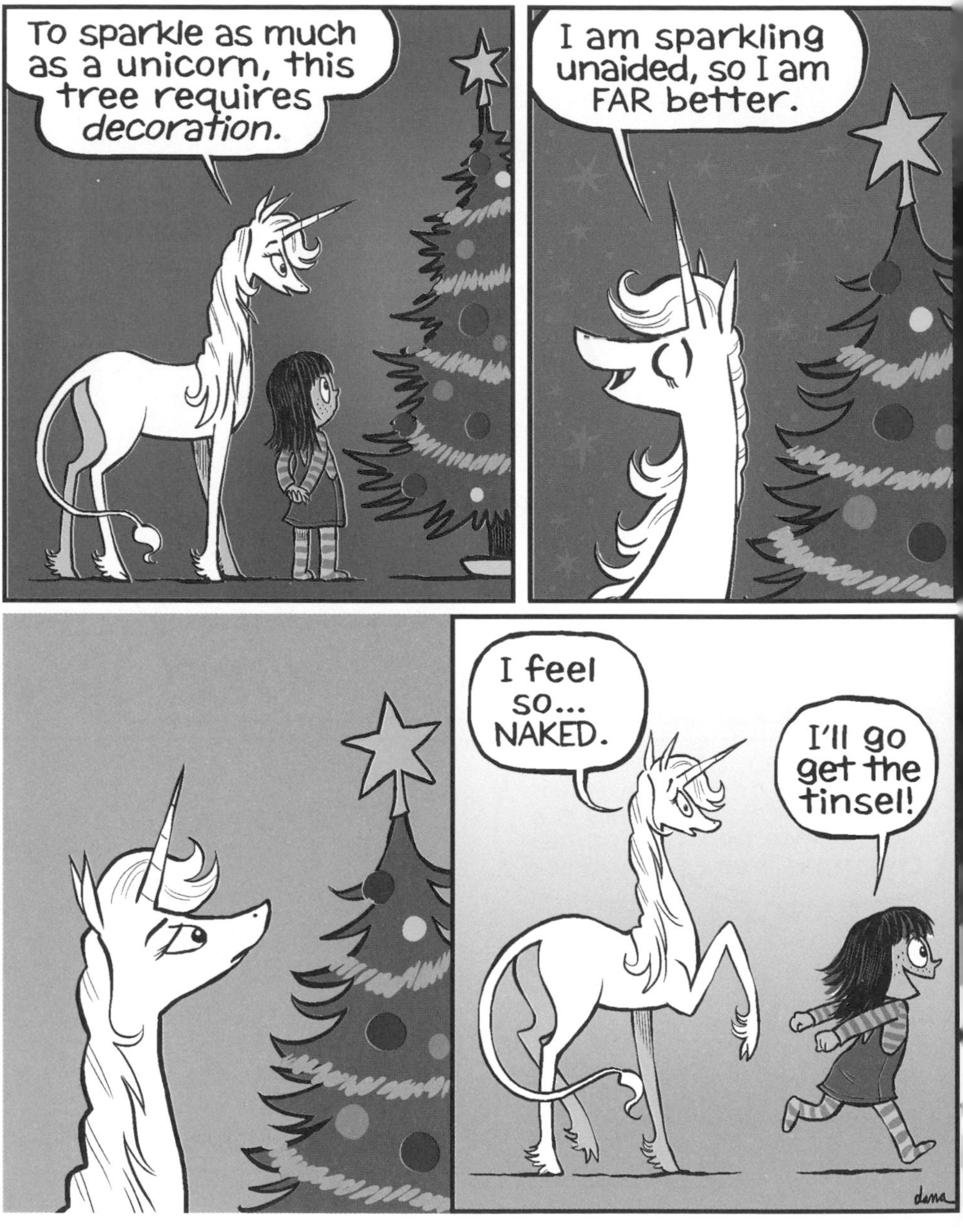
To sparkle as much as a unicorn, this tree requires *decoration.*
I am sparkling unaided, so I am FAR better.
I feel so... NAKED.
I'll go get the tinsel!
dana

It feels wrong to be draped in tinsel.
I am a unicorn, and should not require embellishment.
I encourage you, however, to decorate yourself liberally.
I know you're insulting me, but I feel too sparkly to mind!
Unicorn!

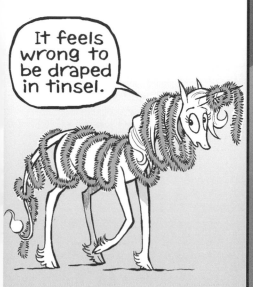

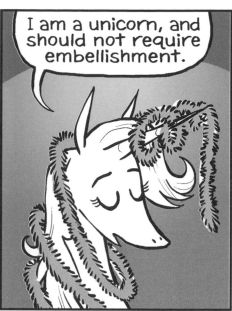

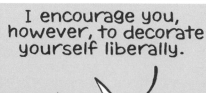

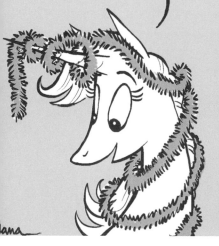

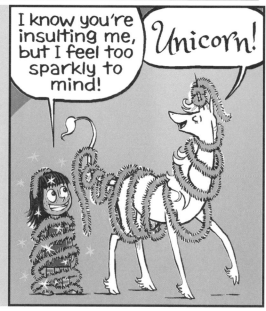

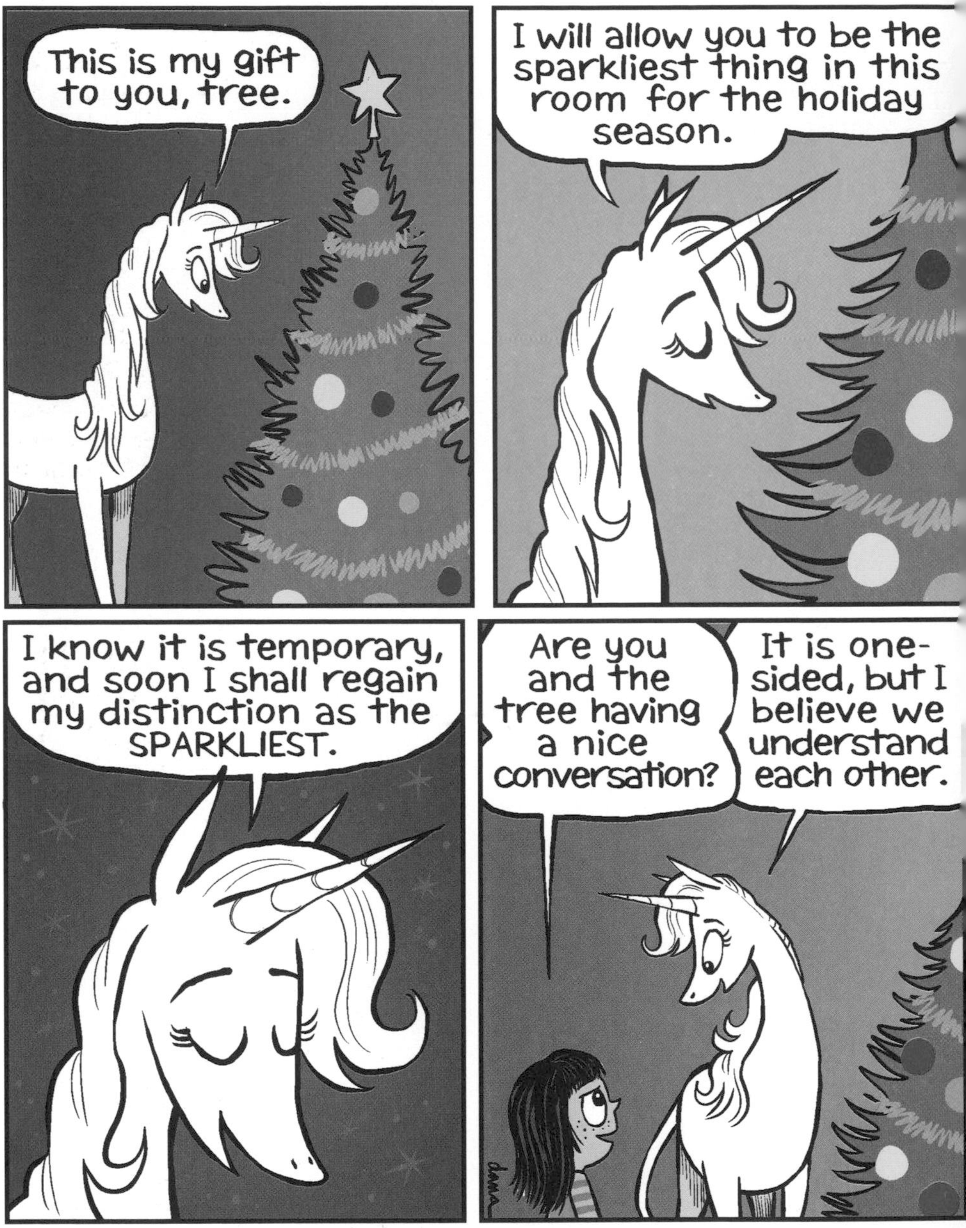
This is my gift to you, tree.
I will allow you to be the sparkliest thing in this room for the holiday season.
I know it is temporary, and soon I shall regain my distinction as the SPARKLIEST.
Are you and the tree having a nice conversation?
It is one-sided, but I believe we understand each other.

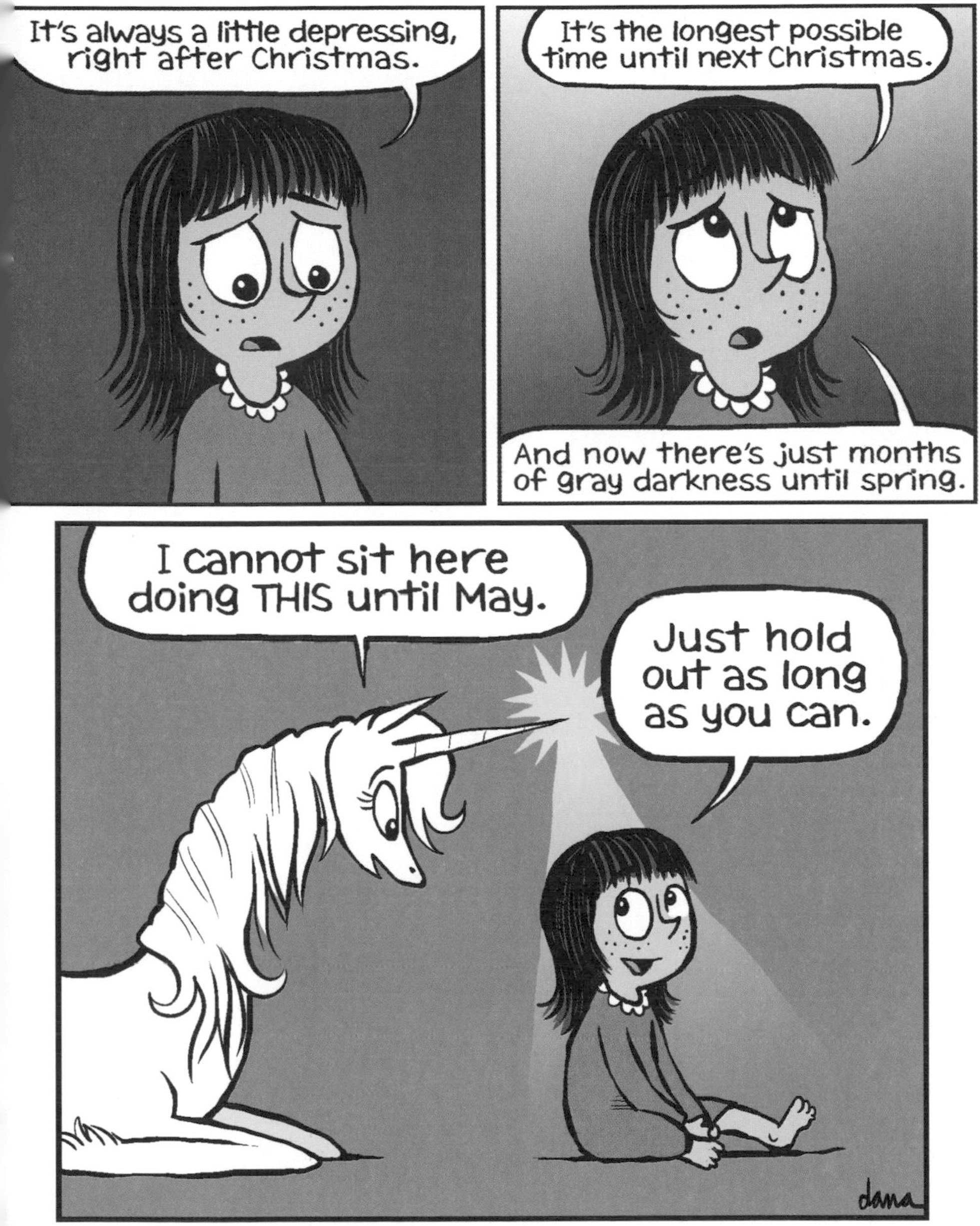
It's always a little depressing, right after Christmas.
It's the longest possible time until next Christmas.
And now there's just months of gray darkness until spring.
I cannot sit here doing THIS until May.
Just hold out as long as you can.
dana

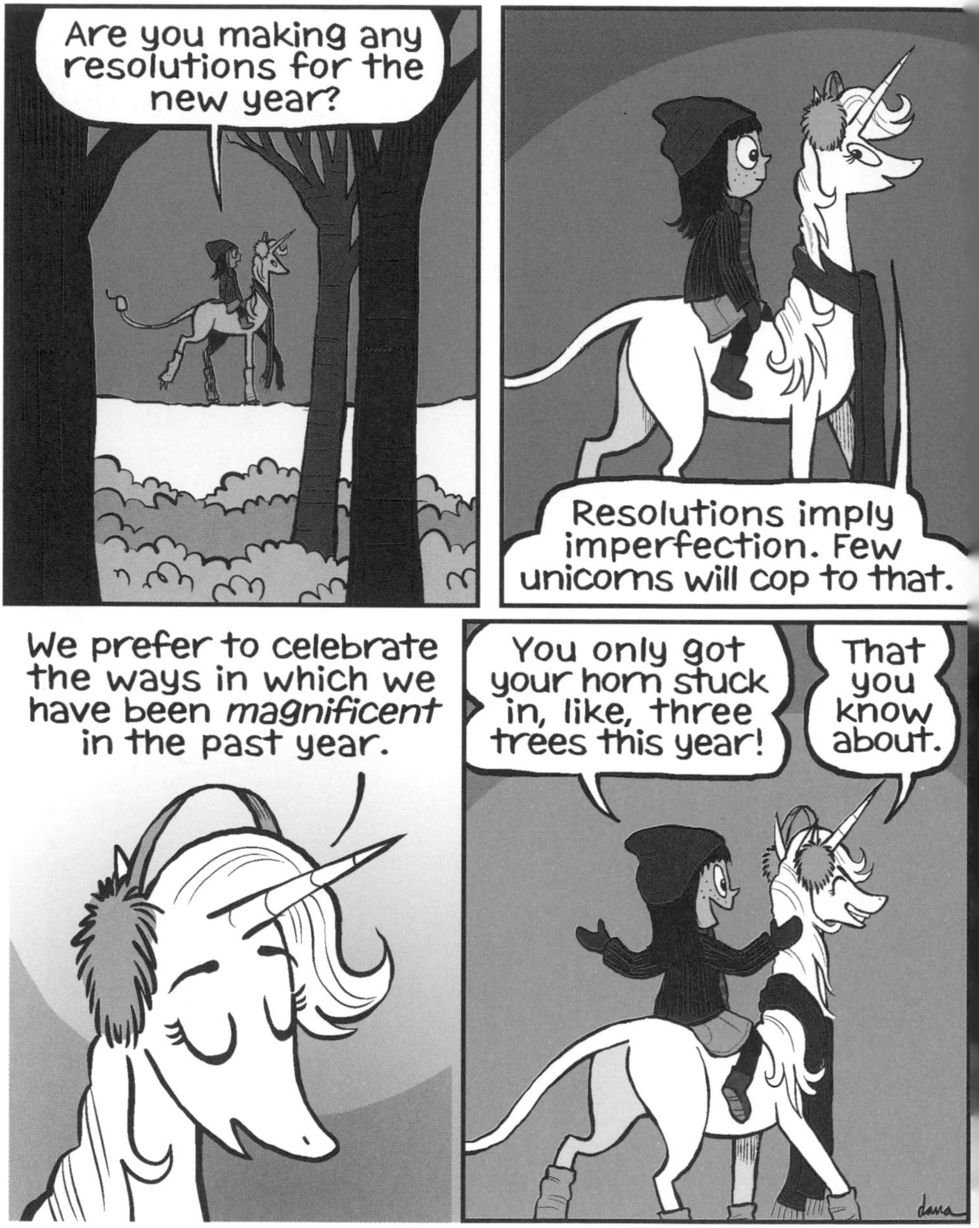
Are you making any resolutions for the new year?
Resolutions imply imperfection. Few unicorns will cop to that.
We prefer to celebrate the ways in which we have been *magnificent* in the past year.
You only got your horn stuck in, like, three trees this year!
That you know about.
dana

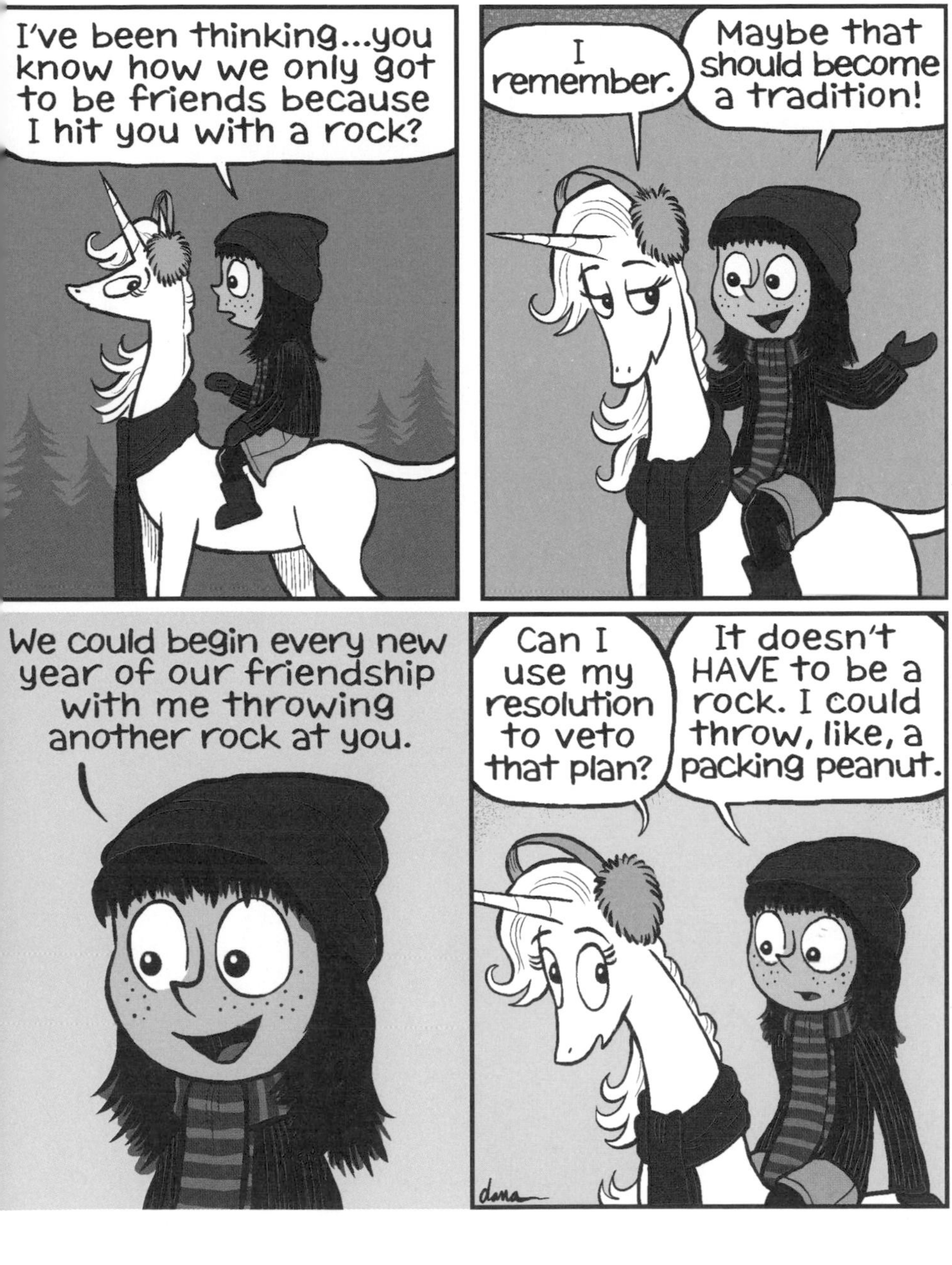
I've been thinking...you know how we only got to be friends because I hit you with a rock?
I remember.
Maybe that should become a tradition!
We could begin every new year of our friendship with me throwing another rock at you.
Can I use my resolution to veto that plan?
It doesn't HAVE to be a rock. I could throw, like, a packing peanut.
dana

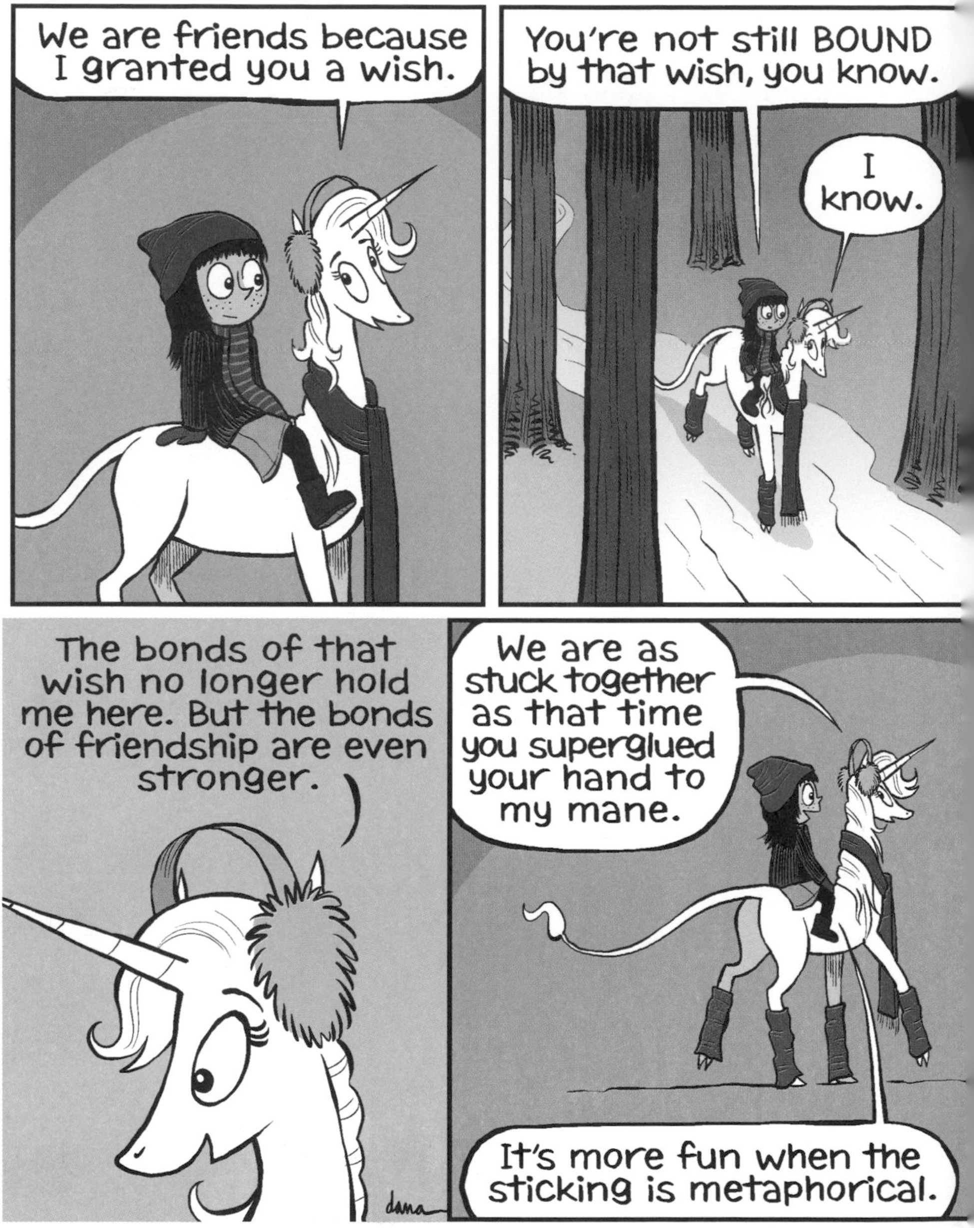
We are friends because I granted you a wish.
You're not still BOUND by that wish, you know.
I know.
The bonds of that wish no longer hold me here. But the bonds of friendship are even stronger.
dana
We are as stuck together as that time you superglued your hand to my mane.
It's more fun when the sticking is metaphorical.

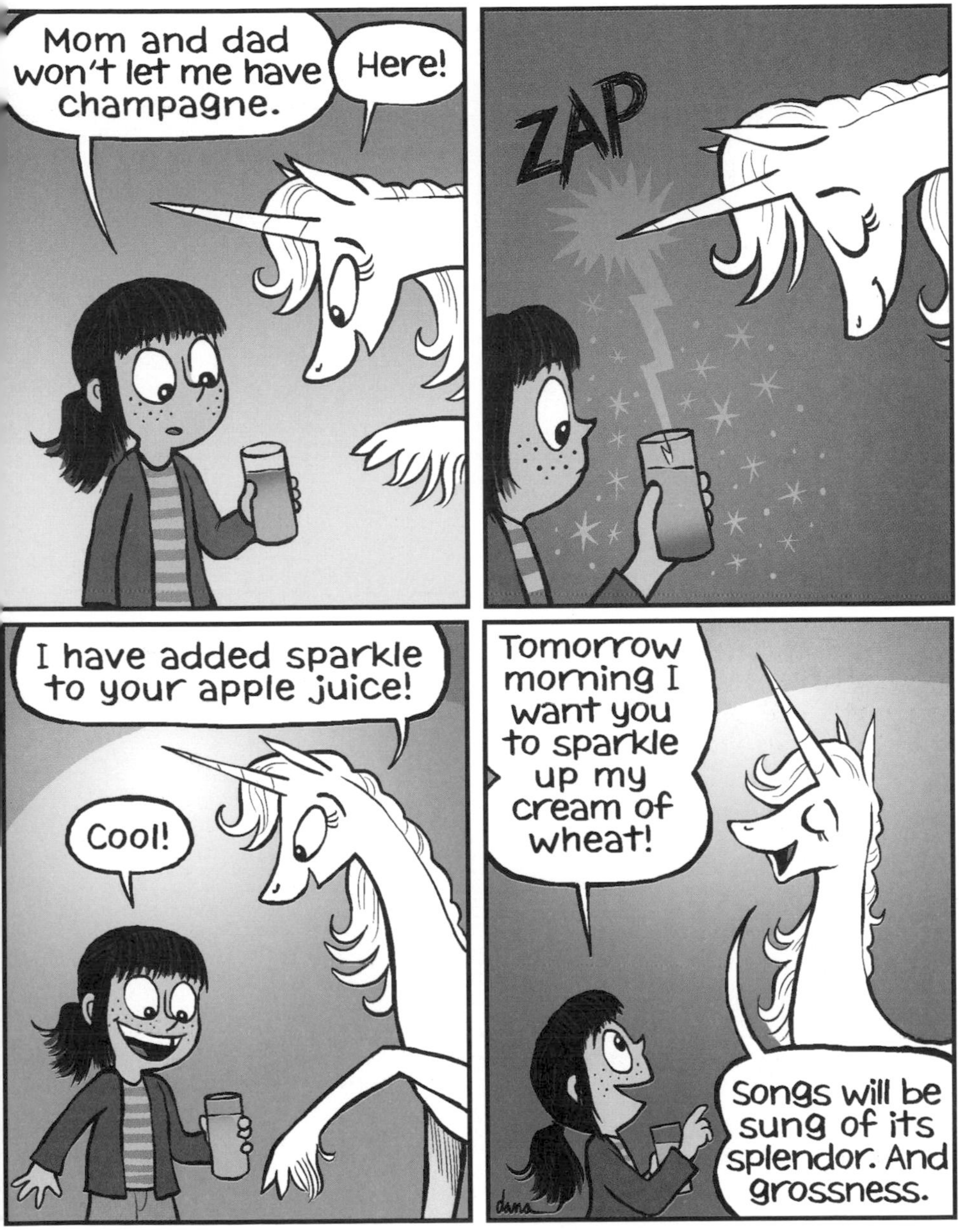
Mom and dad won't let me have champagne.
Here!
ZAP
I have added sparkle to your apple juice!
Cool!
Tomorrow morning I want you to sparkle up my cream of wheat!
Songs will be sung of its splendor. And grossness.
dana

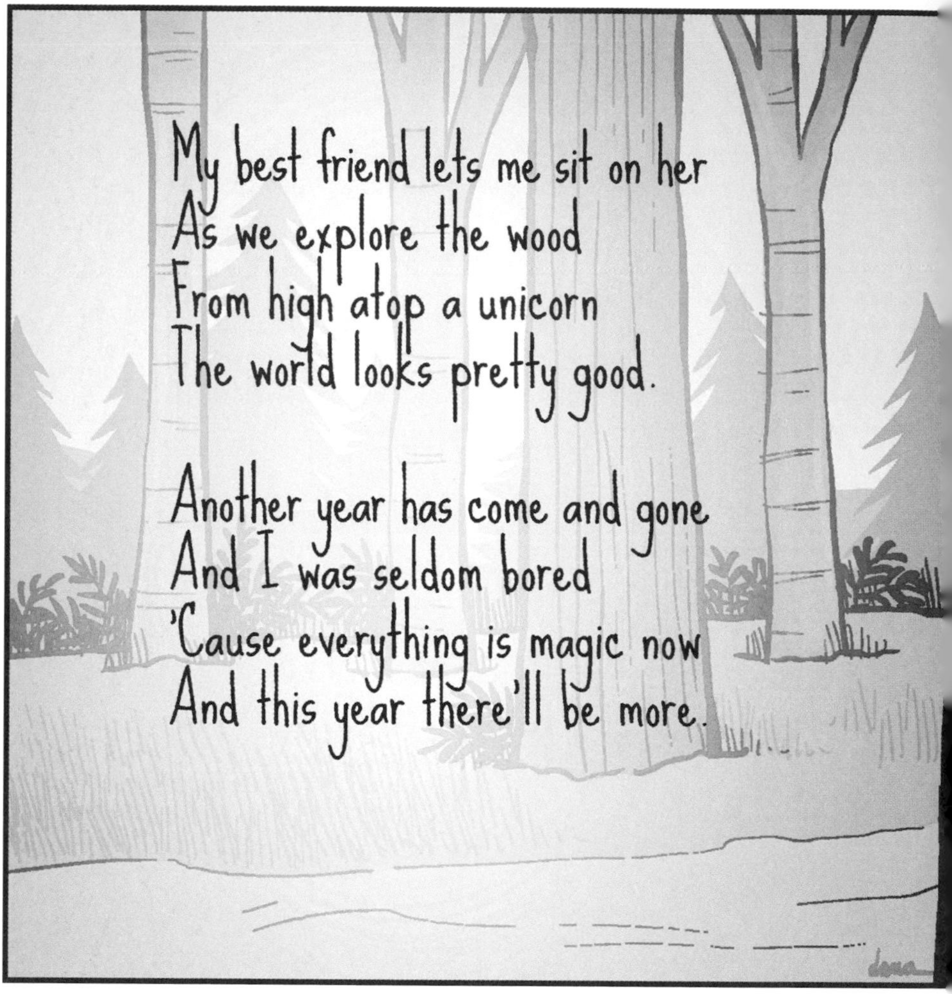
My best friend lets me sit on her
As we explore the wood
From high atop a unicorn
The world looks pretty good.

Another year has come and gone
And I was seldom bored
'Cause everything is magic now
And this year there'll be more.

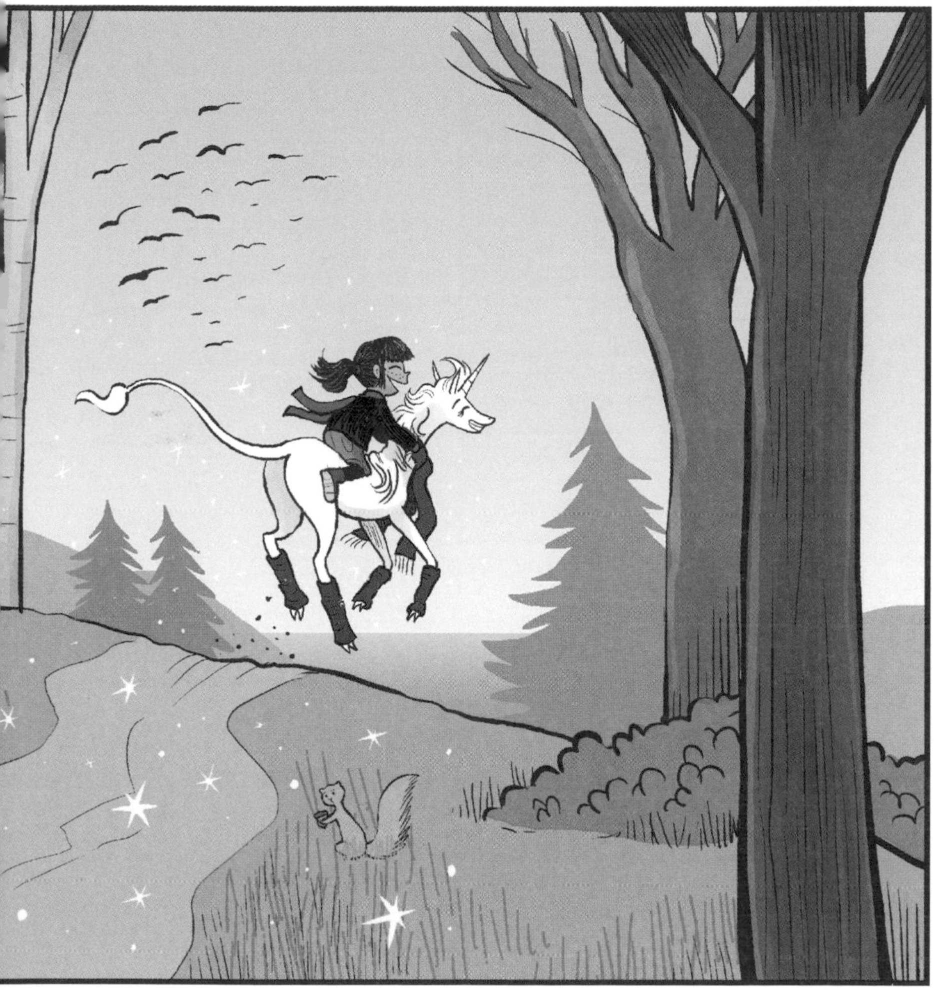

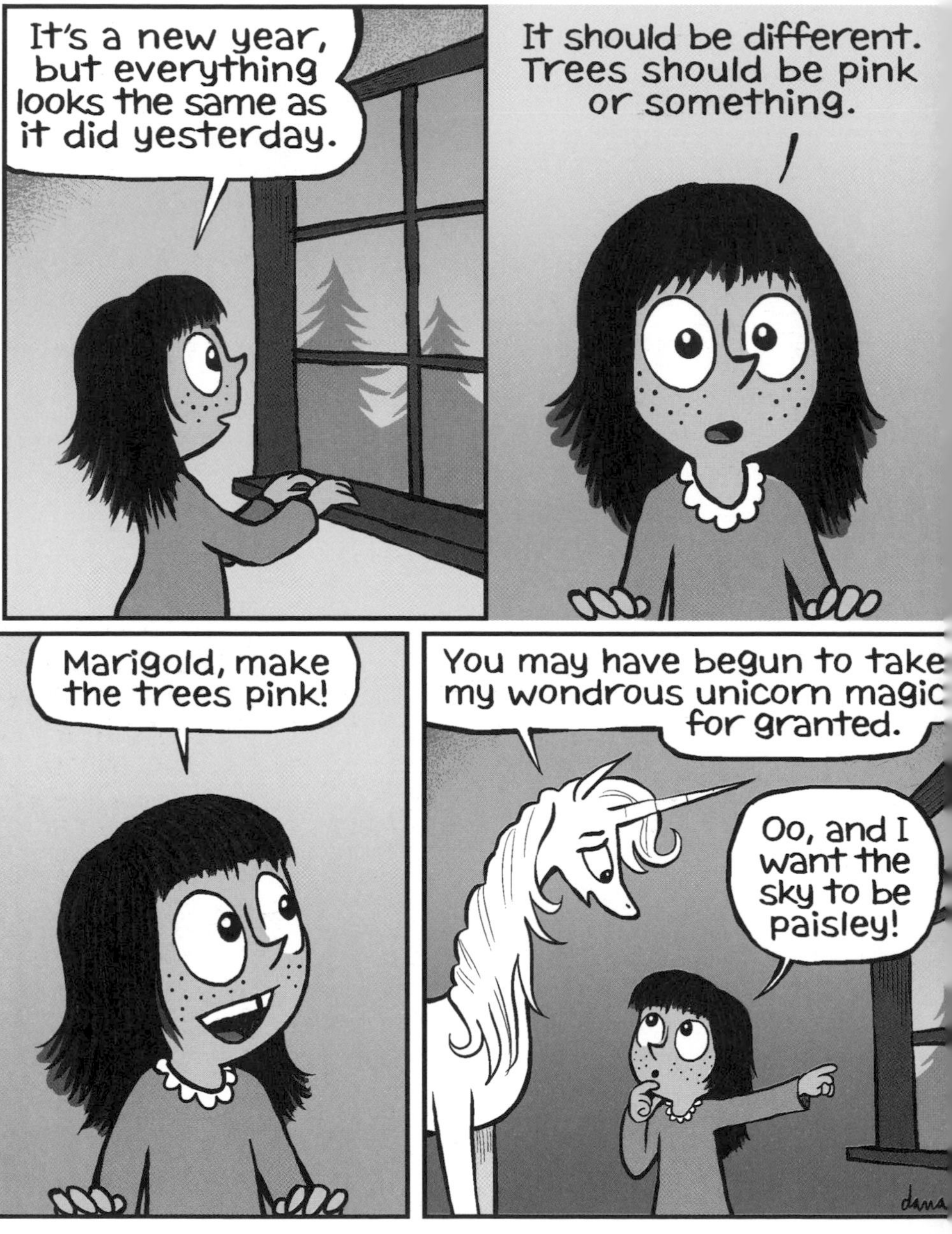
It's a new year, but everything looks the same as it did yesterday.
It should be different. Trees should be pink or something.
Marigold, make the trees pink!
You may have begun to take my wondrous unicorn magic for granted.
Oo, and I want the sky to be paisley!
dana

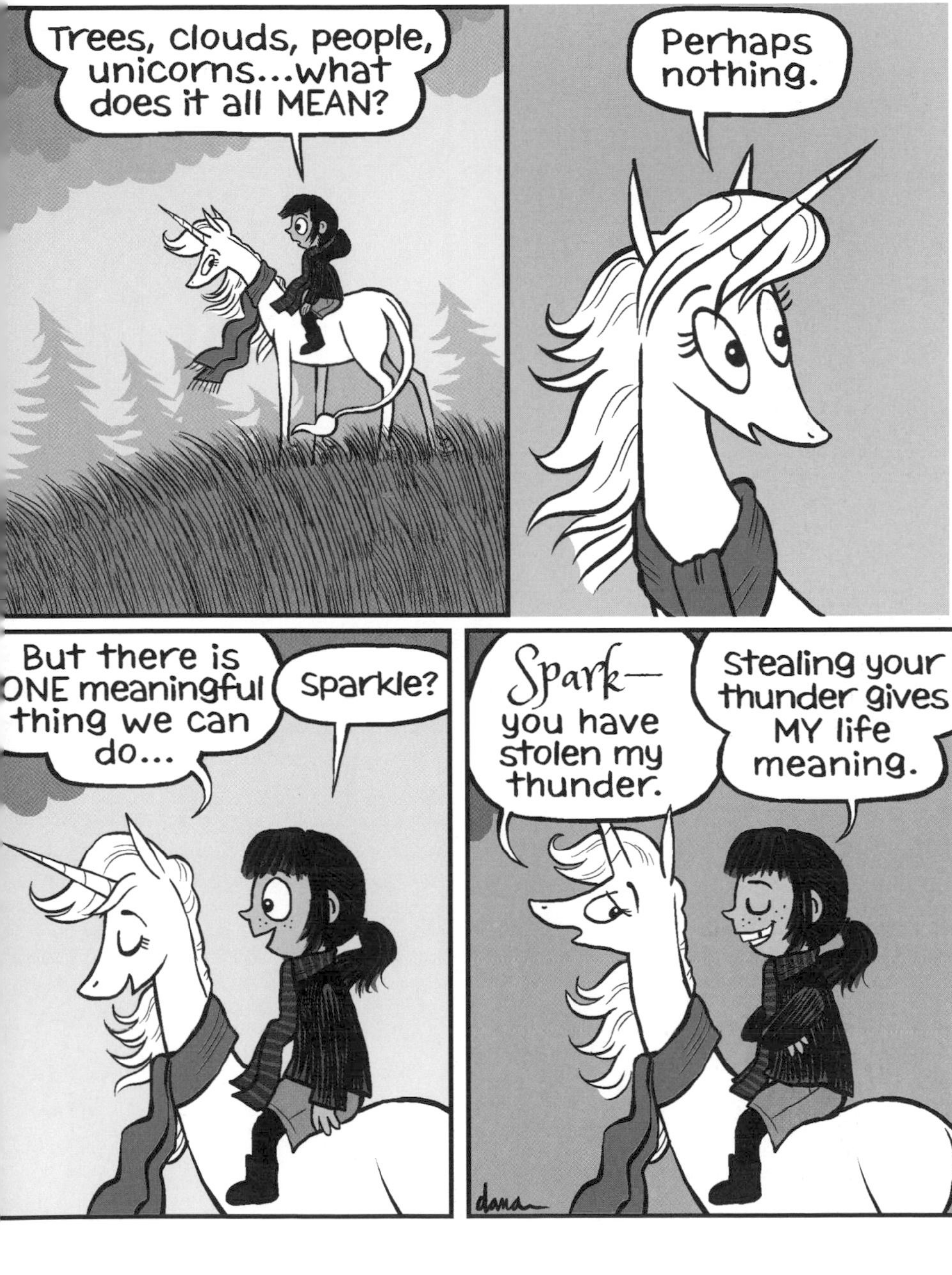
Trees, clouds, people, unicorns...what does it all MEAN?
Perhaps nothing.
But there is ONE meaningful thing we can do...
Sparkle?
Spark— you have stolen my thunder.
Stealing your thunder gives MY life meaning.
dana

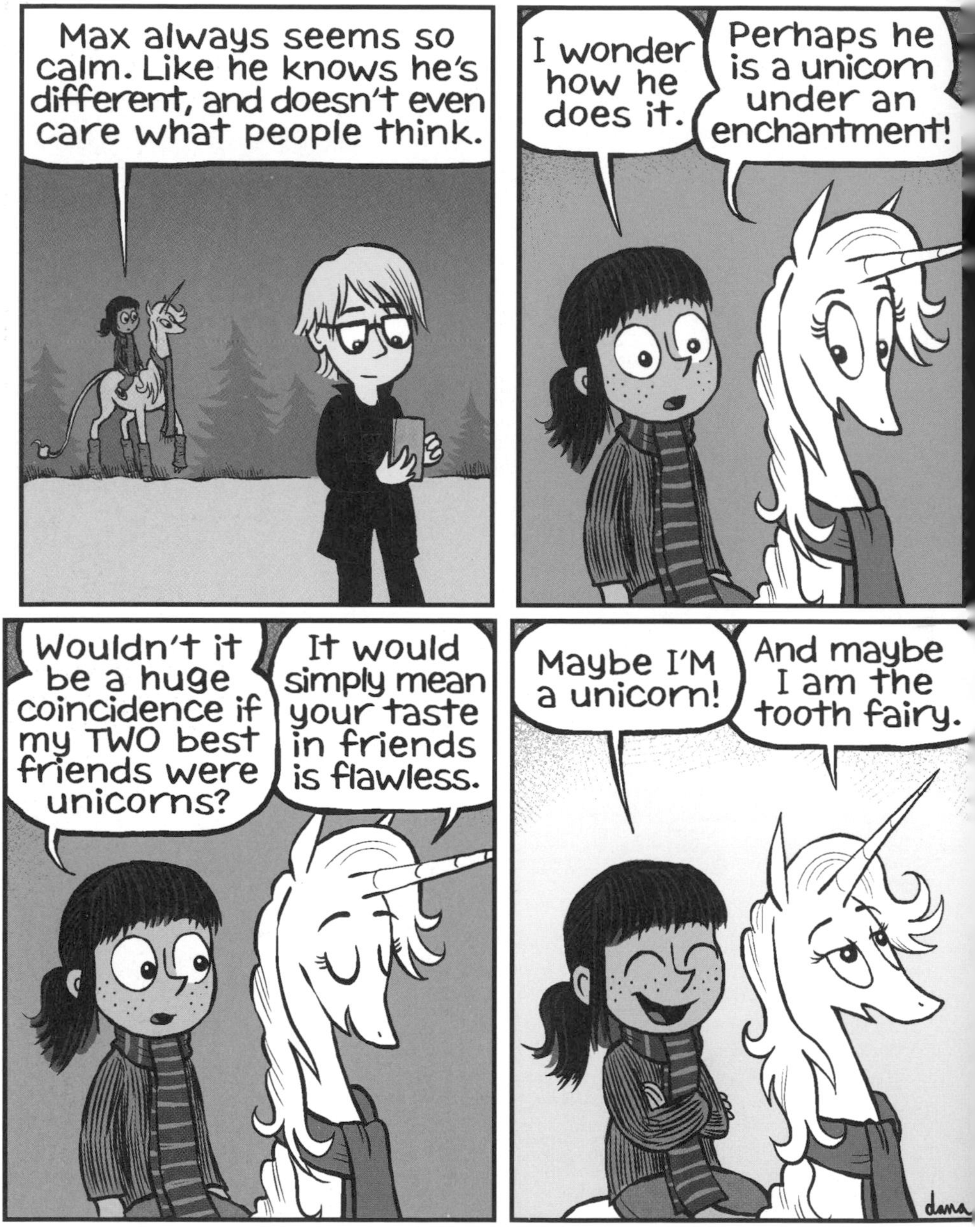
Max always seems so calm. Like he knows he's different, and doesn't even care what people think.
I wonder how he does it.
Perhaps he is a unicorn under an enchantment!
Wouldn't it be a huge coincidence if my TWO best friends were unicorns?
It would simply mean your taste in friends is flawless.
Maybe I'M a unicorn!
And maybe I am the tooth fairy.
dana

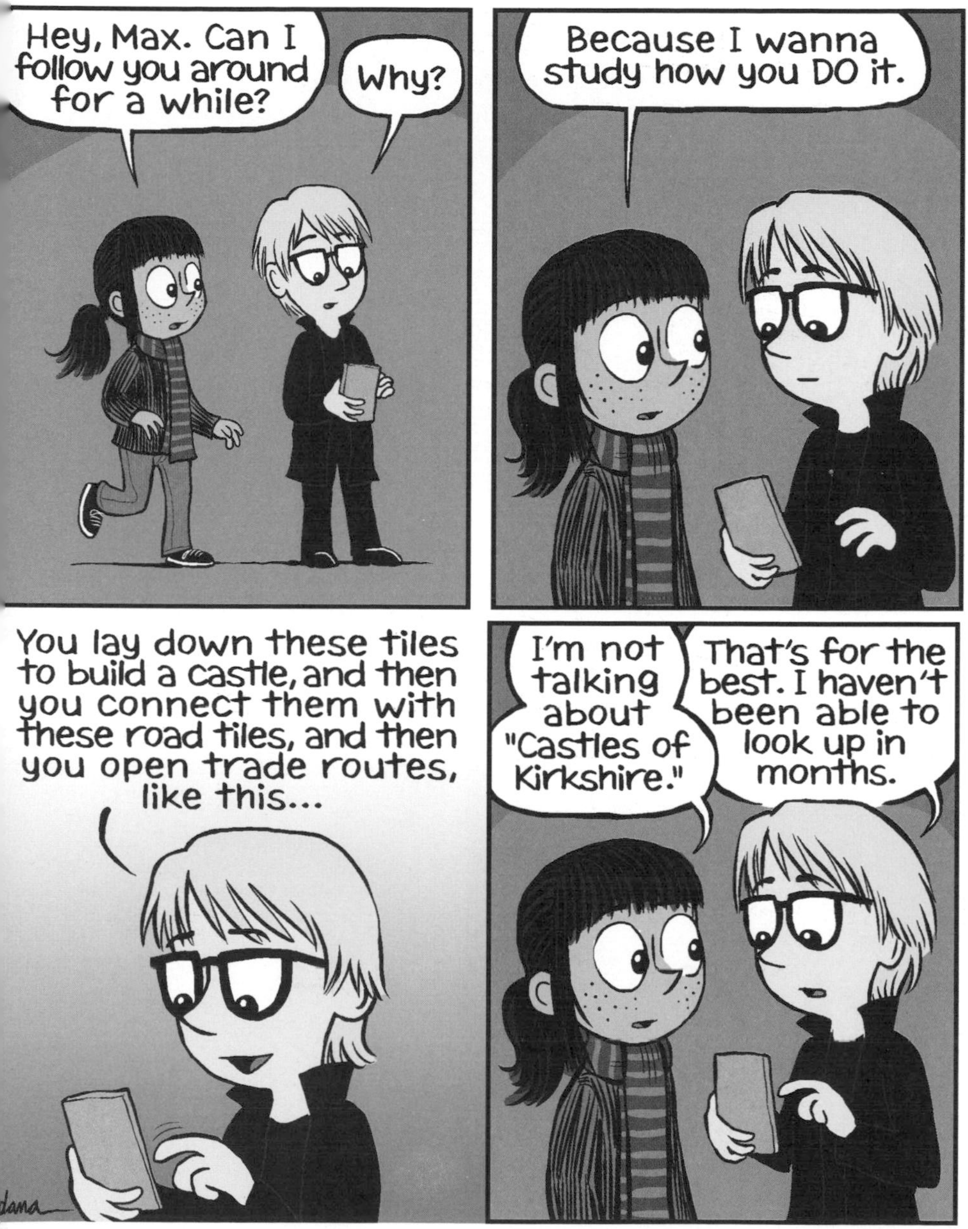
Hey, Max. Can I follow you around for a while?
Why?
Because I wanna study how you DO it.
You lay down these tiles to build a castle, and then you connect them with these road tiles, and then you open trade routes, like this...
I'm not talking about "Castles of Kirkshire."
That's for the best. I haven't been able to look up in months.
dana

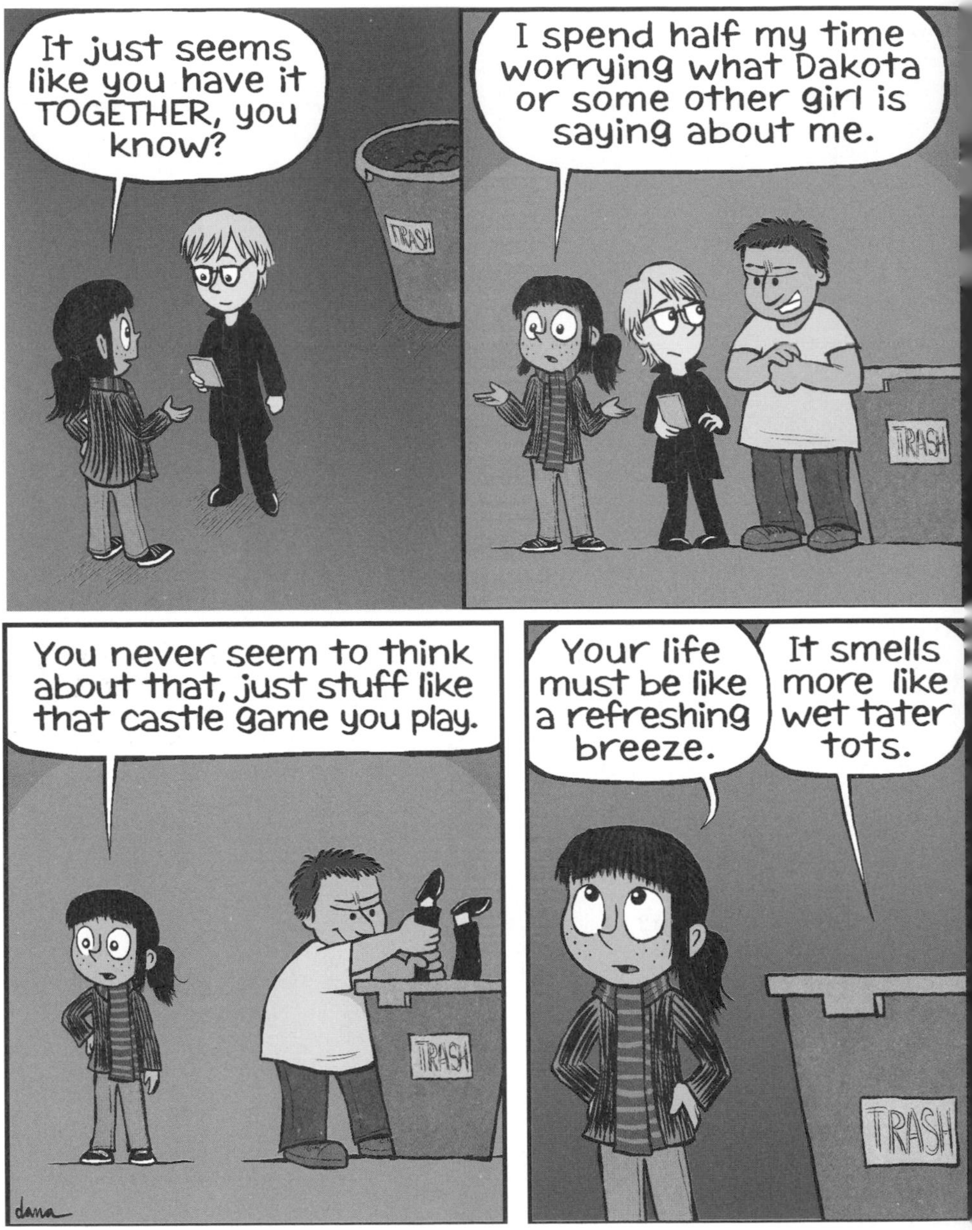
It just seems like you have it TOGETHER, you know?
I spend half my time worrying what Dakota or some other girl is saying about me.
TRASH
You never seem to think about that, just stuff like that castle game you play.
TRASH
dana
Your life must be like a refreshing breeze.
It smells more like wet tater tots.
TRASH

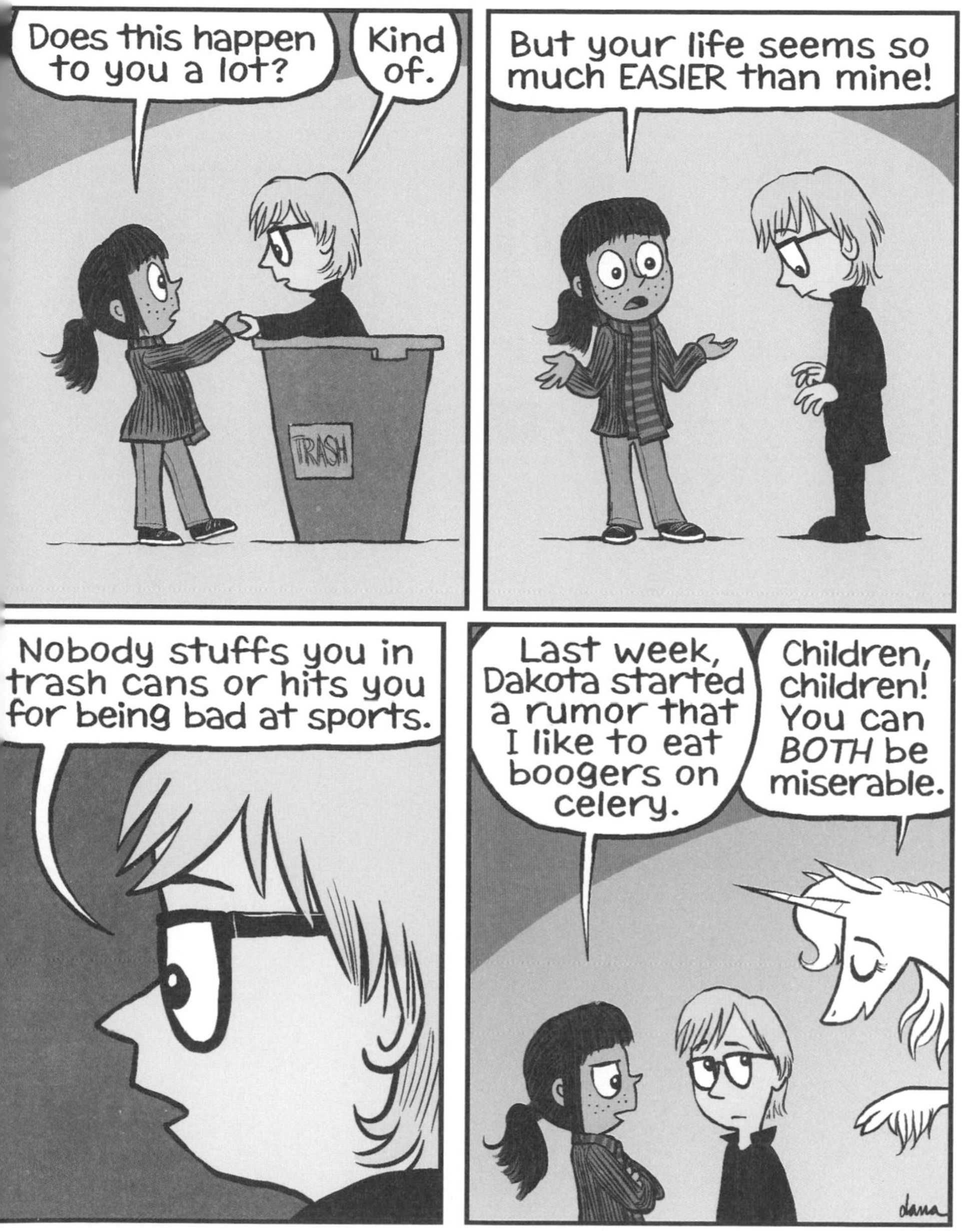
Does this happen to you a lot?
Kind of.
But your life seems so much EASIER than mine!
Nobody stuffs you in trash cans or hits you for being bad at sports.
Last week, Dakota started a rumor that I like to eat boogers on celery.
Children, children! You can BOTH be miserable.
TRASH
dana

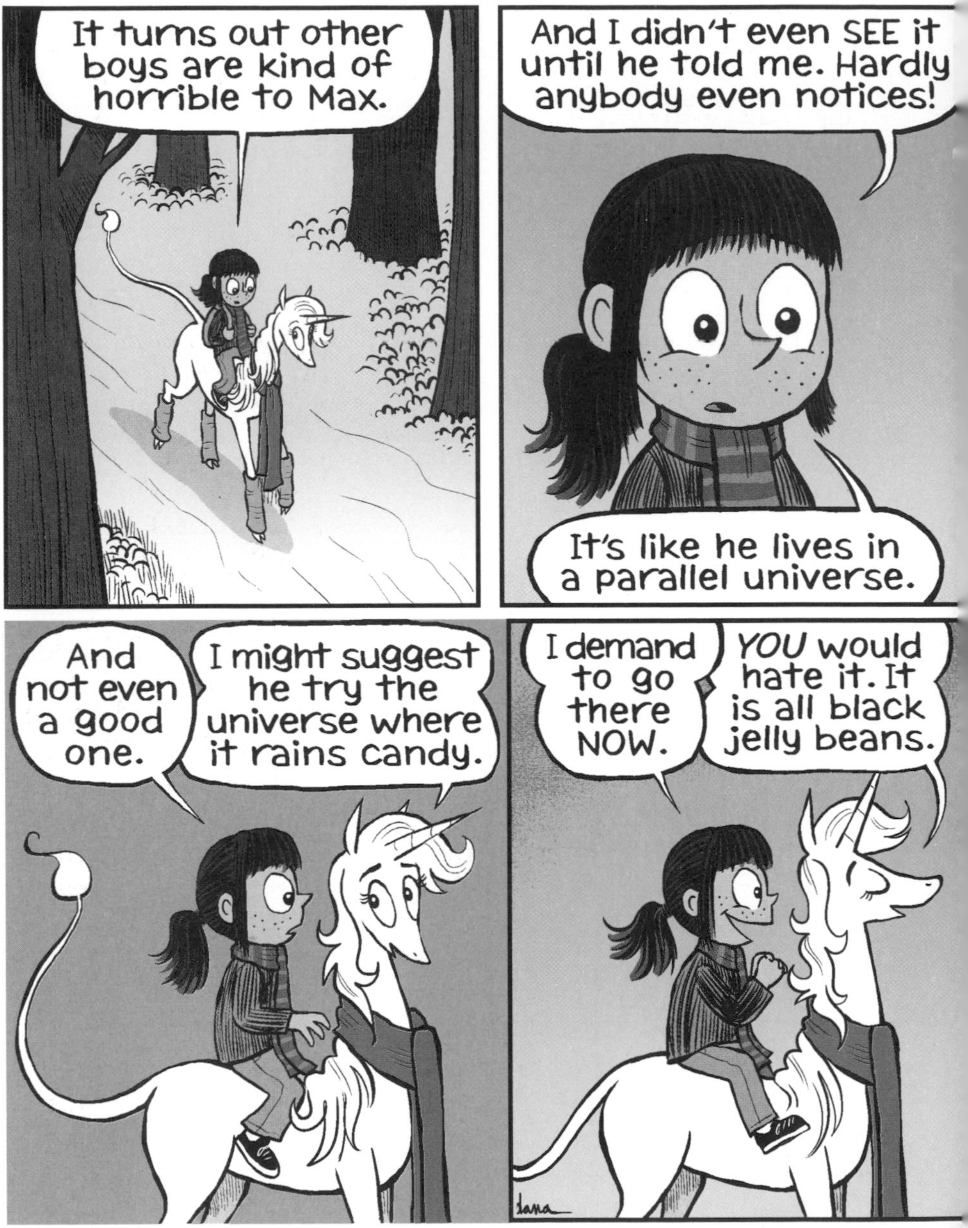
It turns out other boys are kind of horrible to Max.
And I didn't even SEE it until he told me. Hardly anybody even notices!
It's like he lives in a parallel universe.
And not even a good one.
I might suggest he try the universe where it rains candy.
I demand to go there NOW.
YOU would hate it. It is all black jelly beans.
Dana

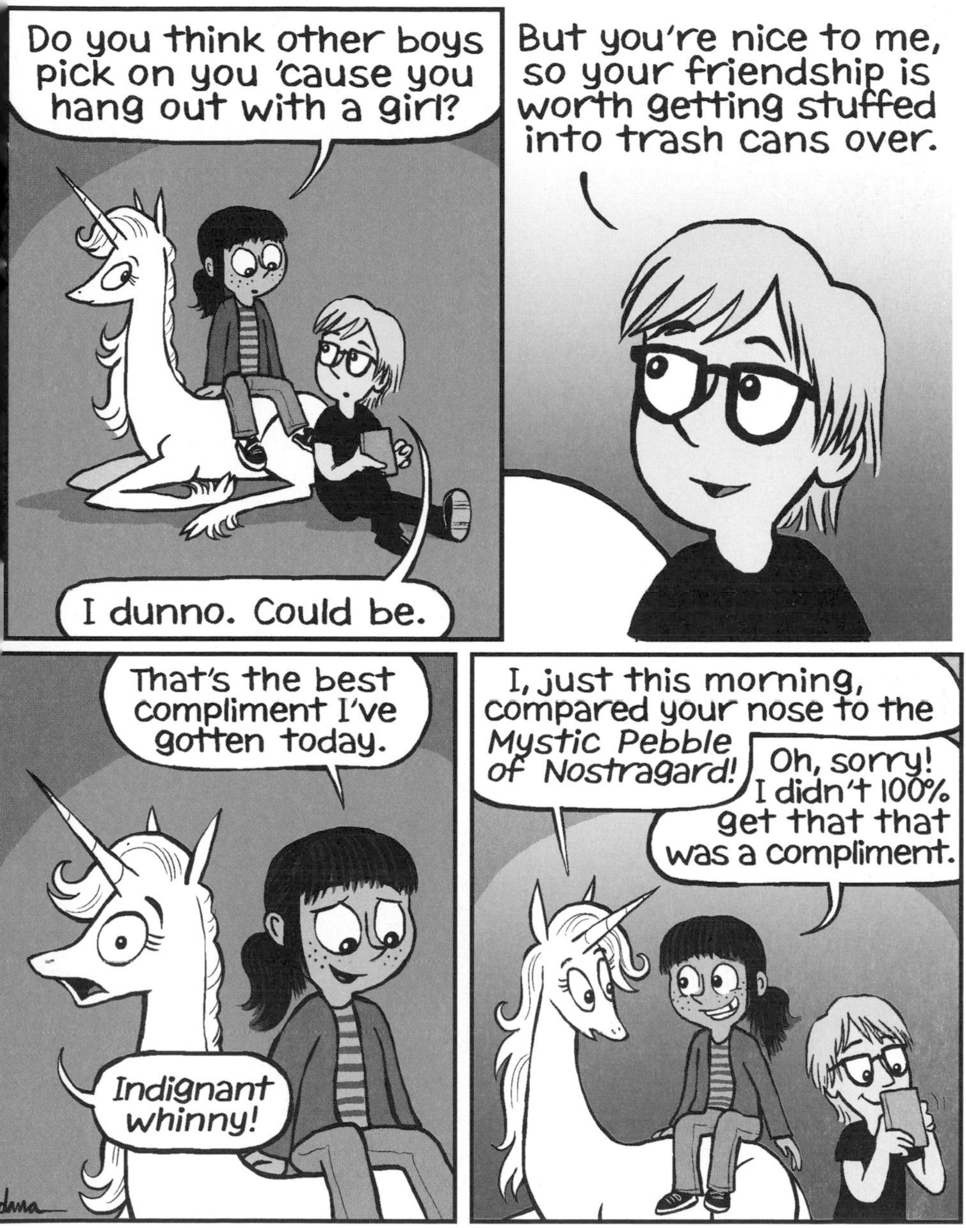

Do you think other boys pick on you 'cause you hang out with a girl?
I dunno. Could be.
But you're nice to me, so your friendship is worth getting stuffed into trash cans over.
That's the best compliment I've gotten today.
Indignant whinny!
I, just this morning, compared your nose to the *Mystic Pebble of Nostragard!*
Oh, sorry! I didn't 100% get that that was a compliment.

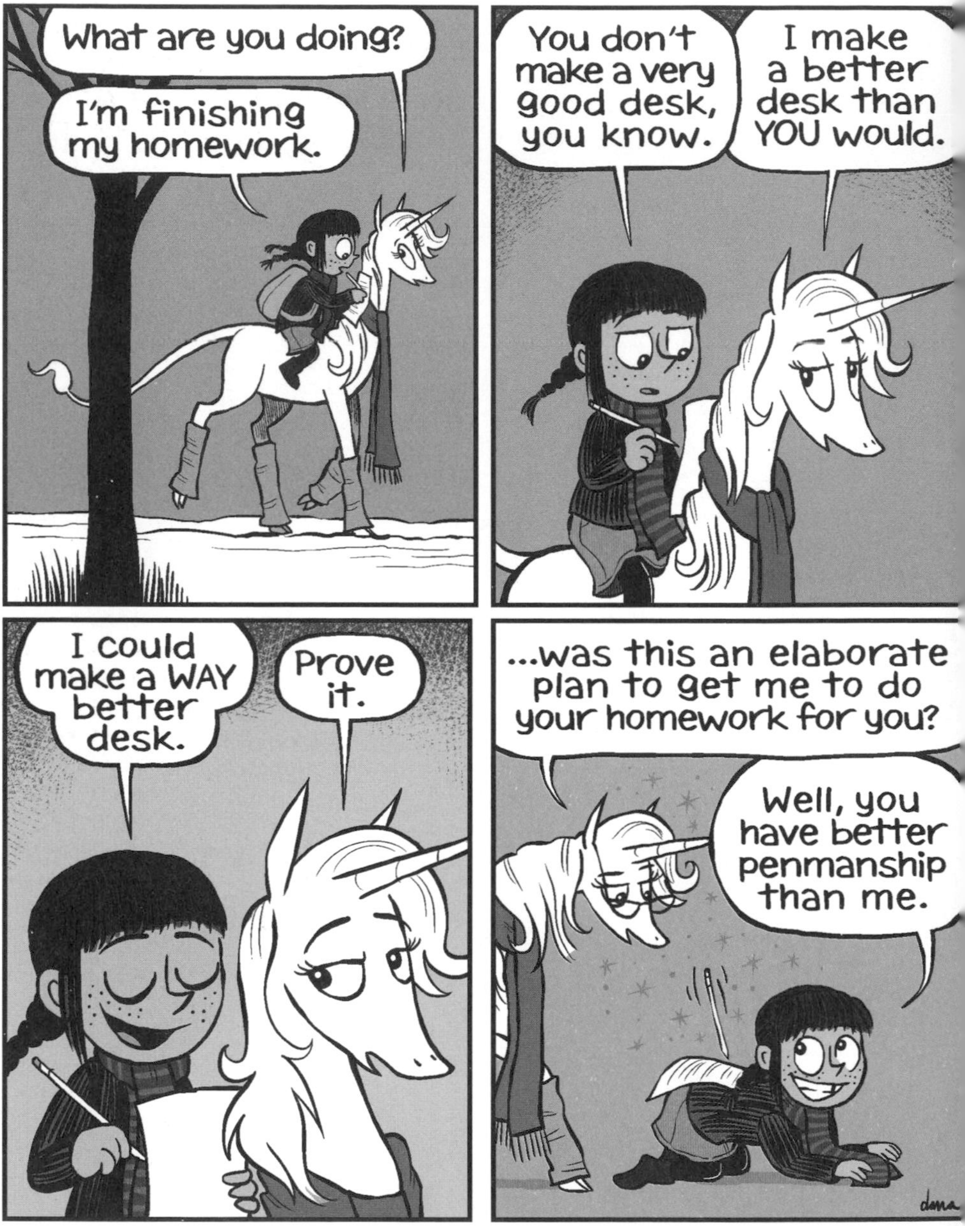
What are you doing?
I'm finishing my homework.
You don't make a very good desk, you know.
I make a better desk than YOU would.
I could make a WAY better desk.
Prove it.
...was this an elaborate plan to get me to do your homework for you?
Well, you have better penmanship than me.

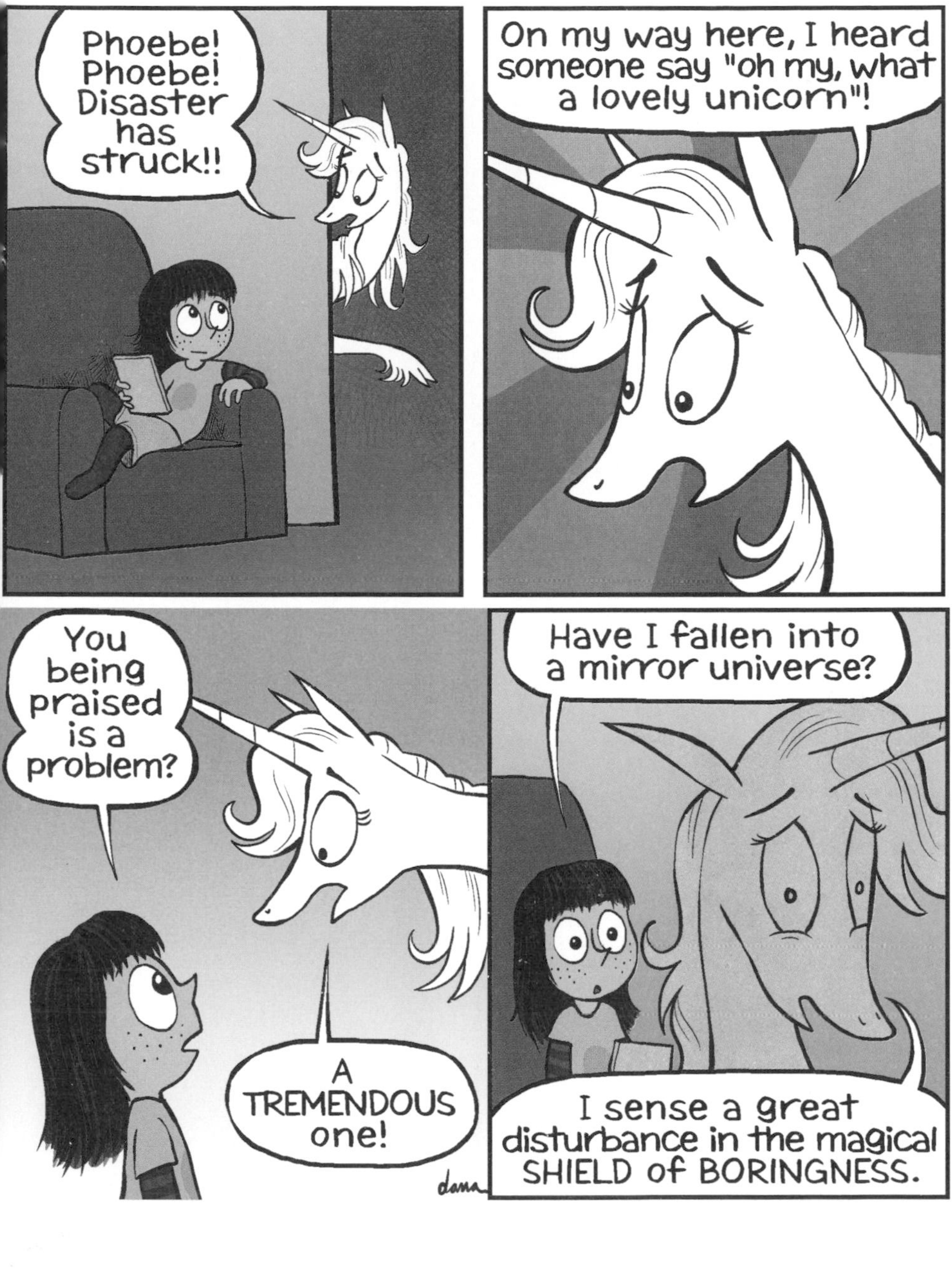
Phoebe! Phoebe! Disaster has struck!!
On my way here, I heard someone say "oh my, what a lovely unicorn"!
You being praised is a problem?
A TREMENDOUS one!
Have I fallen into a mirror universe?
I sense a great disturbance in the magical SHIELD of BORINGNESS.
dana

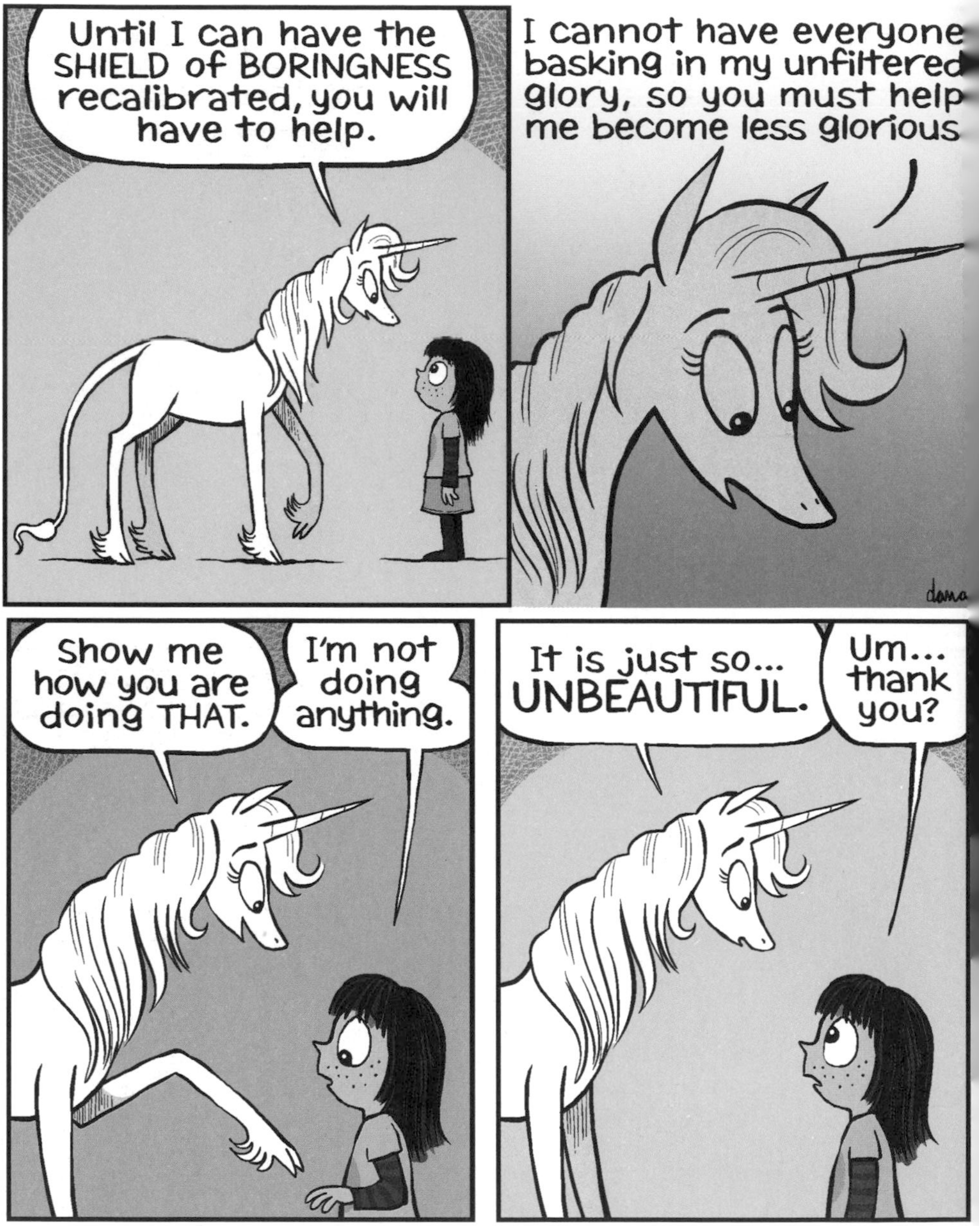
Until I can have the SHIELD of BORINGNESS recalibrated, you will have to help.
I cannot have everyone basking in my unfiltered glory, so you must help me become less glorious
Show me how you are doing THAT.
I'm not doing anything.
It is just so... UNBEAUTIFUL.
Um... thank you?

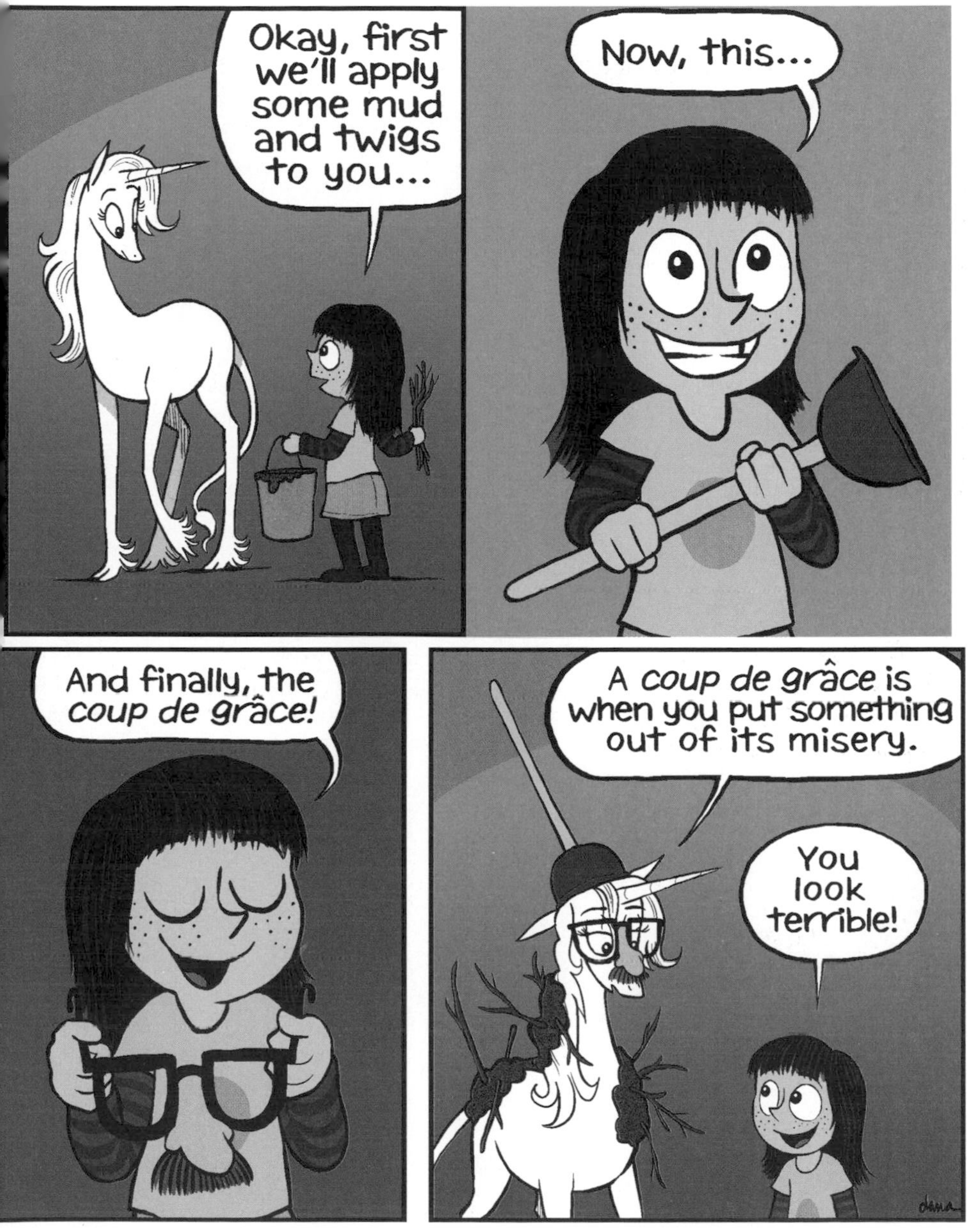
Okay, first we'll apply some mud and twigs to you...
Now, this...
And finally, the *coup de grâce*!
A *coup de grâce* is when you put something out of its misery.
You look terrible!
dana

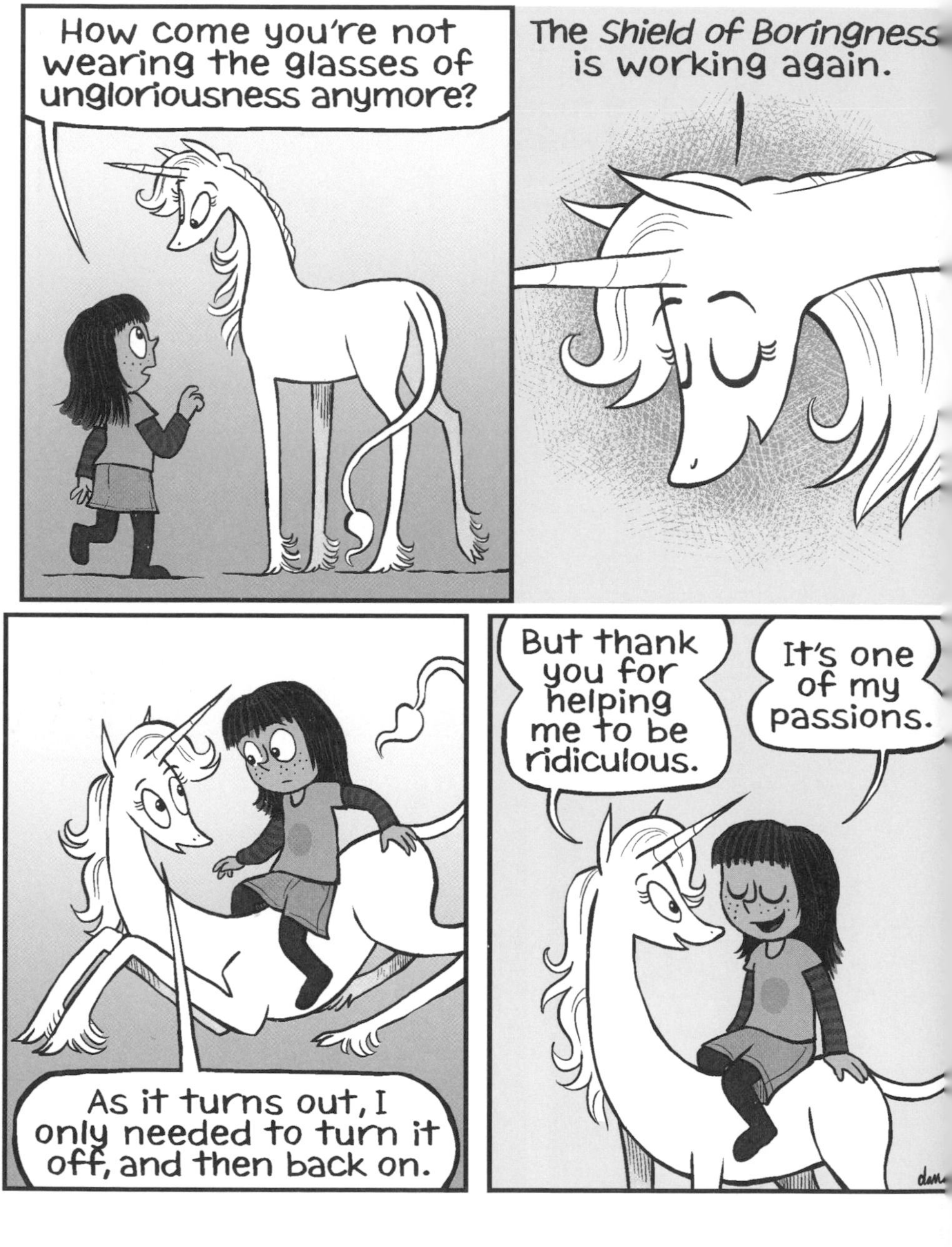
How come you're not wearing the glasses of ungloriousness anymore?
The *Shield of Boringness* is working again.
As it turns out, I only needed to turn it off, and then back on.
But thank you for helping me to be ridiculous.
It's one of my passions.

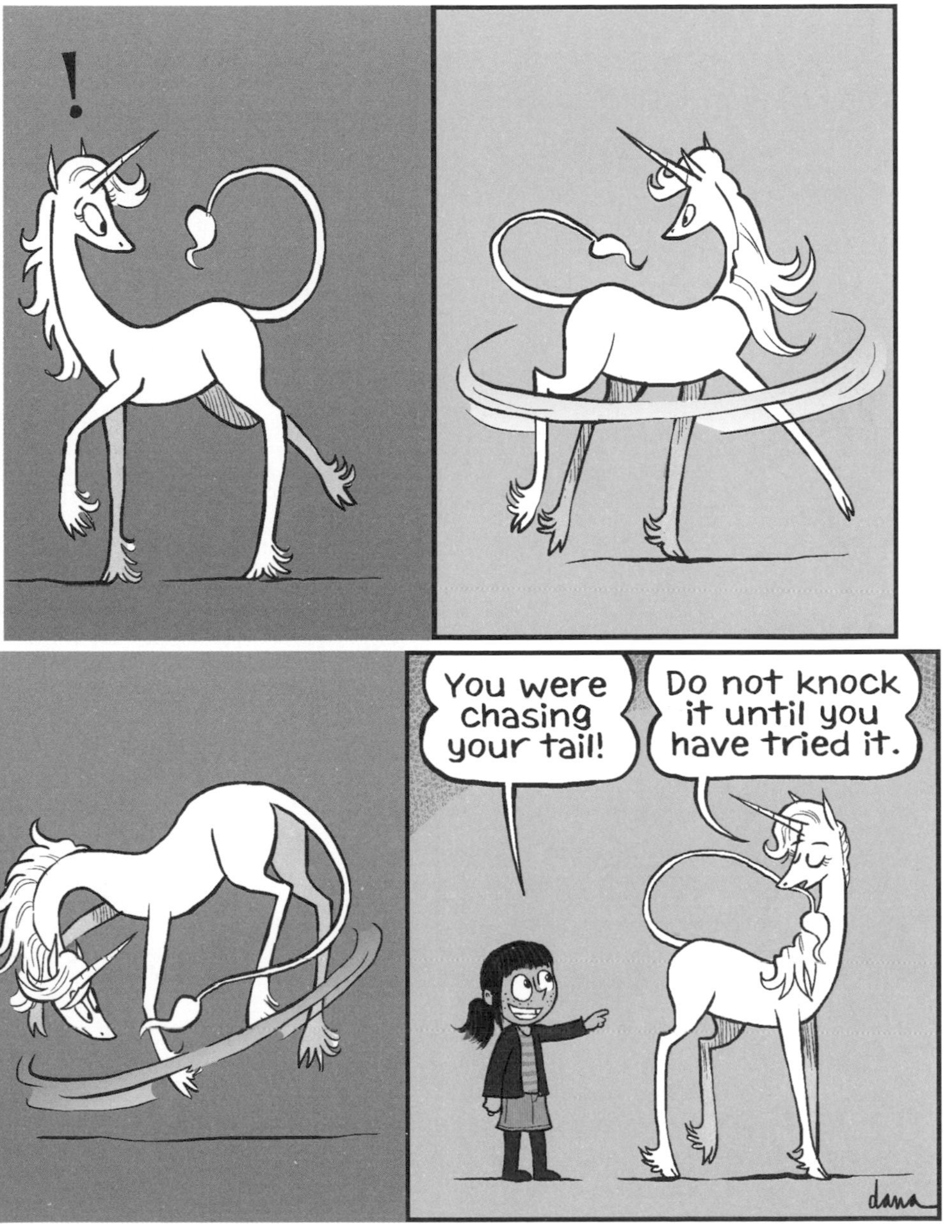
!
You were chasing your tail!
Do not knock it until you have tried it.
dana

MORE TO EXPLORE! A special section featuring words to learn!

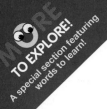

GLOSSARY

abode (uh-bode): pg. 62 – noun / a place where a person lives; home

abomination (uh-bom-uh-nay-shun): pg. 98 – noun / something that is greatly disliked or loathed

askew (uh-skyoo): pg. 60 – adverb / out of position

battering ram (ba-ter-ing ram): pg. 84 – noun / an ancient military machine with a horizontal beam used to beat down walls, gates, etc.

bestower (bee-stoe-ur): pg. 140 – noun / gift giver

compensated (kom-pun-sayt-ud): pg. 11 – verb / made a payment in order to make up for something

conjure (kon-jer): pg. 70 – verb / to produce or bring into being by magic

contention (kun-ten-shun): pg. 119 – noun / a point used in a debate or an argument

countenance (koun-tun-unce): pg. 16 – verb / to approve or support

debacle (duh-bah-kul): pg. 141 – noun / total failure

dirge (durj): pg. 109 – noun / a mournful sound like a funeral song

embellishment (em-bel-ish-munt): pg. 149 – noun / ornament or decoration

extraterrestrial (ek-struh-tuh-res-tree-ul): pg. 45 – adjective / outside the limits of the earth

flaunting (flont-ing): pg. 115 – verb / conspicuously displaying; attracting attention

frolicking (frol-ik-ing): pg. 106 – verb / playing merrily

grackle (grak-uhl): pg. 103 – noun / any of a type of blackbirds with shiny black plumage (feathers)

haggled (hag-uhld): pg. 30 – verb / bargained; wrangled, especially over a price

hypothetically (hi-puh-thet-i-kuh-lee): pg. 133 – adverb / supposedly

liberally (lib-er-uhl-ee): pg. 149 – adverb / freely; abundantly

metaphorical (met-uh-fore-i-kuhl): pg. 154 – adjective / something used in a way to represent something else

notarized (noe-tih-rized): pg. 48 – verb / certified a document through a notary public

notary (noe-tih-ree): pg. 48 – noun / a person authorized to authenticate contracts and other legal documents

ornery (ore-nuh-ree): pg. 127 – adjective / unpleasant; cranky

ostentatious (os-ten-tay-shus): pg. 62, 115 – adjective / showing off wealth or treasure to make people envious; flashy or showy

paisley (payz-lee): pg. 158 – adjective / covered in a pattern of colorful, curvy designs

pandering (pan-der-ing): pg. 83 – verb / doing or saying what someone wants in order to please them

Ph.D. (pee-aich-dee): pg. 43 – abbreviation / Doctor of Philosophy; the highest academic degree awarded by universities

pixelated (pik-suh-layt-ed): pg. 84 – adjective / displayed in a way that individual pixels of a computer graphic are visible

poise (poiz): pg. 107 – noun / a dignified manner

recalibrated (ree-kal-uh-bray-ted): pg. 168 – verb / readjusted something for a particular function

reluctant (ree-luck-tunt): pg. 129 – adjective / unwilling; disinclined

repository (re-pos-it-or-ee): pg. 19 – noun / a place where a large amount of something is stored (like a warehouse, library, or store)

résumé (rez-oo-may): pg. 26 – noun / a brief written account of personal qualifications and experience, prepared by someone applying for a job

sophisticated (suh-fiss-tuh-kay-ted): pg. 66 – adjective / refined; worldly

thesis (thee-sis): pg. 43 — noun / a scholarly paper prepared with original research to prove a specific view

touché (too-shay): pg. 82 — interjection / an expression used to acknowledge something true, funny, or clever

tribbles (trib-ulz): pg. 59 — noun / fictional alien species in the *Star Trek* universe

unionize (yoon-yuh-nize): pg. 11 — verb / to organize into a labor union to protect workers' rights

hoebe and Her Unicorn is distributed internationally by Andrews McMeel Syndication.

Andrews McMeel Publishing
a division of Andrews McMeel Universal
1130 Walnut Street, Kansas City, Missouri 64106

www.andrewsmcmeel.com

19 20 21 22 23 SDB 10 9 8 7 6 5 4 3

ISBN: 978-1-4494-8966-3

Library of Congress Control Number: 2017952108

Made by:
Shenzhen Donnelley Printing Company Ltd.
Address and location of manufacturer:
No. 47, Wuhe Nan Road, Bantian Ind. Zone,
Shenzhen China, 518129
3rd Printing—3/19/19

Check out more *Phoebe and Her Unicorn*

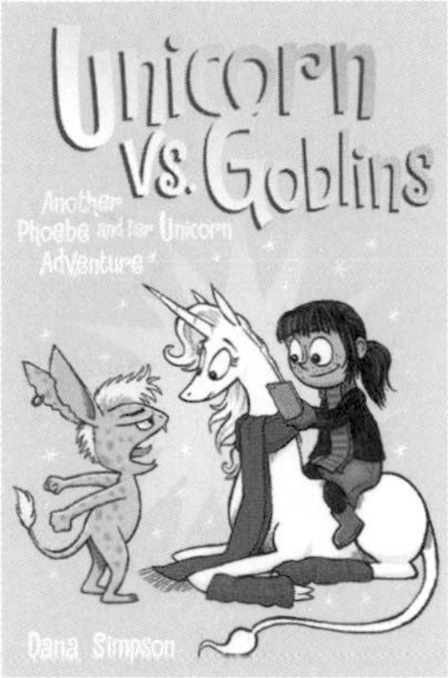
Unicorn vs. Goblins
Another Phoebe and Her Unicorn Adventure
Dana Simpson

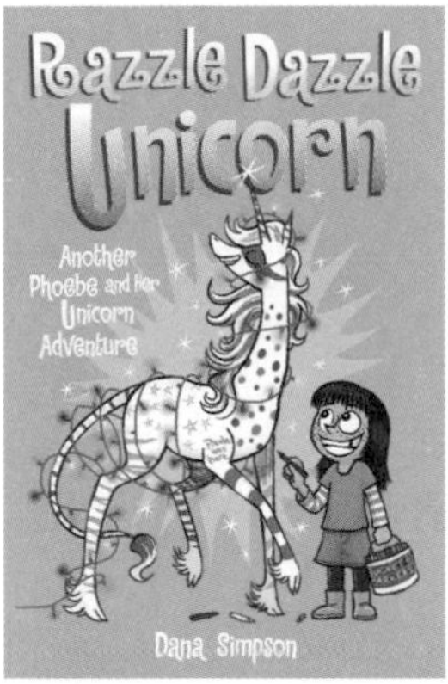
Razzle Dazzle Unicorn
Another Phoebe and Her Unicorn Adventure
Dana Simpson

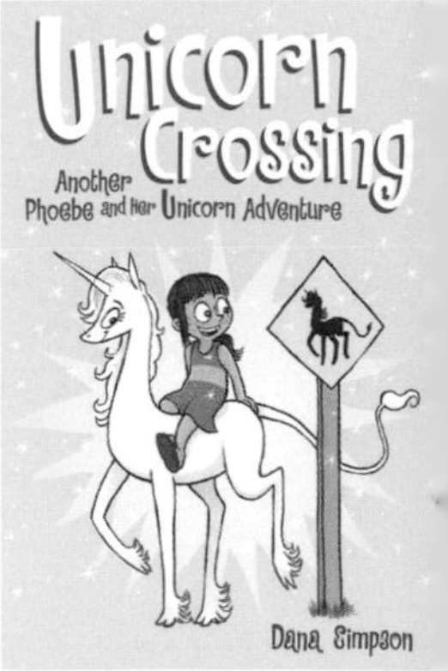
Unicorn Crossing
Another Phoebe and Her Unicorn Adventure
Dana Simpson

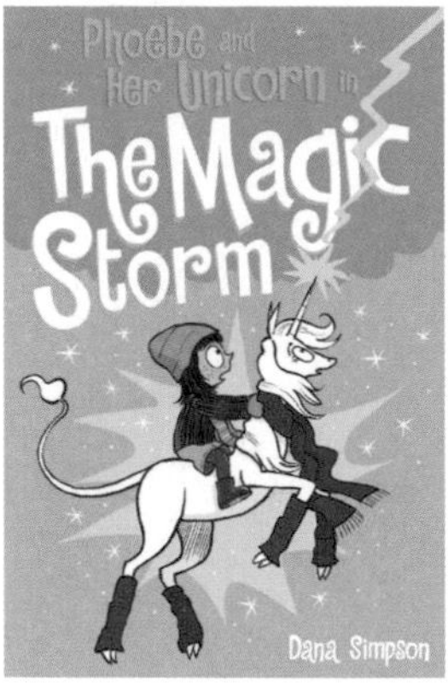
Phoebe and Her Unicorn in
The Magic Storm
Dana Simpson

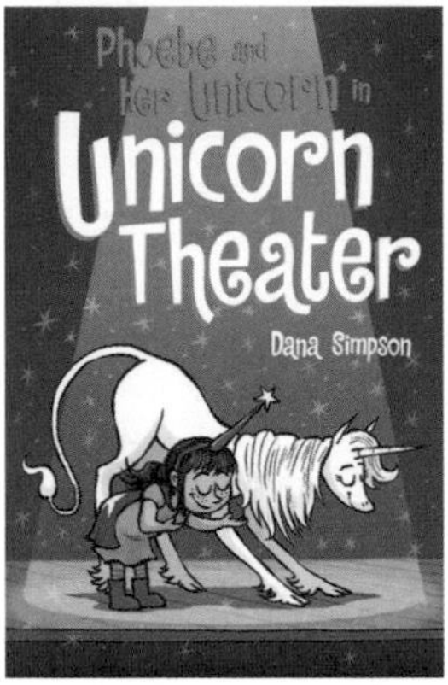
Phoebe and Her Unicorn in
Unicorn Theater
Dana Simpson

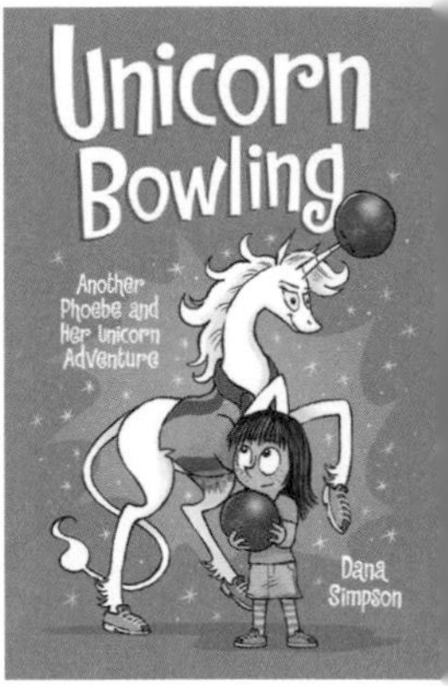
Unicorn Bowling
Another Phoebe and Her Unicorn Adventure
Dana Simpson

If you like Phoebe, look for these books!

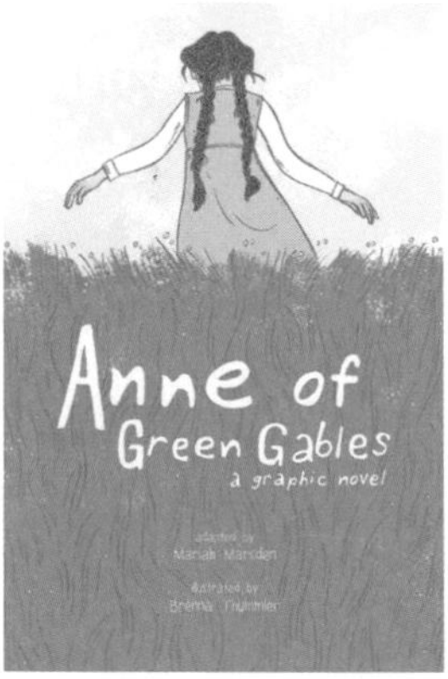
Anne of Green Gables
a graphic novel

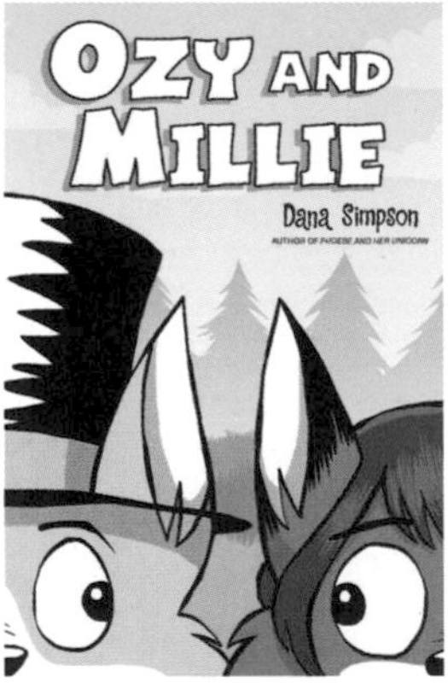
Ozy and Millie
Dana Simpson

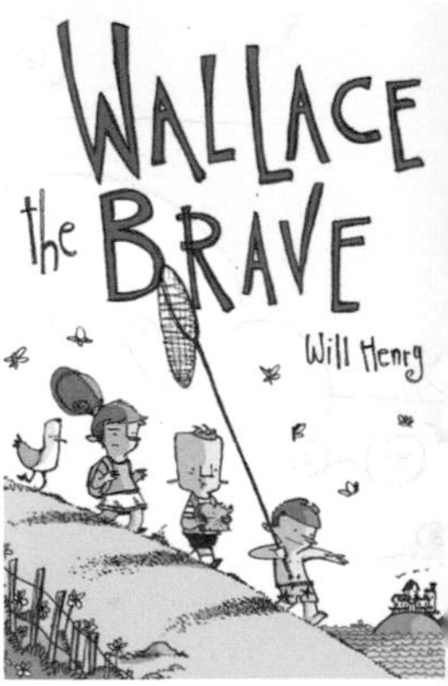
Wallace the Brave
Will Henry